half gir

Chetan Bhagat is the author of six blockbuster books. These include five novels—*Five Point Someone* (2004), *One Night @ the Call Center* (2005), *The 3 Mistakes of My Life* (2008), *2 States* (2009), *Revolution 2020* (2011)—and the non-fiction title *What Young India Wants* (2012).

Chetan's books have remained bestsellers since their release. Several of his novels have been adapted into successful Bollywood films.

The New York Times called him 'the biggest selling English language novelist in India's history'. *TIME* magazine named him amongst the '100 most influential people in the world' and *Fast Company*, USA, listed him as one of the world's '100 most creative people in business'.

Chetan writes columns for leading English and Hindi newspapers, focusing on youth and national development issues. He is also a motivational speaker and a screenplay writer.

Chetan quit his international investment banking career in 2009 to devote his entire time to writing and making change happen in the country. He lives in Mumbai with his wife, Anusha, an ex-classmate from IIM-A, and his twin sons, Shyam and Ishaan.

half
girlfriend

CHETAN BHAGAT

RUPA

Published by
Rupa Publications India Pvt. Ltd 2014
7/16, Ansari Road, Daryaganj
New Delhi 110002

Sales centres:

Allahabad Bengaluru Chennai
Hyderabad Jaipur Kathmandu
Kolkata Mumbai

Lyrics on page 223 have been taken from the song *Don't Wanna Miss a Thing* by Aerosmith (Sony Music); on page 224 from the song *A Thousand Years* by Christina Perri (Atlantic Records); and on pages 253-254 from the song *You're Beautiful* by James Blunt (Atlantic Records). While every effort has been made to trace copyright holders and obtain permission, this has not been possible in all cases; any omissions brought to our attention will be remedied in future editions.

This is a work of fiction. Names, characters, places and incidents are either the product of the author's imagination or are used fictitiously and any resemblance to any actual person, living or dead, events or locales is entirely coincidental.

ISBN: 978-81-291-2402-9

Eleventh impression 2017

15 14 13 12 11

The moral right of the author has been asserted.

Printed at Nutech Print Services, New Delhi

For my mother
For rural India
For the non-English types

Acknowledgements and some thoughts

Thank you, dear reader and friend, for picking up *Half Girlfriend*. Whatever I have achieved today in life is thanks to you. Here's thanking all those who helped me with this book:

Shinie Antony, my editor and first reader since *Five Point Someone*. Her feedback is invaluable.

Those who helped me at various stages of conceptualizing, research and editing—Anubha Bang, Abhishek Kapoor, Anusha Bhagat, Masaba Gupta, Ayesha Raval, Abha Bakaya and Anusha Venkatachalam.

My team—Bhakti, Michelle, Tanya and Virali.

My immediate family—Anusha, Shyam, Ishaan. My mother, Rekha. My brother and his wife, Ketan and Pia. My in-laws, Suri, Kalpana, Anand and Poonam.

Friends who make life worthwhile.

My extended family on Twitter and Facebook.

The entire team at Rupa Publications India.

All those I met in Bihar while writing this book.

And, finally, Bill Gates—and not just for Microsoft Word this time.

I want to share something with you. With this book, I complete ten years as a writer. When I started writing, my motives were different. I wanted to make it. I wanted to prove a point. Today, I write for different reasons. I write for change. A change in the mindset of Indian society. It is a lofty goal, and I am not foolish enough to think I can ever achieve it. However, it helps to have positive intentions and a direction in life, and I am glad to have found mine.

I want to reach as many people as I can—through books, films or other mediums of entertainment. I am human; I will falter and I will have ups and downs. If possible, try to maintain your support and keep me grounded through that process.

One more thing: don't give me your admiration. Give me your love. Admiration passes, love endures. Also, admiration comes with expectations. Love accepts some flaws.

In fact, people sometimes ask me how I would like to be

remembered. While hopefully that is a while away, all I tell them is this: I don't want to be remembered, I just want to be missed.

Welcome to *Half Girlfriend*.

Prologue

'They are your journals, you read them,' I said to him.

He shook his head.

'Listen, I don't have the time or patience for this,' I said, getting irritated. Being a writer on a book tour doesn't allow for much sleep—I had not slept more than four hours a night for a week. I checked my watch. 'It's midnight. I gave you my view. It's time for me to sleep now.'

'I want *you* to read them,' he said.

We were in my room at the Chanakya Hotel, Patna. This morning, he had tried to stop me on my way out. Then he had waited for me all day; I had returned late at night to find him sitting in the hotel lobby.

'Just give me five minutes, sir,' he had said, following me into the lift. And now here we were in my room as he pulled out three tattered notebooks from his backpack.

The spines of the notebooks came apart as he plonked them on the table. The yellowing pages fanned out between us. The pages had handwritten text, mostly illegible as the ink had smudged. Many pages had holes, rats having snacked on them.

An aspiring writer, I thought.

'If this is a manuscript, please submit it to a publisher. However, do not send it in this state,' I said.

'I am not a writer. This is not a book.'

'It's not?' I said, lightly touching a crumbling page. I looked up at him. Even seated, he was tall. Over six feet in height, he had a sunburnt, outdoor ruggedness about him. Black hair, black eyes and a particularly intense gaze. He wore a shirt two sizes too big for his lean frame. He had large hands. He reassembled the notebooks, gentle with his fingers, almost caressing the pages.

'What are these?' I said.

'I had a friend. These are her journals,' he said.

'Her journals. Ah. A girlfriend?'

'Half-girlfriend.'

'What?'

He shrugged.

'Listen, have you eaten anything all day?' I said.

He shook his head. I looked around. A bowl of fruit and some chocolates sat next to my bed. He took a piece of dark chocolate when I offered it.

'So what do you want from me?' I said.

'I want you to read these journals, whatever is readable...because I can't.'

I looked at him, surprised.

'You can't read? As in, you can't read in general? Or you can't read these?'

'These.'

'Why not?' I said, reaching for a chocolate myself.

'Because Riya's dead.'

My hand froze in mid-air. You cannot pick up a chocolate when someone has just mentioned a death.

'Did you just say the girl who wrote these journals is dead?'

He nodded. I took a few deep breaths and wondered what to say next.

'Why are they in such terrible shape?' I said after a pause.

'They are old. Her ex-landlord found them after years.'

'Sorry, Mr Whats-your-name. Can I order some food first?' I picked up the phone in the room and ordered two club sandwiches from the limited midnight menu.

'I'm Madhav. Madhav Jha. I live in Dumraon, eighty kilometres from here.'

'What do you do?'

'I run a school there.'

'Oh, that's...' I paused, searching for the right word.

'...noble? Not really. It's my mother's school.'

'I was going to say that's unusual. You speak English. Not typical of someone who runs a school in the back of beyond.'

'My English is still bad. I have a Bihari accent,' he said, without a trace of self-consciousness.

'French people have a French accent when they speak English.'

'My English wasn't even English until...' he trailed off and fell silent. I saw him swallow to keep his composure.

'Until?'

He absently stroked the notebooks on the desk.

'Nothing. Actually, I went to St. Stephen's.'

'In Delhi?'

'Yes. English types call it "Steven's".'

I smiled. 'And you are not one of the English types?'

'Not at all.'

The doorbell startled us. The waiter shifted the journals to put the sandwich tray on the table. A few sheets fell to the floor.

'Careful!' Madhav shouted, as if the waiter had broken some antique crystal.

The waiter apologized and scooted out of the room.

I offered Madhav the club sandwich, which had a tomato, cheese and lettuce filling. He ignored me and rearranged the loose sheets of paper.

'Are you okay? Please eat.'

He nodded, his eyes still on the pages of the journal. I decided to eat, since my imposed guest didn't seem to care for my hospitality.

'These journals obviously mean a lot to you. But why have you brought them here?'

'For you to read. Maybe they will be useful to you.'

'How will they be useful to me?' I said, my voice firmer with the food inside me. A part of me wanted him out of my room as soon as possible.

'She used to like your books. We used to read them together,' he said in a soft voice. 'For me to learn English.'

'Madhav,' I said, as calmly as possible, 'this seems like a sensitive matter. I don't want to get involved. Okay?'

His gaze remained directed at the floor. 'I don't want the journals either,' he said after a while.

'That is for you to decide.'

'It's too painful for me,' he said.

'I can imagine.'

He stood up, presumably to leave. He had not touched his sandwich—which was okay, because I could eat it after he left.

'Thank you for your time. Sorry to have disturbed you.'

'It's okay,' I said.

He scribbled his phone number on a piece of paper and kept it on the table. 'If you are ever in Dumraon and need anything, let me know. It's unlikely you will ever come, but still...' He stood up, instantly dwarfing me, and walked to the door.

'Madhav,' I called out after him, 'you forgot the journals. Please take them with you.'

'I told you I don't need them.'

'So why are you leaving them here?'

'Because I can't throw them away. You can.'

Before I could answer, he stepped out, shut the door and left. It took me a few seconds to realize what had happened.

I picked up the journals and ran out of the room, but the sole working lift had just gone down. I could have taken the stairs and caught him in time but, after a long day, I didn't have the energy to do that.

I came back to my room, irritated by his audacity. Dumping the notebooks and the slip with his phone number in the dustbin, I sat on the bed, a little unsettled.

I can't let someone I just met get the better of me, I thought, shaking my head. I switched off the lights and lay down. I had to catch an early-morning flight to Mumbai the next day and had a four-hour window of sleep. I couldn't wait to reach home.

However, I couldn't stop thinking about my encounter with the mysterious Madhav. *Who was this guy?* The words 'Dumraon', 'Stephen's' and 'Delhi' floated around in my head. Questions popped up: *What the hell is a half-girlfriend? And why do I have a dead girl's journals in my room?*

Eyes wide open, I lay in bed, staring at the little flashing red light from the smoke detector on the ceiling.

The journals bothered me. Sure, they lay in the dustbin. However, something about those torn pages, the dead person and her half-boyfriend, or whoever he was, intrigued me. *Don't go there,* I thought, but my mind screamed down its own suggestion: *Read just one page.*

'Don't even think about it,' I said out loud. But thirty minutes later, I switched on the lights in my room, fished out the journals from the dustbin and opened the first volume. Most pages were too damaged to read. I tried to make sense of what I could.

The first page dated back nine years to 1 November 2002. Riya had written about her fifteenth birthday. *One more page*, I kept thinking. I flipped through the pages as I tried to find another readable one. I read one more section, and then another. Three hours later, I had read whatever could be read in the entire set.

The room phone rang at 5 a.m., startling me.

'Your wake-up call, sir,' the hotel operator said.

'I am awake, thank you,' I said, as I'd never slept at all. I called Jet Airways.

'I'd like to cancel a ticket on the Patna–Mumbai flight this morning.'

Pulling out the slip of paper with Madhav's number from the dustbin, I texted him: We need to talk. Important.

At 6.30 a.m., the tall, lanky man was in my room once more.

'Make tea for both of us. The kettle is above the minibar.'

He followed my instructions. The early morning sun highlighted his sharp features. He handed me a cup of tea and took a seat diagonally opposite me on the double bed.

'Should I speak first, or will you?' I said.

'About?'

'Riya.'

He sighed.

'Do you think you knew her well?'

'Yes,' he said.

'You feel comfortable talking about her to me?'

He thought for a few seconds and nodded.

'So tell me everything. Tell me the story of Madhav and Riya.'

'A story that fate left incomplete,' he said.

'Fate can be strange indeed.'

'Where do I start? When we first met?'

'Always a good place,' I said.

ACT I

Delhi

1

'Where?' I gasped, trying to catch my breath.

I had two minutes left for my interview to start and I couldn't find the room. Lost, I stopped whoever I could in the confusing corridors of St. Stephen's College to ask for directions.

Most students ignored me. Many sniggered. I wondered why.

Well, now I know. My accent. Back in 2004, my English was Bihari. I don't want to talk now like I did back then. It's embarrassing. It wasn't English. It was 90 per cent Bihari Hindi mixed with 10 per cent really bad English. For instance, this is what I had actually said:

'Cumty room...batlaieyega zara? Hamara interview hai na wahan... Mera khel ka kota hai. Kis taraf hai?'

If I start speaking the way I did in those days, you'll get a headache. So I'm going to say everything in English. Just imagine my words in Bhojpuri-laced Hindi, with the worst possible English thrown in.

'Where you from, man?' said a boy with hair longer than most girls.

'Me Madhav Jha from Dumraon, Bihar.'

His friends laughed. Over time, I learnt that people often ask what they call a 'rhetorical' question—something they ask just to make a point, not expecting an answer. Here, the point was to demonstrate that I was an alien amongst them.

'What are you interviewing for? Peon?' the long-haired boy said and laughed.

I didn't know enough English back then to be offended. Also, I was in a hurry. 'You know where it is?' I said instead, looking at his group of friends. They all seemed to be the rich, English types. Another boy, short and fat, seemed to take pity on me and replied, 'Take a left at the corner of the main red building and you'll find a sign for the committee room.'

'Thank you,' I said. This I knew how to say in English.

'Can you read the sign in English?' the boy with the long hair said.

His friends told him to leave me alone. I followed the fat boy's instructions and ran towards the red building.

◆

I faced the first interview of my life. Three old men sat in front of me. They looked like they had not smiled since their hair had turned grey.

I had learnt about wishing people before an interview. I had even practised it. 'Good morning, sir.'

'There are a few of us here,' said the man in the middle. He seemed to be around fifty-five years old and wore square, black-rimmed glasses and a checked jacket.

'Good morning, sir, sir and sir,' I said.

They smiled. I didn't think it was a good smile. It was the high-class-to-low-class smile. The smile of superiority, the smile of delight that they knew English and I didn't.

Of course, I had no choice but to smile back.

The man in the middle was Professor Pereira, the head of sociology, the course I had applied for. Professor Fernandez, who taught physics, and Professor Gupta, whose subject was English, sat on his left and right respectively.

'Sports quota, eh?' Prof. Pereira said. 'Why isn't Yadav here?'

'I'm here, sir,' a voice called out from behind me. I turned around to see a man in a tracksuit standing at the door. He looked too old to be a student but too young to be faculty.

'This one is 85 per cent your decision,' Prof. Pereira said.

'No way, sir. You are the final authority.' He sat down next to the professors. Piyush Yadav was the sports coach for the college and sat in on all sports-quota interviews. He seemed simpler and friendlier than the professors. He didn't have a fancy accent either.

'Basketball?' Prof. Fernandez asked, scanning through my file.

'Yes, sir,' I said.

'What level?'

'State.'

'Do you speak in full sentences?' Prof. Gupta said in a firm voice. I didn't fully understand his question. I kept quiet.

'Do you?' he asked again.

'Yes, yes,' I said, my voice like a convict's.

'So…why do you want to study at St. Stephen's?'

A few seconds of silence followed. The four men in the room looked at me. The professor had asked me a standard question.

'I want good college,' I said, after constructing the sentence in my head.

Prof. Gupta smirked. 'That is some response. And why is St. Stephen's a good college?'

I switched to Hindi. Answering in English would require pauses and make me come across as stupid. Maybe I *was* stupid, but I did not want them to know that.

'Your college has a big name. It is famous in Bihar also,' I said.

'Can you please answer in English?' Prof. Gupta said.

'Why? You don't know Hindi?' I said in reflex, and in Hindi.

I saw my blunder in their horrified faces. I had not said it in defiance; I really wanted to know why they had to interview me in English when I was more comfortable in Hindi. Of course, I didn't know then that Stephen's professors didn't like being asked to speak in Hindi.

'Professor Pereira, how did this candidate get an interview?' Prof. Gupta said.

Prof. Pereira seemed to be the kindest of the lot. He turned to me. 'We prefer English as the medium of instruction in our college, that's all.'

Without English, I felt naked. I started thinking about my return trip to Bihar. I didn't belong here—these English-speaking monsters would eat me alive. I was wondering what would be the best way to take their leave when Piyush Yadav broke my chain of thought.

'Bihar se ho? Are you from Bihar?' he said.

The few words in Hindi felt like cold drops of rain on a scorching summer's day. I loved Piyush Yadav in that instant.

'Yes, sir. Dumraon.'

'I know. Three hours from Patna, right?' he said.

'You know Dumraon?' I said. I could have kissed his feet. The three English-speaking monsters continued to stare.

'I'm from Patna. Anyway, tell them about your achievements in basketball,' Piyush said.

I nodded. He sensed my nervousness and spoke again. 'Take your time. I am Hindi-medium, too. I know the feeling.'

The three professors looked at Piyush as if wondering how he had ever managed to get a job at the college.

I composed myself and spoke my rehearsed lines.

'Sir, I have played state-level basketball for six years. Last year, I was in the waiting list for the BFI national team.'

'BFI?' said Prof. Gupta.

'Basketball Federation of India,' Piyush answered for me, even though I knew the answer.

'And you want to do sociology. Why?' Prof. Fernandez said.

'It's an easy course. No need to study. Is that it?' Prof. Gupta remarked.

I didn't know whether Gupta had something against me, was generally grumpy or suffered from constipation.

'I am from rural area.'

'I am from *a* rural area,' Gupta said, emphasizing the 'a' as if omitting it was a criminal offence.

'Hindi, sir? Can I explain in Hindi?'

Nobody answered. I had little choice. I took my chances and responded in my language. 'My mother runs a school and works with the villagers. I wanted to learn more about our society. Why are our villages so backward? Why do we have so many differences based on caste and religion? I thought I could find some answers in this course.'

Prof. Gupta understood me perfectly well. However, he was what English-speaking people would call an 'uptight prick'. He asked Piyush to translate what I had said.

'That's a good reason,' Prof. Pereira said once Piyush was done. 'But now you are in Delhi. If you pass out of Stephen's, you will get jobs in big companies. Will you go back to your native place?' His concern seemed genuine.

It took me a few seconds to understand his question. Piyush offered to translate but I gestured for him not to.

'I will, sir,' I finally replied. I didn't give a reason. I didn't feel the need to tell them I would go back because my mother was alone there. I didn't say we were from the royal family of Dumraon. Even though there was nothing royal about us any more, we belonged there. And, of course, I didn't mention the fact that I couldn't stand any of the people I had met in this city so far.

'We'll ask you something about Bihar then?' Prof. Fernandez said.

'Sure.'

'What's the population of Bihar?'

'Ten crores.'

'Who runs the government in Bihar?'

'Right now it's Lalu Prasad's party.'

'And which party is that?'

'RJD—Rashtriya Janata Dal.'

The questions kept coming, and after a while I couldn't keep track of who was asking what. While I understood their English, I couldn't answer in complete sentences. Hence, I gave the shortest answers possible. But one question had me stumped.

'Why is Bihar so backward?' Prof. Gupta said.

I didn't know the answer, forget saying it in English. Piyush tried to speak on my behalf. 'Sir, that's a question nobody can really answer.'

But Prof. Gupta raised a hand. 'You said your mother runs a rural school. You should know Bihar.'

I kept quiet.

'It's okay. Answer in Hindi,' Prof. Pereira said.

'Backward compared to what, sir?' I said in Hindi, looking at Prof. Gupta.

'Compared to the rest of India.'

'India is pretty backward,' I said. 'One of the poorest nations in the world.'

'Sure. But why is Bihar the poorest of the poor?'

'Bad government,' Piyush said, almost as a reflex. Prof. Gupta kept his eyes on me.

'It's mostly rural, sir,' I said. 'People don't have any exposure to modernity and hold on to backward values. There's poor education. Nobody invests in my state. The government is in bed with criminals and together they exploit the state and its people.'

Prof. Pereira translated my answer for Prof. Gupta. He nodded as he heard it. 'Your answers are sensible, but your English is terrible,' he said.

'Would you rather take a sensible student, or someone who speaks a foreign language well?'

My defiance stumped them all. Prof. Fernandez wiped his glasses as he spoke, turning his head towards me. 'English is no longer a foreign language, Mr Jha. It's a global language. I suggest you learn it.'

'That's why I'm here, sir,' I said.

My answers came from the heart but I didn't know if they had any effect on the professors. The interview was over. They asked me to leave the room.

♦

I stood in the corridor, figuring out where to go next. Piyush came out of the committee room. His lean and fit frame made him look like a student, despite him being much older. He spoke to me in Hindi.

'Your sports trial is in one hour. See me on the basketball court.'

'Sir, is there even a point? That interview went horribly.'

'You couldn't learn some English, along with basketball?'

'Nobody speaks it in our area.' I paused and added, 'Sir.'

He patted my back. 'Get out of Bihar mode, son. Anyway, sports quota trials are worth 85 per cent. Play well.'

'I'll do my best, sir.'

2

If she weren't tall I wouldn't have noticed her. It is funny how her height shaped my life.

If she had been four inches shorter, my eyes may never have met hers and everything would have been different. If I had not been bored and arrived at the basketball court an hour earlier, it would have been different. If someone had not missed a pass and the ball had not come out of the court and hit me on the head, I would have had a different life. Tiny bumps in time shape our lives, even though we spend hours trying to make long-term plans. I had no plan to meet the love of my life on a basketball court. I was there only to kill time and because I had nowhere else to go.

A small crowd of students, mostly men, had gathered around the Stephen's basketball court. Girls' sports trials always garnered an audience—there was no better excuse to check them out. Everyone spoke in English. I didn't speak at all. I straightened my back and stared at the court with a sense of purpose, mainly to come across as if I belonged there. As ten girls came on to the court, the crowd cheered. Five of the girls belonged to the existing college team; the other five had applied for admission under the sports quota.

Piyush came to the centre of the court, ball in hand and whistle in mouth. As he blew it, the girls sprang into action.

Five feet, nine inches is tall for an Indian girl. It is tall even for a girl in a basketball team. Her long neck, long arms and long legs held every guy's attention. She was a part of the sports-quota applicants' team. She wore black fitted shorts and a sleeveless sports vest with 'R' printed in yellow at the back. She collected the ball within seconds. She wore expensive Nike ankle-length sneakers, the kind I had seen NBA players wear on TV. Her diamond earrings twinkled in the sun. She dribbled the ball with her right hand. I noticed she had long, beautiful fingers.

'Ten points for looks, coach,' a senior student called out as R passed the ball. The crowd tittered. Well, the men did. The wisecrack distracted R for a moment, but she resumed her game as if she was used to such comments.

The sports-quota girls played well individually. However, they didn't play well as a team.

R dribbled the ball and reached the opposition's basket. Three opponents surrounded her. R passed the ball to her teammate, who missed the pass.

'What the...' R screamed. Too late. The rival team took the ball, passed it to the other end and scored a basket.

R cursed herself, inaudible to anyone else. She then signalled to three of her teammates to cover specific opponents and jogged across the court. When she went past me, I saw her sweaty, flushed face from up close. We made eye contact for nanoseconds, perhaps only in my imagination. But in those nanoseconds something happened to my heart.

No, I wouldn't say I fell in love with her. I wouldn't even say I felt attracted to her. But I felt something deep inside, strong enough for my heart to say, *You have to talk to this girl at least once in your life.*

'Babes, cover her. I said *cover!*' R screamed. Her state of mind was as far from mine as possible. She passed the ball to her teammate, who missed scoring a basket again.

'What are you guys doing?' she shouted in perfect English. I felt nervous; how would I ever speak to her? Her face was grimy, dust sticking to her left cheek and forehead. Yet, it was one of the most beautiful faces I had seen in my entire life. Sometimes it is hard to explain why you find a person beautiful. Was it her narrow face, perfectly in line with her slender body? Was it her flawless skin and complexion, which had turned from cream to pink to red? Or was it not about her looks at all? Was it her passion, her being totally immersed in the game? I didn't know.

Of course, I never actually thought it would lead to anything. She seemed too posh to even give me a second glance.

Destiny, however, had other plans. For why else, in the seventh minute of the first half, would the college team captain overthrow the ball outside the court, where it hit my head as I stood on the sidelines? Why would I grab the ball in reflex? More than anything, why would R come to collect it?

'Ball, please,' she said, panting. I felt paralysed.

'I said ball, please,' she said. I held on to the ball for an extra half second. I wanted to look at her a bit longer. I wanted to take a snapshot of her sweaty face and store it in my mind's camera for life.

I threw the ball at her. She caught it with ease and looked at me. She could tell from my throw that I knew the game.

'Change your point shooter,' I said. For some reason, I had managed to speak in correct English this time.

'What?' she said. She surveyed me from top to bottom. I now wished I had worn better clothes. I had not changed out of my interview shirt and pants, both of which the tailor back home had stitched too loose for me. I looked out of place on the basketball court. With my folder of certificates, I resembled a hero from those Hindi films of the seventies—the one who could not find a job. *I have a Bihar state team T-shirt*, I wanted to tell her. Of course, in the middle of a game, and as a first conversation, this was a terrible idea.

'Your shooter is useless,' I said.

The referee whistled to commence the game. She turned away and forgot about me faster than her throw reached her team member. 'Here, pass it to me,' R shouted as she reached the opposition basket.

Her point shooter held the ball and looked around, confused.

'I said *here*,' R screamed so loudly that pigeons flew off the trees in the lawns. The point shooter passed the ball, R caught it and took a shot from well beyond the three-point line.

Whoosh! The ball went through the basket. The crowd cheered. They already had a soft spot for R anyway.

The referee announced a break at the ten-minute mark. The college team led 12-5. R huddled with her team, figuring out their strategy for the next half. As her team meeting ended, she wiped her face and neck with a towel.

I couldn't take my eyes off her. I forgot I had my own trial in less than an hour. I only wanted to figure out a way to talk to her a bit more. Maybe I could tell her she played well. I wondered how to tell her about my state-level game without coming across as a show-off. And, more than anything, how would I go beyond five words of English?

She caught me staring. I wanted to kill myself. She continued to look directly at me, the towel still around her neck. Then she walked up to me. A shiver ran down my spine.

I didn't mean to stare, I wanted to tell her. I wondered if she would scream at me like she had done during the match.

'Thanks,' R said.

She had walked across the court to thank me?

She was breathing hard. My eyes were glued to hers.

Look away, Madhav, I scolded myself and turned away.

'That was a good tip,' she said to my left profile.

'Welcome... You...are...good,' I said. Uttering each word was like lifting a brick.

'Any other suggestions for the second half? We're losing.'

'Yes,' I said, turning to face her again. I wanted to give her more tips, but couldn't in English. 'You speak Hindi?' I said.

She looked baffled. Nobody in St. Stephen's had ever asked anyone that question.

'Well, yeah, of course,' she said.

'Okay,' I said, and explained in my language, 'they have two strong players. Cover them tight. Don't fix formations for your players. Two of yours should move with them. You become the shooter. Of the other two, one is your defence, the other supports you.'

The whistle blew again.

'Got to go,' she said. 'Catch you later.'

I didn't understand what 'catch you' meant. Did it mean she would catch what I had said later? Did it mean she didn't understand what I had said? Or did she mean she actually wanted to catch me? Like, she liked me so much she wanted to catch me? Of course, this seemed unlikely. But then I *had* given her good tips and you never know with these modern people. You see, my mind has this overdrive switch, especially when it's excited. It starts to get ahead of itself and thinks useless thoughts when I could actually be doing something constructive, like watching the game or finding out that girl's name.

The game restarted. The referee's whistle, the sound of the players' shoes as they run across the court, the shrieks, the yells and the cries of victory and defeat—few things in life match the excitement of a sports court. Basketball, underrated as it might be in this country, packs it all in half an hour. I cannot understand why Indians don't play this game more. It doesn't take up too much space, doesn't need much equipment and a big group can play it all at once.

'Yes!' she screamed as she scored a basket. The ball went in without touching the ring, making the most beautiful sound in a basketball game—the soft '*chhaak*' when only the net touches the ball. Sweat dripped off her face as she ran back to her side of the court.

The match ended 21–15. The newbies had lost, but still kept pace with the college team—a considerable achievement. R, however, seemed disappointed. She wiped her face with a towel and picked up her blue Nike kitbag. A few boys tried to make eye contact with her but she ignored them. I wanted to speak to her. However, no boy from Dumraon has ever had the guts to approach a high-class girl from Delhi. I wanted her to watch my game. There was nothing else I could impress her with. Coach Piyush went up to her. They became engrossed in a conversation. This was my chance. Underconfident guys need a go-between to speak to a girl. I ran up to Piyush.

'My trial now. I change, sir?' I said to him.

Piyush turned to me, surprised, I don't know whether at my English or my stupid question or both.

'Aise kheliyega? Trial-va hai ya mazaak?' he said in Bhojpuri, not even Hindi. He meant: will you play like this? Is it a trial or a joke?

I regretted knowing him.

'I…I…'

Then R interrupted. 'Oh, you are also sports quota?'

Piyush looked at both of us, surprised at the familiarity.

'Yes,' I said, one of the few English responses I could give with confidence.

'State-level player. Watch this Bihari's game and go,' Piyush said and guffawed before he left.

I could have taken offence. He had used the word 'Bihari' as if to say 'Watch, even this poor little Bihari can play', despite being a Bihari himself. However, he had helped me without knowing it, so I was grateful. She looked at me and smiled.

'No wonder you gave those tips,' she said. 'State level, my God.'

'What is your good name?' I blurted out, without any context or sense of timing. Also, who on earth says 'good name' these days? Only losers like me who translate 'shubh naam' in Hindi to English.

'Good or bad, only one name. Riya,' she said and smiled.

Riya. I loved her short little name. Or maybe when you start liking people, you start liking everything about them—from their sweaty eyebrows to their little names.

'Your name?' she said. For the first time in my life a girl had asked my name.

'Myself Madhav Jha.'

That was my reflexive response. It was only later that I learnt that people who construct sentences like that sound low class. You see, we think in Hindi first and simply translate our thoughts, word for word.

'From Bihar,' she said and laughed. 'Right?'

She didn't laugh because I was a Bihari. She laughed because Piyush had already revealed that fact about me. There was no judgement in her voice. I liked her more and more every second.

'Yes. You?'

'From Delhi itself.'

I wanted to continue talking to her. I wanted to know her full name and her native place. That is how we introduce ourselves in Dumraon. However, I didn't know how to ask her in English, the language one needed to impress girls. Plus, I had a selection trial in a few minutes.

The coach blew his whistle.

'I have my trials now, will you watch?' I said.

'Okay,' she said.

I ran—rather, hopped—in excitement towards the changing room. Soon, I was back on court and Piyush started the game.

I played well. I don't want to brag but I played better than any player on the college team.

'Basket,' I shouted as I scored my fifth shot. As the crowd clapped, I looked around. She was sitting on one of the benches, sipping water from a bottle. She clapped too.

I had a good game, but her presence made me play even better.

The score inched forward; I pushed myself harder and scored a few more baskets. When I took a tough shot, the seniors patted my back. Piyush blew the final whistle. Final score: 25–28. We had done it. The newbies had managed to defeat the St. Stephen's team.

My body was drenched in sweat. I felt drained and exhausted. Players patted my back as I struggled to catch my breath. Piyush came running up to me in the middle of the court.

'You scored 17 out of 28. Well done, Bihari,' he said. He ruffled my sweaty hair. I walked out of the court deliberately towards Riya.

'Wow, you really are good,' she said.

'Thanks,' I said, still panting after the game.

'Anyway, I have to go,' she said and extended her hand. 'Nice meeting you. Bye.'

'Bye,' I said, my heart sinking. My head had known it would end like this. My heart didn't want it to end.

'Unless we are both lucky,' she added and grinned. 'And the higher powers here admit us.'

'Who knows,' I said.

'Yeah. But if they do, then see you. Else, bye.'

She walked away. I realized I didn't even know her full name. As she became more distant with every step, I wanted nothing more than to get admission to St. Stephen's.

I walked up to Piyush.

'You cracked it. On fire on the court, huh?' he said.

'Sir, but the interview… My English—'

'Sucked,' he said.

Disappointment slammed into me. His expression suggested 'sucked' meant something nasty.

'But you play bloody good basketball,' Piyush continued. He patted my back and walked away.

I stood alone in the middle of the basketball court. Everyone else had left. I saw the brick-coloured buildings and the greenery around me.

Is this place in my destiny? I wondered. Well, it wasn't just about my destiny. It was *our* destiny.

That is why, one month later, a postman came to my doorstep in Dumraon with a letter from St. Stephen's College. He also wanted a big tip.

3

'Hey,' she said. Her perky voice startled me; I had been scanning the college noticeboard.

I turned around. I had prayed for this to happen. She and I had both made it.

She wore black, skin-tight jeans and a black-and-white striped T-shirt. Without the sweat and grime from court, her face glowed. She had translucent pink lip gloss on, with tiny glittery bits on her lips. Her hair, slightly wavy, came all the way down to her waist. Her long fingers looked delicate, hiding the power they had displayed on court. My heart was in my mouth. Ever since I had got my admission letter, I had been waiting for the month before college opened to pass quickly and to find out if Riya had made it too.

'Riya,' she said. 'You remember, right?'

Did I remember? I wanted to tell her I had not forgotten her for one moment since I left Delhi. I wanted to tell her I had never seen a girl more beautiful than her. I wanted to tell her that the oxygen flow to my lungs had stopped.

'Of course,' I said. 'Glad you joined.'

'I wasn't sure, actually,' she said and pointed to the noticeboard. 'Is that the first-year timetable?'

I nodded. She smiled at me again.

'What's your course?' she asked, her eyes on the noticeboard.

'Sociology,' I said.

'Oh, intellectual,' she said.

I didn't know what that meant. However, she laughed and I guessed it was something funny, so I laughed along. The noticeboard also had a bunch of stapled sheets with the names of all first-year students and their new roll numbers.

'What about you?' I said. I adjusted my yellow T-shirt and blue jeans while she looked at the board. I had bought new clothes from Patna for St. Stephen's. I didn't look like a government office clerk anymore. I wanted to fit into my new college.

'English,' she said. 'Here, see, that's my name.' Riya Somani, English

(Hons), it said. My heart sank. A girl doing an English degree would never befriend a country bumpkin like me.

Her phone rang. She took out the sleek Nokia instrument from her jeans' pocket.

'Hi, Mom,' she said in Hindi. 'Yes, I reached. Yes, all good, just finding my way.'

Her Hindi was music to my ears. So I *could* talk to her. She spoke for a minute more and hung up to find me looking at her.

'Moms, you know,' she said.

'Yes. You speak Hindi?'

She laughed. 'You keep asking me that. Of course I do. Why?'

'My English isn't good,' I said, and switched languages. 'Can I talk to you in Hindi?'

'What you say matters, not the language,' she said and smiled.

Some say there is an exact moment when you fall in love. I didn't know if it was true before, but I do now. This was it. When Riya Somani said that line, the world turned in slow motion. I noticed her delicate eyebrows. When she spoke, they moved slightly. They had the perfect length, thickness and width. She would win a 'best eyebrows' competition hands down—or as we say in basketball, it would be a slam dunk.

Perhaps I should have waited to fall in love with her. However, I knew it was pointless. I had little control over my feelings. So from my first day in college, I was in love. Riya Somani, ace basketball player, English literature student, most beautiful girl on the planet, owner of extraordinary eyebrows and speaker of wonderful lines, had yanked my heart out of its hiding place.

Of course, I could not show it. I didn't have the courage, nor would it be a smart idea.

We walked down a corridor towards our respective classrooms. I had her with me for two more minutes.

'You made friends here?' she said.

'Not really,' I said. 'You?'

'I have some classmates from school in Stephen's. Plus, I am from Delhi, so have many friends outside.'

'I hope I can adjust,' I said. 'I feel I don't belong here.'

'Trust me, nobody feels they do,' she said. 'Which residence did they give you?'

'Rudra,' I said. 'How about you?'

'They don't give one to Delhiites. I'm a day-ski, unfortunately,' she said, using the common term for day scholars.

We reached my classroom. I pretended not to see it and kept walking until she reached hers.

'Oh, this is my class,' she said. 'Where's yours?'

'I'll find out, go ahead,' I said.

She smiled and waved goodbye. I wanted to ask her out for coffee, but couldn't. I could shoot a basket from half-court three times in a row but I could not ask a girl to come to the college cafeteria with me.

'Basketball,' I blurted out.

'What?'

'Want to play sometime?' I recovered quickly.

'With you? You'll kick my ass,' she said and laughed. I didn't know why she felt I would kick her rear end or why she found the phrase funny. I joined her in the laughter anyway.

'You play well,' I said as we stood at her classroom door.

'Okay, maybe after a few days, once we settle into classes,' she said. She walked in for her first English lecture. The joy at the possibility of meeting her again made me forget I had a class. I wanted to dance in the garden.

The bell for the first period rang. 'This isn't sociology, right?' I asked a clueless English student as he arrived late for his own class.

◆

'You are good. Really good,' she said as she wiped her face with a towel.

We had played a half-court game; I defeated her 20–9.

'I'm hopeless,' she said. She took a sip from her water bottle. She wore a fitted sleeveless white top and purple shorts.

'You're fine. Just out of practice,' I said.

She finished the water and shook the empty bottle. 'I'm still thirsty,' she said.

'Café?' I said.

She looked at me, somewhat surprised. I kept a straight face.

'You get good juice there,' I said in an innocent tone.

◆

A swarm of students buzzed inside the cafeteria. Given that it was lunch hour, it took us five minutes to get a table. They didn't have juice, so Riya settled for lemonade. I ordered a mince and cold coffee. I realized both of us had a problem initiating conversation. I couldn't talk because I didn't have the confidence. She, given a choice, preferred to be quiet. Silent Riya, I wanted to call her. I had to break this deadlock if I wanted this to go anywhere. The waiter brought us our food.

'In Bihar, we have aloo chop, in which we sometimes stuff keema. This mince is the same,' I said.

'What's Bihar like? I've never been there,' she said and pursed her lips around the straw to sip her lemonade.

'Not like Delhi. Simple. Lots of rice fields. Peaceful, apart from cities like Patna.'

'I like peaceful places,' she said.

'There are problems, too. People aren't educated. There's violence. I am sure you've heard. Poor and backward state, as people say.'

'You can be rich and backward, too.'

We had an awkward silence for two minutes. Silent Riya and Scared Madhav.

Break the deadlock, I told myself.

'So you live with your family in Delhi?'

'Yes. A big one. Parents, uncles, cousins and a brother.'

'What do your parents do?' I said.

A boy should make more interesting conversation with a girl. But a loser like me had little experience or finesse in this regard.

'Family business. Real estate and infrastructure.'

'You are rich, right?' I said. *Idiot Madhav. Couldn't think of anything better.*

She laughed at my direct question. 'Rich in money, or rich in mind? Two different things.'

'Huh? Rich, like wealthy?'

'Unfortunately, yes.'

'What's unfortunate? Everyone wants to be rich.'

'Yeah, I guess. It just embarrasses me. Plus, all the obsession with money and how it defines you, I just don't get it.'

I realized she and I came from different worlds. Perhaps it was a futile battle to pursue her. Logically, practically and rationally, it made no sense.

'Can I try your mince?' she said. 'I'm hungry.'

I nodded. I asked the waiter to get another fork. However, before he could get one she picked up mine and took a bite.

She took my fork, does it mean anything?

'Where's home for you?' she said.

'Dumraon. A small town, three hours from Patna.'

'Nice,' she said.

'You will probably find it boring.'

'No, no, tell me more. As you can see, I'm not much of a talker. I like to listen,' she said. She seemed genuinely interested. I told her about my life back home, revolving around my mother, her school and basketball. There wasn't much else. My father had passed away ten years ago. He had left us a huge, crumbling haveli, a couple of fields and many legal cases related to property. We had some servants, who stayed in the haveli's servant quarters more out of loyalty than their paltry salaries.

My ancestors were landlords and from the royal family of Dumraon, the oldest princely state in British India. When India became independent, the government took away our family estate and left us with an annual pension that declined with every generation. My great-grand-uncles squandered their money, especially since they all felt they could gamble better than anyone else in the world. Several near-bankruptcies later, the women of the house took charge as the men had all turned into alcoholics. Somehow, the women saved the family pride and the haveli. All of my cousins had moved abroad, and vowed never to return. My father, the only one to remain in Bihar, held the last title of Raja Sahib of Dumraon. Ten years ago, he had succumbed to a cardiac arrest. My mother, Rani Sahiba Durga Jha, was the only strong-willed person left in the family. She brought me up and maintained the few farms left. She also ran the Dumraon Royal School, which taught seven hundred kids from nearby villages.

The noise of air bubbles as Riya sucked up the last of her lemonade made me realize I had spoken non-stop for ten minutes.

'I'm boring you,' I said. I vowed to stay quiet for a few minutes. It had to be Silent Riya's turn now.

'Not at all.'

I smiled. 'Now you speak. If you let me talk, I won't stop.'

'Okay, but wait. Technically you're a prince, aren't you? Or are you the king, Raja Sahib?'

I laughed. 'There are no kings and princes anymore. Only uneducated villagers talk like that.'

'But they do, right? Seriously, am I talking to a prince? Do they address you as Prince?' She widened her eyes. Her award-winning eyebrows moved up and down a little.

'Sometimes they do. Listen, it's not important. We're not rich or anything.'

'You live in a palace?'

'Haveli. It's like, well, a small palace. Anyway, I'm no prince. I'm a Bihari boy trying to graduate. Do I look like a prince from any angle?'

'C'mon, you are tall and handsome. You could be one, if you had some jewellery,' she said. She had said it in jest, but it was the first real compliment she had paid me. Little cupcakes of happiness exploded inside me.

'Did I, a commoner, just play basketball with the Raja Sahib of Dumraon?' she said and burst into laughter.

'I shouldn't have told you.' I shook my head.

'C'mon,' she said and tapped my wrist. My arm went all warm and tingly.

'What about you? Which eighteen-year-old girl comes to college in a BMW and calls herself a commoner?'

'Oh, you noticed. That's my dad's car.'

'You must be so rich.'

'My family is. Not me.'

As she spoke, three girls arrived at our table. 'We've been looking for you everywhere,' one of them said.

'Hey, girls,' Riya said. 'Come, sit with us. Madhav, meet Garima, Ayesha and Rachita, friends from my class. Girls, this is Madhav, my basketball friend.'

I realized my place in her life. *Basketball friend.* Perhaps she had friends for specific purposes.

The girls looked me up and down, down and up, checking me out. 'Not bad, Riya,' Garima said and winked at her. The girls burst out laughing and sat down with us.

'Are you in the college team?' Rachita asked me. She wore a red-and-black bandana on her head.

I nodded, nervous at their bold familiarity.

'Madhav has played state level,' Riya said and looked at me proudly.

'Wow,' the girls said in unison.

'Would you like to order anything?' I said.

The three girls froze and then began to laugh. It dawned on me that they were laughing at me. My English had sounded like this: 'Vood you laik to aarder anything?' I didn't know this was such a cardinal sin.

'What happened?' I said.

'Not a thing,' Garima said and stood up. 'Thanks, Madhav, we just ate lunch. Hey, Riya, let's catch up later, yeah?'

The three girls left. We waved goodbyes.

'What happened, Riya?' I said.

'They're ditzy. Forget them,' she said.

'Ditzy?'

'Silly and stupid. Anyway, I better leave too. My driver should be here.'

We walked out of the cafeteria to the main gate. Her dark blue BMW waited outside.

'So I'm your basketball friend?' I said as we reached the car.

'Well, that, and my lemonade-and-mince friend.'

'How about tea friend?'

'Sure.' She stepped inside the car and sat down. She rolled down the window to say goodbye.

'Or a movie friend?'

'Hmm.'

'What?'

'Need to think about it.'

'Think about what?'

'Will the royal highness condemn me to death if I say no?'

I laughed. 'I might.'

'See you later, Prince,' she said. The car drove off.

I didn't know if I was a real prince or not, but I had found my princess.

4

Three months later

'Did you just put your hand on mine?' she whispered, but loud enough for people around us in the movie theatre to look our way.

'Accidentally,' I said.

'Learning big English words, are we?' she said.

'I'm trying.'

'Mr Madhav Jha, you have come to see a movie. Focus on that.'

'I'm trying,' I said again. I turned my attention back to Shah Rukh Khan. He had rejoined college and was singing 'Main hoon na' to anyone in need of reassurance.

We had come to the Odeon Cinema in Connaught Place. Riya had finally agreed to see a movie with me. She had lost a basketball bet—she had challenged me to score a basket from half-court in one try.

'Now that will be a super shot,' she had said.

'What do I get? A movie treat?'

'You can't do it.'

I had given it a try and failed the first week. Half-court shots are tough. I couldn't do it in the next two weeks either.

'See, even destiny doesn't want us to go out,' she had said.

In the fourth week, I put in all the focus I had and made my shot. The ball hit the ring, circled around it twice and fell into the basket.

'Yes,' I screamed.

Even though she had lost the bet, she clapped.

'So, do I get a date?' I said.

'It's not a date. We just go for a movie. Like friends.'

'Isn't that what high-class people call a date?'

'No.'

'What's a date then?'

'You want to see the movie with me or not?' she had said, her hands on her hips.

The hands-on-hips pose meant no further questions. In the three months I had known her, I knew she hated being pushed. I thought maybe that was how rich people were—somewhat private. We overdid the familiarity in our villages anyway.

Now, as Shah Rukh Khan continued his song, I wondered what I meant to her. We met in college every day, and ended up having tea at least three times a week. I did most of the talking. I would tell her stories from the residences, or 'rez', as the students called them—the fancy word for hostels in Stephen's. I was in Rudra-North, and told her tales of messy rooms, late-night carrom matches and the respect we needed to show seniors. She listened intently, even smiled sometimes. When I asked her about her home, she didn't say much. Back in Dumraon it is unthinkable for friends to not share every detail about themselves. High-class people have this concept called *space*, which means you cannot ask them questions or give them opinions about certain aspects of their life.

Am I special to her? I kept asking myself. Sometimes I saw her chatting with other guys and felt insanely jealous. My insistence on seeing a movie together was to find out what Riya Somani really thought of Madhav Jha. I had held her hand to figure out where I stood. Given her reaction, nowhere.

In fact, she removed her arm from the armrest for the rest of the movie. She seemed upset, even though she never said a word. She kept watching the film.

◆

'Is everything okay?' I said. She sipped her drink in silence. We had walked from Odeon to Keventers, famous for its milkshakes sold in glass bottles.

'Uh huh,' she said, indicating a yes. I hated this response of hers.

We had finished two-thirds of our milkshakes without talking to each other. She looked straight ahead, lost in thought. I felt she would cry if poked.

'I'm sorry.'

'What?' she said, surprised.

'About placing my hand on yours,' I said. I didn't want my stupid move to backfire.

'When?'

'During the movie. You know, I…'

'I don't even remember that,' she said, interrupting me.

'Oh,' I said, and felt a wave of relief run through me. 'Then why do you look upset?'

'Never mind,' she said. Silent Riya's typical response. She brushed aside strands of hair from her face.

'Why don't you ever tell me anything?' I said, my voice a mixture of plea and protest.

She finished her milkshake and placed the empty bottle on a table. 'Ready to go?' she said instead.

'Riya, we never talk about you. Am I only good enough to play basketball with?'

'What?'

'We meet, play, eat and talk. But you never share anything important with me.'

'I don't share much about my life with anyone, Madhav.'

'Am I just anyone?'

A waiter arrived to collect the empty bottles. She spoke only after he left. 'You are a friend.'

'So?'

'So what? I have many friends. I don't share stuff with them.'

'Am I just like every other friend of yours? Is there nothing special about me?'

She smiled. 'Well, you do play basketball better than anyone else.'

I stood up. I didn't find her funny.

'Hey, wait.' Riya pulled me down again.

I sat down with a stern expression.

'Why do you want to know about my life?' she said.

'It matters to me. Unlike your other friends, I can tell if something is bothering you. And, if something is bothering you, it bothers me. I want to know things about you, okay? But getting you to talk is like a dentist pulling teeth.'

She laughed and interrupted my rant.

'I have a fucked-up family. What do you want to know?' she said.

I looked at her, puzzled and astonished at her choice of words.

More than anything, I could not associate any family with a BMW to be fucked up.

Her eyes met mine, perhaps for a final check to see if I deserved her trust. 'Let's go for a walk,' she said.

◆

Her plush car dropped us off at India Gate. The soft evening sun cast long shadows of the monument and of us on the red sandstone pavement. We walked the mile-long distance all the way up to Rashtrapati Bhavan. On these roads, far away from Bihar, India did not come across as a poor country. Pigeons flocked the sky and government babus from nearby offices scurried about, both trying to reach home before it got dark.

We walked together. At least our shadows appeared to hold hands.

'I don't open up to people. At most I keep a journal, and even that is rare. You know I'm a quiet person,' Riya said.

'I understand.'

'Thanks. The problem is my family. They're obsessed with money. I'm not.'

'That's a good thing, right?'

'I don't know. Also, I don't matter. My brothers do, because they will take over the business one day. I'm supposed to shut up, get married and leave. The high point of my life is to have kids and shop.'

'And that's not what you want to do?'

'No!' she almost shouted. 'You know me better than that. Don't you?'

'Sorry.'

'Sucks being a girl in this country, I tell you. Sucks.'

'You seem upset. Did something happen today?'

'I told them I want to study music after college. They want me to marry into some rich Marwari family and live like a queen. I don't want to live like a queen. That is not what I dream of.'

'Trust me, kings and queens are overrated,' I said.

She remained silent.

'What do you want, Riya? Do you have a dream?'

'Well, dreams suck. You get attached to them and they don't come true.'

'Sometimes they do.'

'Not in my case.'

'What is your dream?' I asked again.

She looked at me. 'You'll laugh.'

'Try me.'

She smiled. 'Okay, so, I have this dream. I want to play music and sing...in a bar in New York.'

'Wow.'

'What? You think it's stupid, right?'

'No. That's quite specific. Singing in a bar in New York.'

'Yes. That's it. I don't want to be a famous singer or a rock star. I don't want to marry a billionaire. I just want to sing in peace, surrounded by passionate people. I want to own a house in Manhattan, *my* house, filled with books and music CDs. I want to play basketball on weekends. I don't want to check out a dozen lehengas for my engagement.'

'Sounds like you have it all figured out.'

'Not really. Maybe it's just an escapist fantasy. But I have had it since I was twelve. We had gone to New York. The city blew me away. I saw people who loved what they did. They weren't rich, but happy. And there was this lady in a bar...she sang from her heart, unaware of everything around her.'

The sun was setting, and the sky turned from orange to dark grey. We had now reached the point near Rashtrapati Bhavan where Delhi Police guards tell you to stop and turn around. She continued to tell me about her New York trip.

'In fact, I took up basketball because I saw an NBA game live at Madison Square Garden in New York.'

'You've seen an NBA game live?' I said.

'Yeah. The atmosphere...it's electric. You should see one sometime, Madhav.'

I shrugged. 'Anyway, I like your dream, Riya,' I said. 'It's doable, not unreal.'

'Unreal, like?' she said.

'Like becoming a top actress or the prime minister. You just want something simple.'

She smiled. 'Nothing is simple for a girl in a family like mine,' she said.

We walked in silence for a few minutes.

'I feel better,' she said after a while.

'What?'

She looked at me. The last of the daylight tinted her face orange, making her look ethereal. I wanted to give her a hug.

'I feel better after talking to you. Thanks,' she smiled.

The sun vanished and the road became dark. Her skin glowed in the amber lights of Rajpath. I took a chance and held her hand.

'Another accident?' she said, but did not pull her hand away.

We laughed together. She spoke again. 'Even my uncles are the same. Everyone sides with my parents.'

She continued to talk and I continued to listen, even though my entire attention was on how lovely her hand felt in mine.

5

After our movie date, we started to spend even more time together. During lunch break, we would sit on the college lawns and eat home-cooked food from her house. She brought an elaborate Marwari thali in a three-tiered tiffin box.

'How's the food in the rez?' she said.

'Not as good as the Somani Café,' I said.

We sat facing the red-brick college building. The winter sun warmed us as well as her cold tiffin box. I ate three of her four chapatis, and most of the paalak-daal along with it. She never touched the sweet churma. I ate it with a plastic spoon.

'How's your room?' she said.

'Like any other rez room. Basic. Books, basketballs and bed linen.'

'Do you keep it clean?'

I shook my head and grinned.

'What? You don't clean it regularly?'

'Once a week.'

'Awful.'

'I don't have six servants like you do, Miss Riya.'

'I want to see your room.'

'You can't,' I said. 'Girls are not allowed.'

'I know. Just kidding,' she laughed.

'How's your family?' I said.

'Same. My brothers, male cousins and uncles are busy planning how to increase their wealth. The women are gushing over their last shopping trip or figuring out which marriage to attend next.'

'Good, everything is normal then,' I said.

'I bought a guitar,' she said.

'Nice.'

'Yeah, I barely talk to anyone at home. Me and my guitar, we're happy.'

'You talk to me,' I said.

'Even though you eat all my lunch,' she said and smacked the side of my head.

'Do you like me?' I said. She had heard this too many times.

'Not again, Madhav, please.'

She lay down on the grass. She wore a white-and-maroon salwar-kameez and a black cashmere cardigan, which she had removed and placed on the grass next to her.

She scrunched her eyes to avoid the sun. I shifted and sat in front of her, so my shadow would cover her face.

'Ah, that's nice. Tall shady tree, thank you.'

'People in college talk about us. How we are always together,' I said.

'So? Let them. As long as we know there is nothing between us.'

I tilted my body sideways in protest. The sun was back on her face.

'What?' she said and covered her eyes with her hand. 'Where did my tree go?'

'The tree is not feeling appreciated.'

'What do you mean?'

'Why is there nothing between us?' I said, my upper body still bent to the side.

'Should there be? First, can you sit like you were sitting before, so people don't think you are weird and my delicate skin can be protected from the sun?'

I sat up straight once again.

'Better,' she said. 'I need a pillow. Move forward please, tree.'

She put her head in my lap.

'Nice. Now, what do you want, pillow-tree?'

I'd had many such arguments with her over the past month. She had become an expert at dodging the issue, always getting away with some nonsense, like now.

'Give me your cardigan,' I said.

'Why? Are you cold? It's a girl's sweater, pillow-tree,' she said and giggled.

I placed the sweater over my head. It hid my face.

'What?' she said.

I said nothing.

'Are you sulking, my tall tree?' she said.

I didn't respond. She pulled the sweater towards her so that both our faces came under it.

'Yes? Sulky man, what's the issue?' she said, her face upside-down and huge, given that it was so close to mine.

I did not respond. She blew on my face but I did not react.

'Everyone here must be finding this so creepy,' she said, 'our faces under the sweater.'

'Nobody cares,' I said.

'I thought you said everyone talks about us.'

I let out a grunt of protest. She laughed. I took aim and bent. In a second I managed to place my lips on hers, despite her face being upside-down. Spiderman kisses like that. It isn't easy. I wouldn't advise it if you're kissing someone for the first time.

She sprang up. As she rose, her forehead hit my chin. I bit my tongue.

'Hey,' she said, 'not fair.'

I held my mouth in pain. Her forehead had hurt me badly. Still, the pain paled in comparison to the joy I felt from landing my first kiss.

'Are you hurt?' she said.

I made a face.

'Listen, I'm sorry. But what was that?' she said.

'A kiss.'

'I know. What for?'

'I felt like it.'

She stood up, collected her tiffin box and walked away. I ran behind her. She ignored me and walked faster.

I held her arm. She stopped and glared at me until I let go. She started to walk away again.

'I am sorry, okay?' I said and blocked her way. 'I thought you like me.'

'Madhav, please understand, I'm not comfortable with all this.'

'I really like you, Riya. You mean so much to me. You are the reason I've survived in this place.'

'So appreciate what we have. Don't spoil it.'

'What do we have? What am I to you?'

'If we kiss, we have something; if we don't, then nothing?' she said. I kept quiet.

She looked at me for a few seconds. She shook her head in disappointment, turned and walked off. I saw her reach the main gate and get inside her blue car.

Only then did I realize I still held her cardigan in my hand.

◆

I didn't know if she would come to play basketball with me after the cardigan incident. To my surprise, she did, all svelte in a new Nike top and white shorts. We played without much conversation. Usually, we would stop to chat every five minutes. Today, she focused on the ball like a soldier does in combat with an enemy.

'I am sorry, okay?' I said. Playing with her wasn't as much fun as before.

'It's fine,' she said. 'Let's not talk about it again.'

I put on a sorry face for the next twenty minutes. Finally, I held my ears and stood in the centre of the court.

It did the trick. She smiled.

'Sorry, I also overreacted,' she said.

'Friends?' she said.

Ban this word, I tell you. 'Yes, friends,' I said.

She came forward to hug me. I gently pushed her away.

'What are you doing?' she said.

'I'm not comfortable with this. Please don't spoil what we have,' I said, mocking her high-strung tone. I stomped my feet and walked off the court. She followed me.

Ignore girls and they can't leave you alone. Strange. I didn't look at her.

She spoke from behind me.

'Okay, I get it. I'm a girl. I'm allowed some drama sometimes.'

'Really?'

'Well, I said sorry, too.'

'Whatever. By the way, your cardigan is still with me at the residence.'

'Oh, please get it to college tomorrow. It's my favourite.'

'You want to come pick it up? You wanted to see my room, right?'
I said.

She raised an eyebrow.

'Really? But how?'

'There's a system. It involves me making the guards happy while
you rush inside.'

'You'll sneak me in?' she said, her eyes opening wide.

'You won't be the first girl to come to the residences.'

We walked towards the brick-lined path to Rudra-North. She
stopped a few steps before I reached Rudra.

'What if we get caught?' she said.

'I'll be expelled, but they'll spare you. You're a girl and your father
will have enough contacts.'

'So?'

'Let's do it,' I said.

I went up to the guard. I followed the code: told him to check
out a problem in the bathroom, and slipped him fifty rupees. He had
done it for others before so he quickly understood. He saw Riya in
the distance.

'Is she from outside or a student?' the guard said.

'What do you care?' I said.

'Just in case there's any trouble later.'

'Will there be trouble?'

'No. Make sure she leaves in thirty minutes. No guarantee with
the new guard.'

6

She entered my room and I slammed the door shut behind us.
My room was furnished with the bare necessities—a bed, a desk, an easy chair and a study chair. The walls were lined with certificates and pictures.

'So many certificates,' she said as she scanned them. They began right from the inter-school tournaments I had won in class VIII to the one I had for participation in the national games. (My team from Bihar had come eighth.)

'And are these photos of your friends?'

'Those are friends from my old basketball team,' I said, standing behind her. I stood close enough for her hair to touch me. We had never been alone together before.

'How about family pictures?' she said.

I opened my study-table drawer. I took out a photograph of the Dumraon Royal School's annual day. My mother stood on a stage along with students in red sweaters.

'Your mom?' she said, holding the picture.

'She's the principal.'

'You have more pictures?'

'Not really,' I said and rifled through the drawers. I found another black-and-white photo, but hid it.

'What is that?'

'Nothing.'

'Show, no.'

'It's a childhood picture.'

'Oh, then I definitely want to see it.'

She charged towards me.

'No,' I protested and tried to shut the drawer. She laughed, and tackled me like she did on the basketball court, treating the picture like the ball.

On the court our occasional touches meant little. In the room, her jostling me felt electric. I wanted to grab her tight, but didn't. I didn't want a scene like last time.

I let her have the picture and stepped aside. She looked at it and began to laugh.

'How old are you in this?'

'Four.'

The picture was of my parents and me standing outside the haveli. My mother wore a saree with a ghoongat covering half her face. I wore a vest and little else.

Riya sat down on the bed. She examined the photograph like a detective solving a murder mystery. I sat next to her.

'Is that your haveli?' she said.

I nodded.

'It's beautiful.'

'That's fifteen years ago. Now it's falling apart.'

She looked closer. A cow was visible in the background. Two kids sat under a tree with an old man.

'Who are they?'

'Random people, perhaps some visitors. I told you, people come to us with their problems. For them, we are still the rulers.'

'I'd love to go see it.'

I laughed.

'What?' she said, puzzled.

'You? In Bihar?'

'Yeah, why not?'

I shook my head and laughed again.

'What's so funny, prince?' she said and tickled me.

'Stop it, I'm ticklish,' I said and laughed uncontrollably.

'You think I can't leave my sheltered life, huh?' she said, poking my stomach with her fingers. I grabbed and held her. She realized it only after a few seconds.

'Hey,' she said.

'What?'

'You're holding me.'

'Good observation.'

I looked straight into her eyes. She did not look away. Even though I had zero experience with girls, I could tell this was a good sign.

'What?' she said.

I leaned forward to kiss her. At the last moment she moved her face away and I ended up kissing her cheek.

'Madhav Jha,' she said. 'Behave yourself.'

She said it in a firm voice, though without the anger she had shown that day on the lawn.

'I am behaving like myself. This is what I want to do.'

'All you boys are the same,' she said and slapped my wrist.

'You've experienced all boys?' I raised my eyebrows.

'Shut up. Okay listen, before I forget, I have to invite you to a party.'

'Don't change the topic.'

'Don't stick to one either,' she said and extracted herself from my grip. She shifted into the study chair.

'Come here. Near me,' I said.

'No, sir, I don't trust you.'

'Really? Your best friend?'

'Who is not behaving like a *friend*,' she said, emphasizing the last word.

I lay back on the bed in a sulk, dangling my legs. I picked up a basketball from the bookshelf and spun it on my little finger.

'I said I want to invite you to a party. Are you paying attention?' she said.

'Why do you want attention from someone you don't trust?'

'Next Saturday, my house. At 100, Aurangzeb Road,' she said, palms resting on her lap.

I sat up on the bed.

'Your house?' I said.

'Yes, the party is at my place.'

'You're making me meet the parents?'

'Yeah, why? There are going to be loads of people there. It's a party.'

'Oh, what is the occasion?' I said, back to spinning the ball on my pinkie.

'My birthday party.'

'Your birthday is next month. 1 November. See? I remember.'

'Dad wants me to celebrate it next week. We have family friends in town.'

I nodded and continued to look at the ball. With one swoop of her arm she took the ball away from me.

'Hey,' I protested.

'Is that a yes?'

'Do I have a choice?'

She threw the ball at me. It missed my face and hit my neck.

'You're making it sound like a punishment. It's a party invitation,' she said.

'I'll come on one condition.'

'What?'

'Come sit next to me.'

I patted the bed. She rolled her eyes, stood up and came to sit down next to me.

'Why don't you let me hold you?' I said and took her in my arms again.

'Well, you are now.'

'You don't like it?'

'Madhav...' Her policewoman voice was back.

'What is so wrong with it?'

'I have issues with this stuff. I do.'

'Issues? You know what? Forget it.'

'See, you don't want to listen. Anyway, I am not ready for it.'

'Ready for what?'

She shook her head. I brought my face close to hers. She looked at me.

'There you go again. What is it? A compulsion, huh?' she said. I kept quiet. Her light brown eyes continued to stare me down.

'No woman has ever meant more to me than you.'

She laughed.

'What?'

'That could mean two things. I am really special, or there's not been much choice.'

I couldn't answer. I bent forward and gave her a light peck on her lips. She didn't protest, but didn't join in either. Her lips felt soft and warm. I gave her another peck.

She placed her hand on my chest and pushed me back.

'What?' I said.

'I better leave,' she said and stood up.

'Riya, we kissed,' I said, excited.

She looked at me, her brown eyes a deeper brown than usual.

'You really don't get girls, do you?'

'What?'

'Broadcasting it, like a kid who's found a candy jar.'

'Sort of. Even better than candy though.'

'Nice to know you find me better than a lollipop.'

I laughed.

'Are we dating?' I said.

She grabbed my collar.

'Madhav Jha. Learn about girls, or figure it out. But don't ruin it. Understand?' she said.

I didn't understand at all.

'I do,' I said.

'Bye. Now see me out.'

We tiptoed out of my room and walked to the Rudra exit. We saluted a thank-you to the guard and left.

I had always considered my selection to the Bihar state team as the happiest day of my life. After kissing Riya, the selection day became the second happiest.

7

'A girl in the hostel?' Ashu slapped my back. 'What a stud.'

My hostel mates had come to my room. Fat Ashu sat on my bed, making it creak like crazy. His back slap still hurt.

Ashu, Raman and Shailesh had become my core gang in Rudra. Riya couldn't be with me all the time, and when she couldn't, I hung out with these guys.

'How did you find out?' I said.

'I can still smell the perfume,' Raman said and sniffed like a cartoon character. Everyone laughed.

All four of us came from Bihar or Jharkhand, and none of us were the 'classy' types you find in Stephen's. For instance, nobody in Stephen's would say they watched Bhojpuri movies. We loved them. We liked Hindi music, from Mohammed Rafi in the sixties to Pritam in the here and now. We didn't understand English music beyond one song by Michael Jackson—'Beat it'. Of course, we never admitted all this to the rest of our classmates. We nodded our heads every time someone mentioned a great English movie or brought a rock CD to class. 'Yeah, yeah, cool,' we said.

'Nonsense. Riya and I came straight from the basketball court. No perfume,' I said.

'Even a girl's sweat smells like perfume,' Shailesh said. I threw the basketball at his head. His rectangular-framed glasses flew to the floor. He screamed and held his head in pain.

'You're trying to kill me or what?' he said. I placed Shailesh's spectacles back on his nose.

'Stop talking like that about Riya,' I said.

'Oh my, protective and all,' Shailesh said.

Among the four of us, Shailesh's English was the best. Of course, he preferred Hindi like the rest of us but he could pass off as a 'real' Stephanian when he spoke in English.

'So, are you guys in a relationship? Things seem to be escalating,' Shailesh said.

'What?' I said.

Ashu laughed.

'He's fucking with you,' Raman said. He had just learnt the F-word. He liked using it. A lot.

'Did anything happen?' Ashu said.

I shrugged.

'What?' Ashu said. 'Dude, did you just do it with the BMW 5-series Riya Somani?'

'Nothing much happened,' I said. 'And stop it, all of you.'

'Is she your girlfriend?' Shailesh said. 'Half the college talks about you guys.'

'I don't know,' I said.

'You don't know?' Ashu said.

'She's not sure.'

'And you?'

I kept quiet.

'You love her?' Ashu said.

I smiled at Ashu. He had asked me the most stupid question.

Did I love her? Did the earth go around the sun? Did night follow day?

'Gone, you are so gone. I can see it on your face,' Ashu said. He patted the bed, inviting the others to join him.

My single bed groaned as three boys lay down on it. They stared at the ceiling. As self-styled relationship experts, they offered advice.

'Be careful,' Raman said, 'of this kind of girl.'

'What the...' I said, irritated. 'What kind of girl? And remove your shoes from my bed.'

I sat on the study table and snatched up the basketball again.

'Rich ones. They need toys for time pass. Don't be a toy,' Raman said.

'Toy? I'm her best friend. Besides, she's different. Not money-minded,' I said.

'You know who her father is?' Shailesh said, adjusting his glasses.

'Some big-shot Marwari businessman?' I said.

'Somani Infrastructure. Your lady's dad and his brother have a five-hundred-crore business,' Shailesh said.

Ashu and Raman whistled.

'Five hundred crore!' Raman said. 'Why is she here? Why does she need to study at all?'

I threw a cushion at Raman.

'Shown what a backward Jharkhandi you are? You remind me of villagers back home. People could study for other reasons, no?'

'What reasons?' Ashu said, craning his neck towards me.

'She's figuring herself out. Her dreams, passions, desires…'

'Does she know your desires? Her best friend who wants to do her on his creaky hostel bed.'

Ashu started to move side to side to make the bed creak more.

Everyone laughed.

'Shut up, bastards,' I said.

I needed real advice to make sense of what was happening in my life.

'She's invited me home for her birthday party.'

The three sat up straight.

'Can we come along?' Ashu said.

'No.'

'You're useless,' Raman said.

'The point is, should I go?' I said.

'What?' Raman said. 'Of course you should. Where does she stay?'

'Aurangzeb Road. Where is it?'

'One of the richest areas. In Lutyens' Delhi.'

'See? That's why I am not sure if I should go.'

'Why not?'

'She'll have her clan there. Everyone is going to see me.'

'And you're afraid of that?' Ashu laughed. 'I would be, if I were you.'

'Shut up, fatso,' Shailesh said. 'Listen, you have to go. If you want to get close to this girl, you have to meet these people one day anyway.'

'They will judge me. I can't dress or talk like them.'

'What nonsense. Just wear a nice white shirt. Borrow mine,' Shailesh said.

I kept quiet.

'Better get it over and done with,' Raman said after a pause.

'What do you mean?' I said.

'Boss, her rich and classy Marwari family is never going to approve of a villager. You, me and the rest of us here know that,' Raman said.

'The boy is a state-level basketball player and studies at St. Stephen's College. Isn't that something?' Shailesh said.

Raman smirked.

'Still a Bihari farm boy, no?' he said.

I trembled. The image of rich judgemental parents in a giant bungalow flashed across my mind.

'You're killing his confidence,' Ashu said. 'Damn, he loves her, okay?'

'So?' Raman said.

'She came to his room, no?' Ashu said. 'Madhav, boss, she came to your room right? Knowing you're a Bihari?'

'She wants to visit Bihar,' I said.

'There you go,' Ashu said.

Raman rolled his eyes.

'Go to the party. At least you'll get free food,' Ashu said and 'patted' my back again. Fatso hits so hard, it hurts for days.

8

I took two buses to get to Aurangzeb Road. I couldn't find any regular houses there, only massive mansions. Each building looked like an institution, not someone's private home.

'100, Aurangzeb Road.' I saw the sign etched in gold on a black granite plaque. Concealed yellow lights lit up a nameplate, which merely stated 'Somani'. I had borrowed Shailesh's blazer and shirt. I adjusted my clothes.

Evenings in October had started to turn chilly. I approached the guard.

'What's your name?' the guard said in a Bihari accent. He held an intercom phone in his right hand.

'Madhav, Madhav Jha. I am Riya's friend.'

The guard eyed me up and down. He spoke into the intercom. 'Riya madam's friend. Shall I send him in?'

The guard paused. He looked at me.

'What?' I said.

'Wait. They will respond and approve.'

'Isn't there a party?'

'Yes, in the back garden. The maid has gone to check.'

In college I underwent no layers of security to meet Riya. I felt awkward standing and waiting so I made conversation with the guard.

'Are you from Bihar?' I said.

'Yes, from Munger. You?'

'Dumraon.'

'And you are Riya madam's friend?' he said. I heard the condescension in his voice. A low-class can smell another low-class.

'Same college,' I said. The guard gave me an approving nod. He could now understand how Riya could be friends with me.

The intercom rang.

'Go,' the guard said to me, as if he had received clearance from air traffic control.

I stepped inside. A maid gestured for me to follow her. Five expensive cars—an Audi SUV, two Mercedes Benz, one Bentley and

Riya's BMW—were parked in the compound.

I entered the house, and found myself in a large living room with a shiny white marble floor. Glittering chandeliers hung from the fifteen-foot high ceiling. Three sofa sets, upholstered in expensive silk, were arranged in a U-shaped configuration. A teak and glass coffee table occupied the middle of the room. This is what a real palace would look like if royals actually had any money. I thought of my haveli, with its peeling walls and cracked floors. Forget chandeliers, we felt lucky if we had less than five-hour power cuts.

Suddenly, in this lap of luxury, I felt lonely. I missed home, my hostel room and my mother, all at the same time. It is funny how class works. The moment you are placed in a higher one, a part of you feels terrified and alone.

'Come this way,' the maid said as she saw me stand still.

We reached the back garden. Loud music and a waft of cool breeze greeted me. I saw the manicured, basketball-court-sized garden lit up with small fairy lights. White-gloved servers manned a buffet and bar counter. In the right corner, water shimmered in a small swimming pool. Most of the eighty-odd guests had gathered around the pool. Everyone was dressed as if they had just participated in a fashion show.

People chatted in small groups. Everyone seemed extremely happy.

I looked around for the tall girl who had invited me. However, this party had several tall girls, a lot of them on account of their three-inch heels.

'Hey, Madhav!' I heard her voice.

I squinted to find Riya waving at me from a distance. She walked towards me. She wore a wine-coloured dress which ended six inches above her knees. She had applied light make-up. Her face looked even prettier than it did every day. She wore dangling diamond-and-white gold earrings, with a matching necklace and bracelet. She had dark red lipstick on, making her lips appear fuller than usual. I couldn't believe I had kissed these same lips a week ago.

She hugged me like she always did. It felt odd to embrace in front of so many people.

'Why so late?' she said.

'Took a while to figure out the bus routes.'

'I told you I would send the car. You and your ego hassles,' she said. 'Anyway, come.'

She held my wrist and pulled me towards the crowd. We walked towards the pool where her friends stood.

'Garima, Ayesha and Rachita. You know them, right?' Riya said.

'Yes, from the café.'

'Of course,' Ayesha said. She brushed her hair away from her forehead. The three girls wore expensive dresses and giggled at regular intervals for no apparent reason. Riya introduced me to another girl in a black dress.

'This is Yamini. We were best friends in Modern School,' Riya said, hugging Yamini.

'We *were*. I hear *you* are the best friend now, my competition,' said Yamini, blowing a curly fringe out of her eyes.

'Shoo, Yamini,' Riya said and turned to me. 'She's teasing you. Both of you are my buddies.'

I hated that word—buddies. Buddies felt like a pair of stuffed toys placed next to each other, with no romantic spark whatsoever. I had thought after our first kiss that Riya would be more open about us.

I handed over a present to Riya.

'Oh, thank you,' she said. 'But my birthday isn't until next month.'

She opened the present without asking me.

'What is it?' she said as she fingered the fabric inside, trying to make sense of it.

'It's a shawl,' I said. I didn't have much money to afford a big gift. With winter coming, I thought this would be a nice present. Besides, it was within my budget of five hundred bucks.

'So thoughtful. This will keep me warm,' Riya said with a big smile on her face.

'I hear you play good basketball. Can you beat her?' Yamini said.

'I try,' I said.

'He's being modest. He plays state level. Going to be college captain soon.'

'Handsome college captain,' Yamini chuckled.

A waiter brought over a tray of snacks.

'What's that?' I said.

'Sushi,' the waiter said.

I had never heard that word before. I looked puzzled.

'It's fish on rice,'Yamini said.

I extended my hand to pick up a piece.

'Raw fish,' Riya said.

'What?' I said and recoiled from the tray.

The girls burst into laughter.

'It's okay. Japanese food. Even I don't eat it,' Riya said.

'Your family is vegetarian, right?' I said.

'Yes, but our guests are not. It's for them. Come, let me introduce you to some people.' Riya grabbed my arm.

'Hey, Riya, one second,' Ayesha called from behind.

Riya excused herself and went back. I saw the five girls chat with each other in an animated manner. At one point, everyone apart from Riya laughed; she didn't seem to find the joke as funny as the others.

'Sorry,' Riya said as she rejoined me. 'Are you having a good time?'

'Fancy house you have,' I said as we walked to the other end of the garden.

'My dad's and uncles' house, you mean.'

'Still, great place.'

'Thanks,' she said. 'Are you having a good time?'

'I'm with you. That's how I define a good time.'

She smacked my back with her hand and smiled.

'So, who am I meeting?' I said.

'Dad, Mom and some of their friends.'

'Dad and Mom?' I said.

Every guy has a fear of meeting his girl's parents. Apparently, there is a scientific term for it—soceraphobia.

We reached the bar. A distinguished-looking couple in their early fifties stood with guests.

Riya's parents held a glass of champagne each. They looked like those people in the Titan watch ads. They wore well-ironed clothes with immaculate accessories. Everything they had on was designer, including their smiles. Riya's father wore a black bandhgala and gold-rimmed glasses. Riya's mother wore a gold-coloured silk saree.

'Riya, there you are,' Mr Somani said. He put his arm around his daughter. 'Rohan's been asking for you.'

Riya extracted herself from her father's embrace and moved aside one step.

'Hi, Rohan,' she said. 'When did you arrive?'

Rohan was a handsome man in his mid-twenties with gelled hair. He wore a black formal suit.

'Two minutes ago. The parlour took so bloody long to finish my facial,' Rohan said with a heavy British accent.

Rohan Chandak, I learnt, had come from London three days ago. He and his mother were staying at Riya's house for the duration of their one-week trip. The Chandaks and the Somanis both hailed from Jaipur, family friends for three generations. The Chandaks had a hospitality business in London. I presumed, like the Somanis, they were rich.

'Never mind, young man,' Riya's father said and patted Rohan's back. 'We are so proud of you, beta.'

Mr Somani recited the story of Rohan's father who had died two years ago. Rohan had taken over the hotel business at a young age and was doing extremely well. Riya and Rohan seemed to have heard the story too many times before and looked embarrassed. Mr Somani went on for three minutes. I checked it against my watch.

'It's okay, uncle,' Rohan said. 'I just do it to make my mum happy and proud. That's all.'

Riya's mother stood next to her husband throughout. Like me, she had not said a word.

'So, at just twenty-four, running six hotels in London with four hundred rooms, and planning the seventh. So proud of you, son,' Mr Somani repeated, finally ending his tribute.

I put on an expression of extreme awe and appreciation, as seemed to be expected of me.

'Not that my daughter Riya is any less. Let me tell you...' Mr Somani said. Riya interrupted him.

'Dad. Stop,' she said, somewhat rude and abrupt, considering she was speaking to her father. Mr Somani smiled and let Riya speak.

'Dad, I want you to meet Madhav, a good friend of mine from

college,' Riya said.

Mr Somani looked at me. He paused for a second before saying hello. I had worn Shailesh's best blazer and shirt, but it still didn't match the clothes of the other guests. Mr Somani, with his impeccable taste, had noticed my less-than-designer outfit.

'Hello, Madhav,' Mr Somani said. He shook my hand in an extra-friendly way, as if to compensate for the doubts of a few seconds ago.

'Good to meet you, sir,' I said, my insecurities forcing me to say 'sir'.

'Madhav what?' he said. Indians have to know your last name to place you.

'Madhav Jha,' I said.

'Jha, as in…'

'Bihar. I am from Bihar,' I said, familiar with the upcoming question. Mr Somani didn't answer.

Riya broke the awkward silence.

'And that's Mom,' she said.

Riya's mother smiled and folded her hands. I wished her with a namaste too.

A waiter arrived with a tray of drinks. Rohan took a beer, Riya picked up a glass of wine and Mr Somani helped himself to a whisky. I didn't know what to take so I waved a no.

'Nice party, Somani uncle,' Rohan said.

Mr Somani lifted his glass for a toast. Mrs Somani made an eye movement to indicate that some important guests had just arrived—someone incredibly rich or powerful, or both. Mr and Mrs Somani excused themselves and sidled off.

Riya smiled at me. I smiled back at her, trying my best to fit in.

'So you guys do college together, innit?' Rohan said. His British accent made it hard for me to understand him.

'Yes, different course. Same college,' Riya said.

Rohan was an inch shorter than Riya and five inches shorter than me. However, his age and confidence made us seem like kids answering his questions.

'Basketball, that is wicked,' Rohan said.

'Wicked? Why wicked?' I said.

He laughed, as if he didn't mean it in a bad way. Even Riya smiled.
'What?'

'Nothing. It's such a British English thing,' Riya said.

I guess I didn't understand British or English things.

'How do you like India?' I said, trying to make conversation.

'Grew up here, dude. I left ten years ago,' he said.

I wondered if ten years could completely change a person's accent.

'Stephen's, eh? Top college. You must be pretty damn smart,'
Rohan said to me.

'I entered through the sports quota,' I said.

Riya's eyes shuttled between both of us. She watched our man-to-man equation. He was six years older, insanely rich and far more accomplished. He also had a fancy accent, gelled hair and lived in London. I was nothing compared to him. Yet, there was something jerk-like about Rohan Chandak. Or maybe it was just my imagination. *At least I'm taller,* I told myself to feel better.

'Riya, babe, you only got guy friends? Or you have some lovely ladies to introduce me to?'

'Plenty. Come to the poolside,' Riya said.

'Yeah. Don't make me hang out here with the oldies.'

Riya and Rohan turned towards the pool.

'Hey, Madhav,' Riya said.

'Yeah?'

'Stop looking so lost.'

We rejoined Riya's gang.

'Ah, so this is where the loveliest ladies in Delhi hang out,' Rohan said.

Why couldn't I think of clever lines like that?

Riya introduced Rohan to everyone. Rohan held each girl's hand for a second, lifted it and said 'a pleasure to meet you' or something like that. It was too much, if you ask me. However, the giggly girls liked it.

'So you are the London hot-shot,' Yamini said.

'From London for sure, madam, but not a hot-shot,' Rohan said.

Everyone laughed. I think when rich guys say something, girls find it extra funny.

'Wait a minute, guys,' Rohan said as he took out his phone from his pocket. 'Yes, Mummy ji. Everything okay, right? When will you be here? Everyone is asking for you... Okay, don't be too late. The party can't start without you.'

I watched Rohan's face as he stepped aside to take his call. It glowed, perhaps due to the facial he had mentioned, or maybe it was just his mother's voice.

'You ladies like to party? Is there a nightclub for afterwards?' Rohan said when he came back.

'There's Agni at the Park,' Ayesha said, playing with her hair.

I wondered why on earth anyone would leave such a fancy party and go anywhere else. However, rich people like to have options and try different things.

'You've known Riya a long time?' Rachita asked Rohan.

'Since she was a little girl,' Rohan said. 'I used to be able to lift her easily.'

'Hah. I was two, you were eight, Rohan,' Riya said.

'Yes. Let me try that now.'

Rohan put his glass down. He bent forward and took hold of Riya's waist. Riya was too startled to protest. A surge of anger ran through my entire body. My fists and face tightened up in a primal response.

Leave her alone, you bastard, I said in my head.

Rohan lifted her off the ground. The girls giggled. He placed Riya back down. It all lasted only two seconds. However, my insides continued to burn long after it was over.

'You are the quiet type, mate,' Rohan said to me. 'What's up? Need another drink?'

Yeah, I need to drink your blood.

Rohan beckoned to a waiter with drinks and passed me a beer without me asking for it. I didn't need a beer. I needed to whack this NRI's head like a slam-dunk shot. I needed alone time with Riya. I needed another accent.

I chugged the beer down in one shot. I did it to assert my fast-diminishing manliness in the group. Everyone watched me in surprise.

'Mate, that's rough. Go easy,' Rohan said.

Riya understood I wasn't being myself. She looked at me as if to ask what the matter was. I turned the other way to avoid eye contact.

The girls gathered around Rohan. He told them stories about his adventures at Indian airports.

'Madhav, can I talk to you for a second?' Riya said.

We stepped away from the group.

♦

We sat opposite each other on plush white sofas in Riya's drawing room. Two waiters hovered around us.

'Can't we just...' I said and fell quiet. A waiter brought us a tray of spring rolls.

'Madhav, so many guests. How are we supposed to be more private?'

'Yeah, fine, I understand,' I said. I picked up two spring rolls.

'Besides, I will see you in college on Monday, right?' she said.

I nodded as I ate the spring rolls. A part of my frustration came from hunger. I felt better after the snack.

'I understand how you feel. In some ways, even I feel like a tourist at these parties,' Riya said.

'What?'

'It's not real. All this. I've lived with this fakeness all my life,' she said.

'And why did you speak to your dad so rudely?'

'Did I? Whatever. He's another fake.'

'C'mon Riya. Don't talk like that.'

'You hate it here, don't you?'

'No, I'm fine. What a grand house you live in. I still can't get over it,' I said, in an attempt to change the topic.

'I hope it doesn't affect us. I'm still the same Riya who plays with you on the dusty court,' she laughed.

'What is "us", Riya?'

'Us. You and me. Our friendship.'

'Riya, we are more than friends.'

'Are we?' She looked at me as if genuinely confused.

'I've never kissed anyone before,' I said.

'Madhav.'

'What?'

'People can hear us.'

'Nobody can hear us.' The loud music in the garden ensured nobody could hear anything.

'We'll talk about this later.'

'You never do,' I said.

'I will, I promise. Please cheer up now.'

'What's with Mr London? What was he lifting you for?'

Riya laughed. 'Oh, Ro. Ro is an old buddy. He's mad.'

She even had a nickname for him. Ro. It means 'cry' in Hindi. I wanted Ro to ro.

'Are you jealous?'

'Not at all.'

'Yes, you are.'

'Whatever, let's go back in.'

She stood up. 'You liked my parents?'

I nodded. You can't say you didn't like someone's parents.

'Good. Come, let's go in before they start getting ideas.'

Ideas? What ideas? I wanted to ask her.

We walked into the garden. The music drowned out my thoughts. The younger crowd danced around the pool. Rohan danced with Riya's friends. He called out to us. I wondered if I could pretend to dance and kick Ro into the water.

Of course, I didn't do that. I refused to dance. I couldn't embarrass myself in front of this crowd. In Dumraon, we danced like mad people. We played loud music and moved our bodies frantically. Also, men and women never danced together. Here, Rohan danced with each girl for a few seconds. Sometimes, he would hold their hand while dancing, and the girl would be all giggles. What is so funny about a rich guy holding your hand? He even held Riya's hand once. She twirled around him. My internal organs twirled inside me. I couldn't do anything but look away.

A waiter came up to me.

'Are you Madhav Jha, sir?' he said.

'Yes,' I said, surprised he knew my name.

'I am from Dumraon, too.'

'Oh, how do you know I am from there?'

'The guard outside told me. Nice to meet you, sir. Feels like I've met someone from home.'

The waiter spoke to me for few minutes, shook my hand and left.

Riya raised her eyebrows from the dance floor, wondering what I was doing with the waiter. I shook my head and smiled.

There are things some people can never understand. There's no point telling them.

9

'Even I have no fucking idea what sushi is,' Ashu said.

'It's Japanese food. How the fuck are we supposed to know? Do they know our litti-chokha?' Raman said.

He dug his fork deep into the mound of biryani piled high on his plate. We were in the dining hall for Sunday dinner and a post-mortem of Riya's party.

'Sushi is no big deal. The bigger deal is she didn't make you feel special,' Shailesh said.

He adjusted his spectacles and drank a glass of water. Shailesh, always the straight talker, had silenced everyone with his statement. The sound of cutlery filled the awkward silence.

'Trouble, brother, trouble,' Shailesh said, after a minute.

'But she kissed him,' Ashu said.

'Toys. Told you about rich people and their toys,' Shailesh said.

I ate my food. My friends further analysed the situation. In my heart I knew Riya didn't see me as a toy. We had a connection. But my heart can be over-imaginative and stupid.

'I'll talk to her,' I said.

'What? Enough talking. Now do,' Raman said.

'Do what?' I said.

Raman shook his head. Everyone smiled.

'Listen, Madhav, I don't want to break your heart. But you do know such a girl is beyond you,' Raman said.

'What do you mean?' I said, putting my fork down on the table.

'Look at them. Look at you. You forgot your aukaat or what?'

Raman had spoken in a flat, controlled voice. However, it hurt. It hurt like he had taken his blunt fork and jabbed it into my chest. It hurt because he didn't think I deserved Riya. It hurt because he had spoken the truth.

'Why does she hang out with me all the time?' I said. 'She can have all the rich friends she wants. In fact, she does.'

'You are the new exotic creature in her life. She's bored with **everything else,**' Raman said.

'Are you always this pessimistic?' Ashu said. Only the fat kid supported me. I transferred the gulab jamun from my plate on to his.

'The statistical probability is low,' Shailesh said, in his academic voice. 'However, my friend Raman should know that love does happen between classes.'

'If this is love, why is she avoiding a relationship?' Raman said. He stood up to leave. He had finished his dinner and what he wanted to say.

Ashu thanked me for the gulab jamun. 'Raman has no experience with girls. You are doing well. Take it slow. Everything will be fine,' he said.

'What do you think, Shailesh?' I said.

Of the four of us, I trusted Shailesh's judgement the most. He topped the class and was the most well-read. Of course, like us, he had little experience with women. He drank another glass of water.

'Yes, don't rush it. However, don't stall it either,' Shailesh said.

'What does that mean?' Ashu said on my behalf.

'Keep it slow, but keep escalating,' Raman said.

'Escalating? What? How?' I said.

'What's the clearest sign a girl likes you?' Shailesh said.

'She spends time with you?' I said.

'Wrong,' Shailesh said and stood up as well.

'So then?' I said.

'You know the answer. Now do it,' Shailesh said and left.

◆

'What do you want to talk about?' Riya said.

She had worn a lemon-coloured chikan salwar-kameez to college that day. We sat under the big banyan tree in between classes. Her hair blew in all directions in the afternoon breeze.

'Thanks for the party,' I said.

'You are welcome. Like I told you, it isn't really my scene but my parents wanted to do it.'

'Riya, that's your world. It was me who didn't fit in.'

'I can fit in, but I can't relate to it. I'd rather have a meaningful conversation over chai than catered sushi with plastic smiles.'

'How's Rohan? Sorry, Ro,' I said.

'He made quite an impression on you. He's cool, no?'

'See, you find him cool. That is your world,' I said.

'He's over the top and a bit of a show-off. But at least Rohan's fun. The rest are all boring businessmen who only talk money and property.'

'Go have fun then,' I said and looked away from her.

She tugged at my elbow.

'Anyway, forget the party. Eye contact, please.'

Eyes squinting against the mid-morning sun, she draped her yellow dupatta around her face. She looked like a bunch of yellow flowers. I had to be firm. I ignored how cute she was, lest it weaken my resolve.

'What did you want to talk about?' she asked again.

'The kiss,' I said.

Riya giggled. 'I can't believe I am the girl and you are the guy. The guy wants to talk about it.'

'Very funny. Now can we discuss it?'

'What about the kiss? You forced it on me.'

Her answer stumped me. I didn't know what to say.

'I…I did it because…' I fumbled for words.

'Yes, why? Why did you do it, Mr Jha?'

'Because I…I love you.'

Riya burst out laughing. I didn't like her laughter this time.

'Can you please be serious? Your casual behaviour hurts me,' I said.

She composed herself and sat cross-legged under the tree.

'Okay, fine, Madhav, I will be serious. I laughed because I don't think you are in love with me.'

'Oh, really? How do you know that?'

'Have you been in love before?'

'No.'

'So how do you know it's love?'

Her confusing words left me tongue-tied.

'How do you know it's not?' I said after half a minute.

'I know it is not. We are both too young, inexperienced but

curious. Sure, we like each other. But love? Please.'

'Riya, you have no idea how much you mean to me. I would do anything for you. Anything,' I said.

Our eyes locked. For a few seconds, even the articulate Miss Riya Somani didn't have words.

'Madhav, you mean a lot to me too. But…'

'But what?'

'I am not sure if I want a relationship right now. With anyone.'

How does one answer that? I had no idea.

'I don't mean that much to you then,' I said.

'We hang out all the time. Aren't we almost a couple?'

'So what's wrong with the next step?'

The bell rang for class. We stood up to leave.

'What's the next step, Madhav?' she said, as we walked towards class.

I scratched my head to think of an answer.

'Become my girlfriend.'

'Oh. And what does that involve? Getting physical?'

'Maybe. That's often part of it.'

She smiled and shook her head in an all-knowing manner.

We stopped as we reached our respective classrooms.

'Please, Riya,' I said. 'Please be my girlfriend.'

'Is this a proposal?' she said.

'If that's how you see it.'

'I'll think about it.'

'You'll tell me after class?'

She grabbed my shoulders and turned me towards my classroom.

◆

Riya didn't come to college the next day. I briefed my friends-cum-relationship-experts about the proposal while eating lunch in the dining hall.

Shailesh felt I had come across as desperate. Ashu thought I had handled it well.

'Well, did she tell you her decision afterwards?' Raman said.

'No. And today she is absent,' I said.

'See? Desperate. She's skipped college to avoid you,' Shailesh said.

'To avoid me?'

Shailesh shrugged.

'You better get an answer,' Raman said.

'You better *do* it with her,' Shailesh said. Everyone fell silent.

'Do what?' I said. The boys guffawed.

'You guys are sick.'

'She's using you. Time pass until a real guy comes along,' Shailesh said, picking his teeth with a toothpick.

'Ignore Shailesh. Find out why she's absent. Message her,' Ashu said.

'Should I? She's supposed to answer my question,' I said.

The boys didn't answer either. I came to my room after lunch. I had a mobile phone now. Even though expensive, I would use it sometimes to call Riya.

I composed a message. Did not see you in college. Everything OK?

I deleted the text and re-typed it three times. Finally, I pressed send.

The worst wait in life is waiting for someone to text back. Riya didn't answer for an hour. It felt like a week. After that one hour, I sent the same message again. That way, it would come across as a double delivery rather than me being desperate. It is funny how, when friendship moves towards a relationship, every message requires awareness and strategy. The second message went, disguised as a screw-up of Airtel.

She didn't reply for another hour. I wanted to call her. It felt lame. I had proposed to her. The least she could do was give me a reply.

I also felt scared. *What if she said no?* Maybe her silence meant no. *What if she stopped talking to me?* Panic gripped me. I wondered if proposing to her was the worst mistake of my life.

I decided to call her. I typed her number six times. But I did not press the green call button. I didn't have the courage.

My phone beeped. I had a new message. My heart beat fast as I opened it.

Am sick ☹. Viral fever. Resting at home.

Relief coursed through me. She had sent back a normal, harmless message. I wanted to ask about the proposal, but it felt like a bad time. Unsure, I froze. *Why don't they teach us how to talk to girls?*

Get well soon, I sent after rigorous analysis and deliberation in my head.

Thanks, she said.

Miss you, I typed. Before I could think I pressed send.

She didn't respond for a minute. It felt like a decade. *Had I messed up again? Was it not the right thing to say?*

Then come home. Cheer me up.

Her message felt like a thousand red rose petals on my face. I checked my timetable. Damn, I had four important, un-skippable classes. I couldn't go.

See you in an hour, I said. Classes can wait. Love can't.

10

I knocked on the door of Riya's bedroom, located on the first floor of her house.

'Come in, Madhav,' Riya said and sniffled. 'Meet your sick friend.'

She was in bed, leaning against the backrest with her legs stretched out. She wore a white night-suit with pink dots all over it. She looked like candy, more cute than ill. Viral fever suited her.

'Wait. Come back in again. I should sit with a thermometer in my mouth,' she said.

I smiled and sat on a chair near her bed.

'How are you feeling?' I said.

She shifted to the side and bent to look under the bed. She pulled out a guitar. Strumming it once, she started to sing.

'Terrible, I feel terrible. And I need a hug.'

I looked at her, surprised.

'Because I'm sure. That is my only cure.'

She saw my shell-shocked face and winked at me. Even though she sang as a joke, I loved her voice and the goofy lyrics of her song.

'You sing well,' I said, 'and the guitar-playing is not bad either.'

'Ha ha. I feel terrible. I also sing terribly,' she said.

'No you don't. You're good,' I said.

She smiled and kept her guitar aside. She spread her arms.

'What?' I said.

'I said I need a hug.'

It is funny how women feel they have the right to demand physical affection whenever they want, but men can't. Like a trained pet, I stood up and bent to embrace her.

'You don't have fever,' I said as I held her. Her body felt cold, in fact.

'I did a few hours ago. I took a nap and now I am better.'

'You are fine.'

She mock-frowned. 'I am a sick girl. Please take care of me,' she said in a baby voice.

I took that as a sign that she was in a good mood. I voiced what had been haunting me for the past twenty-four hours.

'You didn't answer my question,' I said.

'What?'

'The proposal.'

'Baby, why are you doing this to us?'

'I can say the same thing to you.'

We locked eyes for a few seconds. I came forward to kiss her. She ducked, and my lips landed on her forehead.

'What?' I said.

'That was sweet. I like forehead kisses,' she said.

I gently took hold of her chin and raised her face. Our eyes met again. I leaned forward to kiss her again.

She moved her face away with a jerk.

'What, baby?' I said. If she could call me baby, I could too.

'No. No, Madhav, no.'

'Why not?'

'I don't want to. I'm not comfortable.'

'We did it earlier.'

'Yes, okay, we did. But I thought about it and I don't want to.'

'You don't want to be with me?'

'I didn't say that.'

'Well, are you my girlfriend?'

'No.'

'What are we then?'

'Friends?'

'You allow friends to hold you like this?'

I had not let her go. She gently moved away.

'Okay, I'm your half-girlfriend.'

'What?'

'Yeah. I'm close to you. We spend time together. We can have affectionate hugs. But nothing more.'

'Nothing more? What is more?'

'Well, you know what constitutes more.'

We heard a knock on the door.

'It's the maid. Can you sit on the chair again, please?' she said.

I moved back to my seat. The maid brought in a tray with two glasses of orange juice. Riya and I took one each. We sipped our drinks in silence.

I wondered what she meant when she said 'half-girlfriend'. Where was my expert panel when I needed it?

'What were you saying? Half?' I said after the maid left.

She nodded. She seemed clear on what she had in mind.

'So we are more than friends?' I said.

'Well, more than just casual friends.'

'But I don't get to kiss you?'

'You are obsessed with kissing, aren't you? Is that all I am to you, a pair of lips?'

She finished her glass of juice. It left a thin orange moustache on her face. Yes, I wanted to kiss that orange moustache.

The maid knocked on the door again. She brought in a giant bouquet. It had three dozen fat pink roses with thin silk ribbons tying them together.

'Wow,' Riya said. 'Who sent these? You?'

I shook my head. I couldn't afford such fancy flowers.

The maid placed the bouquet on the bedside table and left.

'It's Rohan,' Riya said, reading the 'get well soon' tag.

'Isn't he in London?'

'Yes, but he has contacts here.'

'Are you in touch with him?'

'Aha, my half-boyfriend is already possessive.'

'I'm just asking.'

'Not really. Dad must have told him I'm sick.'

'Why is he sending you flowers?'

'Don't read too much into it. He owns hotels. It's easy for him. His secretary must have asked a hotel in Delhi to send them.'

I remained silent. I had no idea. Maybe rich people found it normal to send flowers across continents to other rich people who had viral fever. I stood up to leave. She came to the door to see me off.

'So, we cool?' she said.

I nodded. In reality, I didn't know what to say. I needed my friends, like, *now*.

◆

I summoned my expert panel for an urgent meeting. All of us sat cross-legged on the grass lawns outside Rudra. I narrated my conversation with Riya, my failed attempts at kissing her, her frequent hugs and finally the deal on the table—half-girlfriend. I skipped the flower delivery, though. I didn't want to bring another variable or person into the picture.

'Half isn't bad. Depends on how you look at it,' Ashu said. 'Half-empty or half-full.'

I idly tugged at blades of grass, waiting for everyone in my expert panel to make their opening remarks.

'Pretty sucky, if you ask me,' Shailesh said.

'Pessimist,' Ashu said. 'Always glass is half-empty.'

'No. The half that is missing is pretty vital,' Shailesh said.

'Raman?' I said.

Raman let out a deep sigh. 'Fuck, if a girl won't get physical with you, it's a warning sign,' he said.

'Hell, it's more than a warning sign,' Shailesh said. 'It's a fire brigade siren on maximum volume using thousand-watt amplifiers. Don't you get it, Mr Dumraon? She is playing with you.'

'Ashu, you agree?' I said.

The fat Bihari, always soft and supportive, looked me in the eye.

'Do you like her?' he said.

'Yes,' I said.

'Do you trust her?'

'I think so. The way she hugged me again and again. Or how she called me home. Or how she sits in her night clothes in front of me. I don't know. It means something, right?'

'What is your gut feeling?'

'My gut is bloody confused. That's why I am asking you guys.'

An army of intellectual men cannot solve the riddle created by an indecisive woman. My limited-experience panel struggled for words.

'Say no. No half-girlfriend. All or nothing,' Shailesh said.

'All means what?' I said.

'All means she is your girlfriend, in private and in public,' Raman said.

I pondered over their advice. At one level they made sense.

However, when I was with Riya, she also seemed to make sense.

'What do I do? She asked if we were cool and I nodded,' I said.

'This stuff is not discussed. This stuff is done,' Shailesh said.

'How?'

'Call her to your room.'

'And then?' I said.

The three boys looked at each other and smiled meaningfully.

'And then *what*?' I said.

'Make Bihar proud,' Raman said and squeezed my shoulder.

11

We had practised for less than ten minutes when she got a stomach cramp. She held her stomach and gestured to stop the game.

'I'm not fully okay after the viral attack,' she said.

She walked off the court and sank to the ground. She buried her face in her hands.

'I need to rest. And I'm a little cold in these.' She pointed to her extra-small red shorts. They barely covered her upper thighs.

'You should have told me. We need not have played today,' I said.

'I'll be fine,' she said. She removed her hands from her face and smiled at me.

It had been a week since my panel recommended taking Riya to my room again. 'Make Bihar proud, else you don't matter' is what they had repeated to me all week. Today, I had the chance.

'Hey, you want to rest in my room?' I said.

'Sneak in?'

I played it cool. 'Yeah. You rest. Take a nap. I can study, or will even leave the room if you want me to.'

'You don't have to leave your own room.' She stood up.

She had said I didn't have to leave. It meant she had agreed to come to Rudra. Girls never tell you anything straight out anyway. You have to interpolate and extrapolate their responses to figure out what's on their mind.

◆

I smuggled her in again. As I shut the door of my room, I knew my moment of truth had come. *Make Bihar proud, make yourself count,* I repeated in my head.

Riya sat on the bed, legs extended straight.

'Lie down,' I said.

'I'm not that sick. Just need to rest,' Riya said and smiled. 'I see you've cleaned up your room.'

'Well, it's still not as fancy as yours.'

'It's a room in my father's house. How I wish I could stay in a hostel like you.'

'Hey, would you like to change?' I said, switching topics. 'You said you were cold.'

She had a change of clothes in her rucksack.

'Where?' she said. 'I can't use the bathroom here.'

'You could change here.'

'Ha ha, nice try, mister.'

'I meant I could leave the room.'

'Oh, really? Such a gentleman.'

I had learnt to ignore her sarcasm. I shrugged.

'I'm fine in these,' she said.

'I'm not,' I said.

'Why?'

'Those shorts. They distract me.'

'These red shorts?'

'Well, the legs, to be precise. The legs the shorts are unable to hide.'

Riya laughed. She took a bedsheet and covered herself.

'Here. Better, mister? Now what? You want to study?'

Damn, I had lost my view.

'Yeah. You'll rest?'

'Yes,' Riya said and sniggered.

'What?'

'Like that's going to happen.'

'Of course it is,' I said and turned away from her. I sat on the chair, switched on the table lamp and opened my sociology textbook.

Riya sat on the bed. She seemed amused and somewhat stumped at me letting her be. A few minutes later, she lay down on the bed.

'What are you studying?' she said, her eyes closed.

'Social uprisings in the early twentieth century.'

'How are your grades?'

'Not bad, but I'm no topper.'

I went back to my book.

'What do you want to do after graduation?' she said. Girls cannot stand being ignored, that too for a textbook.

'I've told you fifty times. Work in Delhi for a few years and then go back to Dumraon.'

'Hmm,' she said, her eyes still closed. She sounded like the nosey uncles who ask you questions only to dismiss your answers with a 'hmm'.

'Let me study, Riya. You also rest.'

I didn't have a strategy, but I did have an intuition on how to proceed. *Don't act too interested at first; she will just launch into a lecture.*

My curt responses puzzled her. I shut her up whenever she tried small talk. Finally, she grew quiet.

'I'm tired,' I said, after half an hour of silence.

'I'm sleeping. Don't disturb,' she said. It was her turn to act pricey.

'I also want to sleep.'

'Stay there. I'm a patient. The patient is resting,' she said, suppressing a smile.

I shut my textbook. I went to the side of the bed and sat down.

'Riya?' I said, my voice soft.

She didn't respond, as if asleep. I lifted the quilt covering her. Her tiny shorts had bunched up even further. I couldn't help but stare at her legs. She pulled the quilt back over her as a reflex. A girl knows she is being stared at, even in her sleep. I lay down next to her. I took care to have the least amount of body contact. I shared some of the quilt and shut my eyes.

We lay still for two minutes. She turned to her side. Her nose poked into my right shoulder. Her hand touched my elbow. Even with my eyes closed, I felt her warmth next to me. I turned to face her, pretending to be asleep. Casually, I placed my left arm on her. She didn't protest. My left hand touched her long hair. Her nose was now buried in my chest and I could feel her gentle breath on me. I slid my hand down her back and moved her closer towards me.

She continued to sleep, or continued to pretend to sleep.

I placed my leg over hers, my boldest move yet. The smooth bare skin of her leg touched mine. Electric sparks shot through me. I resisted the urge to kiss her. I let my hand slide further down her back. As I reached her lower back, her voice startled me.

'Mr Jha,' she said.

'Yes, Miss Somani.'

'This is not called sleeping.'

'You can sleep.'

'Oh, really? How do you expect me to with you all over me?'

I laughed. I brought her closer and lifted her face. I tried to kiss her but she turned away.

'Control yourself, Madhav,' she said.

She tried to extricate herself. I didn't let go.

'Why?' I said.

'That is what we agreed to.'

'But why?'

'Just. Oh my God, I just felt your... Madhav, let me go.'

'Riya, come on.'

'Can you just let me go? You are hurting me.'

I let her go. She slid to the edge of the bed, away from me.

'I want you.'

'No.'

'Please let me.'

'No.'

'You have to.'

'What do you mean I have to?' she said.

She sat up on the bed. She glared at me, her posture stiff. However, I was too consumed with my own feelings to cave in at this point. I had waited and played the patience game for too long. I expected her to yield to me now.

'What is your problem?' I said.

'What is *your* problem? I'm not a release for your horniness.'

'I didn't say you were.'

'So why can't you just stick to what we discussed? Nothing physical. Just close friends.'

'That doesn't work.'

'Fine, maybe we can't even be friends.'

I couldn't answer her. I had run out of strategies and clever responses. She stepped off the bed, straightened her clothes and picked up her rucksack to leave.

Anger mixed with desire. I grabbed her hand.

'You can't just play with me. I'm not your toy.'

'Toy?'

'You are using me. Until another guy comes along.'

'Whatever. You are trying to use me. Ruining a perfect friendship. Bye.'

I pulled her close to me. She sat on the bed again, right next to me.

'It isn't a perfect friendship. I am not fully satisfied.'

She didn't like my answer.

I bent forward to kiss her. She moved her face again.

'Only once.'

'No.'

'Please.'

'I said no,' she said, her voice firm.

'I'm at my limit, Riya.' I grabbed her shoulders.

'Madhav, I haven't seen this side of you. You are using physical force on me.'

'I want to say something.'

'What?'

'Deti hai to de, varna kat le.'

'What?'

I had said it in coarse Bhojpuri-accented Hindi. I had said: 'make love to me, or leave'. Actually, that sounds respectable. If I had to make an honest translation, I would say: 'fuck me, or fuck off'. Hell, even that sounds way better than how I said it.

I don't know what came over me that day. Maybe I just couldn't wait anymore. Perhaps I felt insecure and scared. Most likely I am a crass Bihari from Dumraon whose true animal nature had come out. I realized I had spoken filth. I tried to take it back.

'What the hell did you just say?'

'Nothing. Listen, I just…'

I released my grip. Before I could collect my thoughts, Riya Somani had collected her belongings and left.

◆

She refused to take my calls. She didn't reply to any of my twenty-seven messages. I waited for her at the college entrance every morning.

She stepped out of her BMW, ignored me and walked quickly into her classroom.

During breaks she surrounded herself with her girlfriends. When I approached her in the cafeteria, she took out her phone and pretended to be on a call.

'That was a bit much,' Shailesh said. I had told my friends about the debacle in my room. They had listened with much interest, hoping for a story with titillating action. Instead, they heard of a total fiasco. When I repeated the 'deti hai...' line I had said to Riya, even my thick-skinned friends cringed. We spoke filth sometimes but nobody would ever talk like that to a girl. I, the idiot, had spoken like that to the woman I loved, worshipped, adored and respected more than anyone else on earth.

'Fix this disaster, rather than focusing on intimacy right now,' Ashu had said, his tone irritated.

Well, I had tried to fix it. Riya just wouldn't meet me. Helpless, I had no option but to stalk her. I had to talk to her alone. I swore to myself not to say a word of Hindi, lest it come out crudely again.

I did find her alone, finally. She sat in the library, immersed in her textbook, poring over the history of European literature. She wore a red-and-white salwar-kameez with black earrings.

'Riya,' I whispered.

She stood up to change her seat.

'Two minutes, I beg you,' I said.

She ignored me. She moved to another table full of students. I couldn't talk to her there.

'I'm waiting outside,' I said. Ten students looked up at me, startled. Riya continued to read the same page.

I waited outside the library for two and a half hours. When she came out, she saw me and walked in the other direction.

'Two minutes,' I said as I ran up to her.

'I don't want to talk to you, at all. Understand?'

'I'll keep following you. Might as well talk.'

She glared at me and stood still, her hands balling into fists.

'Your time has started,' she said.

'Listen, I am really, really sorry.'

She crossed her arms, textbook still in hand.

'Don't waste your time. Sorry is not going to work.'

'I didn't mean it.'

'Why did you say it? Do you know how it made me feel?' She stared into my eyes. I looked away. 'I'm a reserved person, Madhav. I have issues opening up to people. I trusted you. And you...' She bit her lower lip.

'I just...'

'Just what? The stuff you said. I may not speak much Hindi, but I do understand it, Madhav,' she said and turned her face sideways. Then she said as if to herself, 'My friends had warned me about you.'

'I just love you, Riya.'

'Yeah, right. Indeed a classy way to show love.'

'I said it in anger.'

'Let me be clear. I have never, ever been spoken to in such a cheap manner in my life. I let you into my world. We had something together.'

'We do.'

'No, we don't. If you could speak to me like that, I wonder how you think of me in your mind.'

'I wanted to be close to you. Never let you go.'

'You said "deti hai to de, varna kat le". Does that sound like being close?'

'It's my useless friends, they provoked me. They said, sleep with her or else she'll never be yours.'

'You discussed this with your friends first?'

'Not everything but...'

'But stuff like "let me go fuck her today".'

Before I could respond she raised a hand to silence me. 'I'm going to say something now. Listen carefully. Okay?' she said, her voice shaky as she tried to maintain her composure.

'Sure.'

'One, don't ever try to talk to me. Two, we are not friends anymore. I have promised my friends and myself I will choose my friends carefully. Three, stop hounding me, it's disturbing. I don't want to tell my parents or the college authorities.'

'Riya…'

'Please go now,' she said and folded her hands, as if pleading with me.

I took one last look at her—the beautiful but angry and sad face, the long hair I had stroked, the lips I had kissed once—and turned around. I heard the sound of her footsteps get fainter as she walked away.

12

Six months later

After my break-up, or half-break-up, with Riya, my personality changed. People in college started to call me SSS, or the Silent Saint of Stephen's. I attended every class and sat in the front row. I took notes like a court stenographer. I never asked the professor any questions. I would sit with my friends in the residences but not contribute to the conversation. Initially, they tried to cheer me up. They gave me copies of *Playboy* and arranged booze parties to help me get over Riya. However, just like their earlier advice, their break-up cures were useless too. The only thing that helped somewhat was basketball. Every time I thought of her, I hit the court. Three hours of dribbling and shooting temporarily cured my heartache, if only because it left me physically exhausted. Frankly, I went to the courts in the hope she would come to practice. She never did. Perhaps her father had built her a court in the backyard of 100, Aurangzeb Road.

Sometimes I lurked in the college corridors, waiting for her class to end. I stood far away and avoided eye contact. I would watch her come out of class, only to disappear into a crowd of friends. Once she did see me. She didn't smile or turn away. She didn't even look angry. She didn't react at all. It killed me. If she had come forward and slapped me or yelled, I would have been okay. However, she looked right through me, as if I didn't exist.

Nights hit me the hardest. I couldn't sleep. I lay on the same bed where I had messed it up with her. The same place where I had spoken like a Bhojpuri movie villain. I wished I had a time machine to undo my actions. I didn't want a time machine to predict the stock market or buy property cheap. I only wanted it to un-say that sentence. I had said it in a combined state of horniness, bravado and stupidity. Well, it is also the state in which men are most of the time.

I tossed and turned. I couldn't sleep. I bounced my basketball on the room's wall back and forth until the student in the adjacent room shouted curses. I studied my course books to distract myself. I found books in the library on psychology, relationships and love. Through these I tried to figure out women. Either the English was too tough or the books gave contradictory ideas. I ended up being more confused than ever. Women like to nurture and have long-term relationships, one study said. However, I had wanted exactly that. So why did the study fail to explain this? Anything I read about women in newspapers I connected with Riya. If an actress gave an interview saying she was moody, I nodded and felt that, yes, even Riya was moody.

I had to get this girl out of my head. I couldn't.

A few months later it was my birthday. I sat with my friends in the cafeteria. As luck would have it, Riya entered at the same time with her friends. My friends wanted to see if she would wish me. They started singing, 'Happy birthday to you, Madhav', even as I cut a mince cutlet. The girls noticed but ignored us. Riya didn't even flinch. My heart crumbled like the mince cutlet.

'You're lucky. It's best such an insensitive girl is out of your life,' Raman said.

One afternoon, after college ended, I was sitting outside on the main lawn. Students turned their gaze to the main gate as a car entered the college.

It was a beautiful car. It looked expensive even from twenty metres away.

'It's a Bentley. Costs over two crores,' a boy sitting close to me told his friend. A young man stepped out of the car. He wore shades. He walked as if he owned the college.

Riya Somani emerged from the main building and walked towards the Bentley. I stood up and walked towards the driveway. I ensured I could not be seen; not that anyone was interested in me.

The man's face seemed familiar. Riya went up to him. They hugged. I noticed the man was an inch shorter than Riya.

Rohan Chandak, the name popped into my head. *What's this asshole doing here?* It's amazing how quickly the mind switches from figuring out a situation to commenting on it.

I had no idea why Rohan had come to college. Maybe he wanted to buy the building and turn it into a hotel. Well, that seemed unlikely as he didn't enter the building. Both of them got into the Bentley and it drove off, with Riya's BMW tailing Rohan's car. The students in the lawns released collective oohs and aahs.

'I also want a loaded boyfriend,' I heard a girl near me say.

'Is he her boyfriend?' I asked her. I shouldn't have but I did. Like I'd proved earlier, my impulse control is rather weak.

'How do I know?' she said and walked away.

I could still smell the burning fumes from Rohan's Bentley long after he had left. Or maybe it was my burning insides.

◆

I had to talk to Riya. I decided to do it during Harmony, the annual cultural festival of St. Stephen's. It would be my final attempt to rescue our friendship. The festival had various cultural competitions such as choreography, music, debates and treasure hunts. Students, including the day-skis, stayed in the college until late at night. Riya had already won the music competition in the solo English vocals category. She was also taking part in Western choreography.

I took my place in the audience early, sitting in the front row facing the makeshift choreography stage on the front lawns. Boys from all over Delhi University had gatecrashed. They sat at the right vantage points to ogle at the St. Stephen's chicks. Some of these boys resembled men back home. They spoke loudly in Hindi. They whistled every time a pretty girl came on stage. Stephanians, of course, hated all this. We were way too dignified to express our lecherous feelings in such a public manner. We ogled nonetheless, but in a dignified way.

A dozen girls wearing pink tights and silver-grey tops came on stage. Riya, the tallest amongst them and the easiest to spot, stood in the centre. Stage lights changed colours. A commentator spoke in a husky self-important voice. He spoke about evolution and how all life emanates from nature. It is stuff that sounds profound when you hear it but is total bullshit when you look back and think about it.

Riya's lean frame, athletic body and stunning looks meant most men had their eyes on her. Of course, another girl with a massive bust had her own set of fans.

As the commentator spoke his lines in a sexy voice, I rehearsed mine in my head.

'Riya, I think people deserve a second chance.'

Riya did cartwheels on stage with incredible grace. The crowd burst into applause as she did a perfect cartwheel.

Inside my chest, my heart did the same.

'Riya, not a day—*not a day*—passes when I don't think of you,' I said to myself. I deleted it from my mental shortlist. It sounded too keen. Girls are difficult. It is all about finding the right balance. You can neither be too pushy, nor come across as too cool to care. I suck at this fine balance.

In the last act, Riya took a handheld mic and sang the two closing lines about nature and how we need to protect it. Her clear and tuneful voice earned a round of spontaneous applause.

The show ended. The girls came forward to take a bow. The crowd cheered. I slipped out and then sprinted to the classroom converted into a green room. Finger-combing my hair, I knocked on the door.

A female student peeked out.

'What?'

'I need to talk to someone.'

'Sorry, only girls allowed inside.'

'Is Riya Somani there?'

'She is changing. Wait.'

I had little choice. I sat on a ledge opposite the classroom. I waited for thirty minutes. A group of girls came out, giggling for no particular reason. Riya didn't.

Forty-five minutes later, dressed in black jeans with silver buttons and a tight black top, Riya stepped out. In a deliberate act, she took brisk steps away from me.

'Riya,' I said.

She stopped. However, she didn't turn towards me. Her hands froze, as if uncomfortable.

'Please,' I said.

She semi-turned towards me.

'Hi, Madhav.'

I stood squarely in front of her.

'I want to talk. Five minutes,' I said.

'Anything important?'

'To me it is. Five minutes?'

'I'm listening.'

We stood in a dark corridor, facing each other stiffly, as if in confrontation. It didn't seem like the right place to talk. I saw her face. She was still the most beautiful woman in the world to me. Even though we were in the middle of what seemed like a world war, I wanted to kiss her. That is how sick the male mind is. It can forget the entire context of a situation and follow its own track.

'I said I'm listening,' she said. I flushed out the sick thoughts from my mind.

'Not here. Somewhere private?'

'Oh, really?' she said.

I realized it had come out all wrong.

'Sorry, not like that. Somewhere we can sit, face to face. And it isn't so dark.'

'The café?' she said.

'Now? It's packed with the DU crowd. You won't get a table.'

'Listen, I have plans. I have to go,' she said.

'Okay, the café then. Fine.'

We walked to the café. As expected, lines to enter extended all the way outside.

'It is crowded. Is it okay if we talk in my car?' she said.

I looked at her. She seemed to have calmed down a little.

'Yeah. The driver will be there, right?'

'I'll send him away. Actually, let's go to the car. I need to give you something, too.'

13

We walked out to her car. She handed her driver a fifty-rupee note.

'Driver bhaiya, can you go and buy a few packets of Parle-G biscuits for me, please?'

The driver looked puzzled.

'Madam, we will buy it on the way?'

'No, go now. Leave the keys. I'll wait inside.'

The confused driver handed the keys to Riya and left.

Riya and I sat in the backseat of her BMW. A fat armrest separated us. She switched on the reading light and slipped her feet out of her shoes. Turning sideways, she leaned back against the window to face me. She tucked her feet under her legs on the seat.

I sat stiffly. The BMW reminded me how out of place I was in her world.

'So?' Riya said.

'You were really great on stage. And congrats on winning the English vocals.'

'Oh, thank you. That's nice of you, Madhav, to congratulate me.'

'Amazing show,' I said, clearing my throat.

'Thanks. Is that all you wanted to say to me?'

I shook my head. I hated it when she adopted this formal tone.

'So let's skip the small talk. Say what you want to.'

'I'm sorry.'

'Have heard it a million times from you.'

'Forgive me.'

'I have forgiven you. I have also moved on. It's past. It's over. So, that's it?'

I looked into her eyes. In the dim reading light of the BMW, I could not spot any emotion on her face. I felt weak in her presence. I fought back tears.

'I want us to be friends again,' I said.

'Why?' she said, her voice as cold as Delhi's foggy winter night.

Did she miss nothing about me or what we had?

Because I miss you, damn it! I wanted to scream at the top of my voice. Of course, I couldn't. I had lost the right to express any words, let alone any emotions, to her. I had to say something reasonable, underplaying what I felt.

'So I have a chance to show you I am not a jerk,' I said.

'I am sure you are not. I take your word for it. You don't have to show me.'

Riya is too clever, too smart and sometimes too icy. She left me speechless. I had a sinking feeling something was not going right.

However, she touched my hand on the armrest. Her soft fingers pressed into my wrist, as if checking my pulse.

'Listen, Madhav,' she said. 'I am sorry I am being this way. Cold and aloof.'

Her warm touch melted my resolve to keep my composure. I loved her touch but I wished she would remove her fingers. I didn't know if I could hold back my tears anymore.

'Please,' I said. It sounded needy. I hated myself for saying it.

'Madhav, I'm not angry with you anymore. It is anyway not possible for us to be friends again. I am leaving.'

'What?'

'I'm leaving college.'

'What? Like quitting?'

She nodded.

'I'm dropping out.'

'You're in the second year. You won't finish your degree?'

'Never cared much for formal education.'

I looked at her, shocked.

'Of course, I can say that because my dad's rich. It's okay if you think that I'm a quitter.'

'No, I didn't think that. All I'm thinking is, why?'

She shrugged.

'You're dropping out of St. Stephen's. There must be a reason.'

Our eyes met. Maybe it was my imagination but, for a moment, I felt the same connection to her as I had in the past.

'I don't think you want to know.'

'I do,' I said. 'Of course I do.'

'You will judge me.'

'Have I ever?'

She kept quiet.

'Riya, have I ever judged you? You judged me and threw me out of your life.'

'Madhav, please.'

'Let's not go there. Yeah, fine. Anyway, are you still thinking about quitting or is it final?'

'Pretty final.'

'Why?'

She took a deep breath.

'Open the glove box.'

'What?'

She pointed to the storage box below the dashboard. Puzzled, I reached over and opened it. It had three red cardboard boxes inside.

'Take one,' she said.

I picked up a box and sat back on my seat. The velvet-lined red box had golden leaves embossed on it.

'Open it.'

I switched on the reading light on my side of the car. I lifted the red-gold lid of the box.

Inside, I found a red envelope on top of a silk pouch. The card and the pouch had 'R and R' on it.

'What?' I said.

She gestured with her eyes that I look further.

I held the envelope in one hand and the pouch in the other. The pouch contained pieces of chocolate wrapped in silver paper. I put the pouch aside and opened the card.

I read a couple of lines. My head swam.

'What?' I turned to Riya.

'I told you, you don't want to know.'

I composed myself and summoned the resolve to read the full card. It went like this:

Shri Vishnu Somani and Shrimati Kala Devi Somani
humbly invite you to the wedding of
their granddaughter
So. Riya Somani
(d/o Mr Mahendra Somani and Mrs Jayanti Somani)
with
Chi. Rohan Chandak
(s/o Late Shri Manoj Chandak and Jamna Bai Chandak)
on 25 January 2007 at 8 p.m.
at the Taj Palace Hotel, Delhi
Programme and RSVP details attached. Request no gifts.

I didn't read the other cards in the box, which had details of the other ceremonies. I simply sat there frozen. I clutched the silk pouch like a stress ball and looked straight ahead.

'It happened so fast,' Riya said.

I remained quiet. Shock waves ran through me. Numb, I traced the golden embroidery on the pouch.

'A part of me can't believe it is happening,' she said, to fill the awkward silence.

'You're getting married?' I whispered, my tone unusually calm, my gaze still averted.

'In two months.'

I smirked and turned to her. 'Wow, Riya. I've never faced such a dodge, even on the basketball court.'

'What do you mean?'

'I wanted us to be friends again. But you are leaving college. Getting married.'

'That's life, I guess.'

'You're nineteen.'

'Will turn twenty after the wedding, later the same year.'

'Have you gone mad, Riya?'

'You've lost the right to talk to me like that,' she said.

'I'm sorry.'

'It's fine. Madhav, it is my choice. Nobody is forcing me. I want to leave.'

'Why?'

'I never wanted to do this course. I don't want to be near my sexist relatives.'

'You could finish your degree. Go abroad later to study. Why marriage?'

'I want adventure, travel and excitement. Rohan promises all that.'

'Are you sure?'

'Yeah. He's crazy. He keeps me entertained. He's also well settled. What's wrong with marrying him?'

'He's rich.'

'So? Is that his only flaw? So am I.'

'Not a flaw. Just an observation. He couldn't wait for you to finish college? He wants you to drop out?'

'Well, he doesn't care either way. It's his family. They want him to get married soon. My parents don't want to risk losing a match like him, too.'

'Riya, nobody drops out of college like this.'

'People abroad do it all the time.'

'Not in India.'

'Oh, come on. Most of India needs a degree to get a job and make a living. I don't need that, right?'

She wasn't wrong. Losers like me need to study, else we have no future. People who are born at 100, Aurangzeb Road can do whatever they want in life.

'Even Rohan joined an MBA and never finished it.'

'Is Rohan your boyfriend?'

'Well, he will be my husband,' Riya said.

'That's not what I asked.'

'We are getting closer. Of course, I always called him Rohan bhaiya when I was growing up, so it's an adjustment,' she said. She laughed at her own joke. I wished someone had strangled Rohan at the 'bhaiya' stage. That bastard had seemed like trouble right from Riya's party.

I wanted to say something sensible. I wanted to turn the tide even somewhat in my favour. Of course, God had not given me the brains to do so. Neither was my timing right. A girl giving you her wedding card is basically like a giant 'Game Over' sign flashing in a video game. It is not the time to say you want her back. Or that you love her more than anything else on earth. I wondered if I should act supportive. I wondered if I should ask her about the preparations, or if she needed any help. I stopped myself. I could not sink that low.

The situation reminded me of what my friends used to tell me. I was indeed a toy. I felt like Woody from the movie *Toy Story*. In the film, Woody, a neglected toy, cries alone because his owner grows up and no longer plays with him.

'Say something,' she said.

You bloody bitch, my impulsive mind suggested. I controlled myself.

Please don't do this. I love you so much, said the emotional side of my mind. I realized my head was a mess right now. Given my track record, saying anything would only mean regretting it later.

'What do I say? Surprised. Shocked. I don't know.'

'People normally say congratulations.'

'Yeah,' I said, but didn't congratulate her.

'I hope we can move past whatever happened. We can, right?' she said.

I nodded.

'You will come?'

'Where?'

'The wedding. I just invited you.'

I wanted to throw her over-the-top wedding invitation box-cum-card at her.

'Let's see,' I said. I patted myself mentally. I had responded with more dignity than I thought I had. 'Go fuck yourself' would have been a more natural response.

'Please do come,' she said.

'Are you sure you're doing the right thing?' I managed to say one more time.

'I'm following my heart. That's usually doing the right thing, right?'

'I don't know. Sometimes following your heart leads you nowhere.'

I looked at her to see if she understood my sly comment. She did, and gave a wry smile.

'I am sorry, Madhav, if I hurt you.'

I nodded to reassure her that hurting me was no big deal. Pretty girls have the right to hurt men. I found it hard to breathe. I switched off the reading light. That way, in case I started crying, my tears would not be visible.

I heard a knock on the car's door. The driver was back.

'Here, madam,' the driver said. He handed her four packets of Parle-G.

She passed the biscuits to me. 'Please take them for Rudra. I'm addicted to these. If I keep them in the car I'll eat them all.'

'You asked him to get it.'

'Only so he would leave us alone.'

I kept the packets, my consolation prize. Rohan gets Riya. Madhav gets biscuits.

I opened the car door and stepped out.

She stepped out from her side and walked up to me.

'Bye,' she said.

'Bye, Riya,' I said. It was hard to hold back my tears forever. I wanted her to leave.

'Hey, you forgot something,' she said.

'What?' I said.

'Your card.'

She reached into the car and handed me the evil red box once again, with the cards and the chocolates. I somehow managed to hold everything along with the biscuit packets.

'Oh, thanks,' I said. I wondered where the nearest dustbin was.

'Take care then,' she said and came forward for a basic goodbye hug.

I stepped back. I didn't want any more fake hugs.

She understood my hesitation and withdrew with grace. She smiled at me one last time and slid into her car. The BMW slipped away with its silent elegance, as if nothing had happened.

The car took a left turn from Hindu College and was soon out of sight. I sat down on the road. The red box and its contents lay around me, almost like hardened blood.

I cried. The desolate campus road meant nobody could see me.

I let it all flow out. Months of pain condensed into tears. A car passed by. I probably looked like a Delhi beggar, complete with biscuit packets around me.

After a while, I collected everything from the road and stood up. I walked up to the dustbin outside the main gate of the college. I removed the chocolates and biscuits and stuffed them in my pocket. I threw away everything else.

Even though I was in pain, I remembered the golden rule: if you live in a hostel, never throw away food.

14

One year and three months later

'So tell us why you're here,' said a thirty-year-old man. He wore a red tie and a crisp white shirt.

I was at HSBC's placement interview, facing a panel of three bankers. Each wore a pained and bored expression. They had heard over forty Stephanians talk nonsense about their greatness. Each candidate had solved all the problems India faced, redesigned the bank's strategy and promised to work harder than apartheid-era slaves. Why do companies bother with such interviews? Perhaps it makes them feel better to talk about the problems of the world, even though the actual job involves sitting at a desk and punching formulas into spreadsheets.

I had no answer for my panel. I didn't know why I had applied to them, or for any job at all. I hated Delhi. I flashbacked to my college life. Yes, I'd loved it when I had first joined college. The first year had gone by so quickly it had felt like a vacation. The second year was painful, with Riya breaking up with me. However, she was at least around. I could steal a glance at her every now and then, be rejected every couple of months and still remember the good times. I had something then that keeps people going during the worst times—hope.

I dreamt Riya would come around one day. She would realize I was her perfect partner—in terms of height, basketball, mental connect, how hours felt like minutes when we were together and how little we cared about the rest of the world. She never did. She slapped a wedding card on me and left. My Bihari gang had made me swear on my mother I would never contact her again. I didn't. She quit college in a couple of weeks. She had a lavish wedding, Stephanians who attended it said afterwards. I'm sure Rohan spent the college's entire annual budget on the wedding reception. I overheard that Riya had gone to Bora Bora for her honeymoon. The name of the place sounded like it was in Bihar. However, I googled it and discovered it was a set of beautiful islands in the Pacific Ocean, some reachable only by private plane. Which ruled out me going there and murdering the groom.

However, the pain of the second year felt like a tickle compared to the third year. Third year sucked. I had zero ability to get over her. I couldn't believe a girl who had left me a year ago had such a grip on me. We had not even slept together. However, it mattered little. She was the only girl I had played, walked, eaten, talked, studied and had fun with. I had peeked into Silent Riya more than anyone else, or so I thought. How could I forget her?

Well, I could not forget her from two years ago, but I had forgotten the interview room I had entered two minutes ago.

'I said, what brings you here?' the interviewer repeated and sipped from his bottle of water.

'Yes, sir. I am here because…' I fumbled to remember the company's name. 'Because HSBC is a dynamic place to work in and I want to be a part of it.'

Given my cut-paste answer, I thought he would splash his water on my face. However, he didn't.

'Madhav Jha, right?' said another member of the panel, reading my résumé.

'State-level basketball, impressive. Shortlisted for national team trials last year. Did you make it?'

'No, sir.'

'Why not?'

I hesitated for a second and then gave my answer. 'I didn't go for the trials.' Basketball reminded me of her. After she left, I never went to the court.

'Why?' all three of them asked together.

'I couldn't. I was under stress.'

'What kind of stress?' said the first interviewer.

'Personal.'

The other interviewers cleared their throat. They nodded their heads at each other, communicating the need to skip that question.

'Why do you want to do banking?' the third panellist said.

'Because that is what you want me to do.'

'Excuse me?' The panellist blinked.

'Well, I need a job. Yours is one of those available. And you pay well. So yes, I'll do whatever you want me to.'

'You don't have a preference?'

'Not really.'

I don't know what made me talk like this. Perhaps it was the fact that I had given eight interviews over the past two weeks and I had lied in every one of them. I had finally had enough. I didn't want to be in Delhi anymore. I missed my mother. I wanted to call her right now.

'Madhav, do you want this job?' the first panellist said.

'What's your name, sir?' I asked instead.

'Shukla. I am Pramod Shukla. Regional manager for North India.'

'Mr Shukla, are you happy?'

'Excuse me?'

'You don't look happy. None of you look happy. Nobody wants this job. Everyone wants the money you offer. You see the difference?'

The panellists looked at each other. If I had a camera, the picture of their priceless expressions could have won any photography competition.

'I like you. The first honest candidate we have had. I will hire you,' Pramod said.

The other two looked shocked. However, they were too junior to counter the boss's whim.

'But I don't want it,' I said and stood up.

'Why?' Pramod said. 'Private banking in Delhi. Top clients. Six lakhs a year.'

'No, sir. I am done serving rich people,' I said and left the room.

◆

As I walked back to my residence after the interview, for the first time in a year, I felt respect for myself. I decided not to be a doormat anymore. I decided to stop moping over a rich girl who had left me. I had had enough of Stephen's and trying to be upper class.

You belong to Dumraon in Bihar. That is who you are, Madhav Jha, I told myself, *and that is all you will ever be and need to be.*

I called my mother.

'How are the interviews going?' she said.

'One company offered me a job.'

'Who?'

'HSBC.'

'What do they do?'

'Bank.'

'They have a branch in Patna?'

I laughed. 'No, it is an international bank. The job is in Delhi,' I said.

'Oh,' my mother said and her voice dropped. 'You will have to be there then.'

'I said no.'

'What?' she said, surprised.

'I didn't want the job. My heart is not here anymore.'

'Where is your heart?' My mother chuckled.

London, said a voice in my head.

'Dumraon. I'm coming back home.'

I could sense the wide smile on her face through the phone.

'You'll come back to Dumraon? After finishing Stephen's college?' she said, her voice bright.

'Yes. It is my home, after all.'

'Of course. Everyone keeps asking about you: "Where is our prince, the rajkumar?"'

'Please, Ma, I hope all that nonsense won't start there.'

'What do you mean, nonsense? You are the prince of Dumraon. People want to do your rajyabhishek ceremony.'

'Ma. I don't like such traditions. Royalty is dead in India.'

'It's just a way they express love. We know, and they know, we don't have power. But we help keep the community together. You shouldn't shrug it off.'

'Anyway, I arrive in three weeks. I need to find something to do there.'

'You can help with the school.'

'You are running it well.'

'For how long? Plus, there are so many issues I can't solve at this age. Should I focus on the teaching or repair the roof? From teachers on one side to labourers on the other, everyone eats my head.'

I laughed.

'I'll take care of the roof and any upkeep issues. You run the school.'

'Really?'

'Yes, Ma.'

'How much would it have paid you? The job you left?'

'Let it be, Ma. How does it matter now?'

'Tell me.'

'Fifty thousand.'

'A year?'

'A month.'

My mother gasped so loudly my eardrum hurt.

'You really refused that job to come and help in a village school?'

'Yes, Ma. I told you. I'm booking a ticket on the Magadh Express. See you in three weeks.'

'I know what made you do this.'

My heart stopped.

'What?'

'Your royal blood. You are different. You deserve to be a prince.'

'Prince has to go. Doesn't have balance in his prepaid phone.'

My mother laughed as I hung up. Most Indian mothers would slap a child if he left a high-paying job like that. My mother wouldn't. She knew life involved things greater than money. She had seen the lavish life. She had also seen her wedding jewels pawned to loan sharks. None of this mattered. What mattered to my mother, the Rani Sahiba of Dumraon, was respect.

'Beyond a point, people want money to buy respect,' she would tell me when I was a kid. 'Respect, however, can't be bought. You have to earn it.

'Live with dignity. Live for others, that is how one earns respect,' she used to say. She was right. Dumraon's people loved her. Not because she was the Rani Sahiba, but because she was the Rani Sahiba who cared. For the past fifteen years, she had given her all to the Dumraon Royal School in Nandan village, on the outskirts of Dumraon.

I felt homesick. The dusty lanes of Dumraon felt more enticing than the colonial lawns of St. Stephen's. I couldn't wait to be home.

ACT II

Bihar

15

Dumraon, District Buxar, Bihar

I wanted to surprise my mother, so I told her I was arriving a day later than the actual date. I reached the Dumraon railway station after a fourteen-hour train journey from Delhi.

As I walked out of the station, the familiar smells of my childhood hit me straightaway.

There is nothing spectacular about my hometown. It is a small place, less than three kilometres across on any side. Its only claim to fame is being one of the oldest princely states of India. My family had something to do with that achievement. However, I don't know if I can feel proud for what my ancestors did ten generations ago.

Dumraon is in Buxar district, around sixteen kilometres from Buxar town on the banks of the Ganges. If you were not sleeping in history class you would have heard of the Great Battle of Buxar in 1764. Frankly, it should be renamed the Embarrassing Battle of Buxar. The battle was fought between the British East India Company and the combined armies of three Indian rulers—Mir Qasim, the Nawab of Bengal; Shuja-ud-Daula, the Nawab of Awadh; and the Mughal king, Shah Alam II. The Indian side had forty thousand troops. The British had less than ten thousand. Guess what happened? The British clobbered us. How? Well, the three Indian kings ended up fighting with each other. Each Indian king had cut a side deal with the British and worked against the other. In a day, the British had won the battle and taken control of most of India. I don't think Indians have learnt much since that day. We remain as divided as ever. Everyone still tries to cut a deal for themselves while the nation goes to hell.

Anyway, there is a reason I am telling you this. You may think things are not connected, but think about this. If there was no Battle of Buxar, or if it had had a different outcome, the British may not have ruled India like they did. There would be none of the 'English high class, rest low class' bullshit that happens in India. There would not even be a St. Stephen's College. Just imagine, if only the jokers in

Buxar had done things a little differently, maybe the white man would be speaking Hindi and Bhojpuri would be the new cool.

I took an autorickshaw. 'Raja ki haveli,' I told the driver. He put the auto in first gear and drove off. In Dumraon, our house is a landmark by itself.

It was the bumpiest ride ever. A cloud of dust surrounded us as we drove through the city.

'What happened to the road?' I asked the auto driver.

'There are no roads,' he said and laughed.

◆

Twenty minutes later, the auto reached the haveli's main entrance. Fifteen years ago, we had a guard post here. Now, we just had pillars on each side. Along with my three fat suitcases I stood in the central quadrangle, once a beautiful garden. My childhood picture, which Riya had seen, had been taken here. I noticed a stack of bamboo poles and bundles of cloth kept in the quadrangle. Two labourers sat in a corner, smoking beedis.

'What's this?' I said.

'We are putting up a tent,' said one of them.

◆

Ma wasn't home when I arrived. I entered my old room. The large wooden doors creaked more than before. The cupboard doors had become stiff. I opened the windows. Sunlight fell on the posters of Shaquille O'Neal and Magic Johnson stuck on my wall for the last five years.

I lay on the bed, staring at the basketball champions. I wondered if I should have focused more on the national trials.

A few hours later my mother returned from school. 'Ma,' I screamed from the window.

My mother saw me as she entered the haveli gate. She waved at me. I rushed downstairs and gave her a big hug. Girlfriends come and go but, thank God, mothers don't break up with you.

'You said tomorrow,' she said. We sat on one of the living-room sofas, frayed but still elegant.

'I thought I would surprise you,' I said.

'That's nice. But you spoilt our surprise.'

'How?'

Savitri tai, one of my mother's oldest helpers, brought in tea and sweet litti.

'Your coronation. You saw the tents outside, right?'

'What?' I said, a half-eaten litti ball in my hand.

'It's an auspicious day, Ashad Krishna.'

'Ma, I don't want this drama.'

'It isn't drama. It's tradition,' my mother said in a low, emotional voice, the perfect starting point for female drama.

'I'll feel like a joker, being anointed a prince in a democracy.'

My mother stood up and walked to the dining table, her back to me. She remained silent, her most potent weapon. Standing tall at five feet, eight inches, in her starched saree, my mother did look royal. She clenched her fists tight.

I walked up to her.

'Ma, you shouldn't have sent me to college if you wanted me to keep following such rituals.'

My mother spoke, her back still towards me. 'Funny, I was thinking the same thing.'

I went around the dining table to face her. 'We have an MLA,' I said. 'What's his name?'

My mother looked at me in defiance.

'What's his name, Ma?'

'Ojha. Useless fellow.'

'Yes, Ojha. We also have an MP in Buxar and a CM in Patna.'

'The villagers still care for us. You know why?' she said.

'Because they are old-fashioned and uneducated?'

My mother looked at me sharply. 'You've become like them.'

'Like whom?'

'The over-educated idiots in big cities. Whenever they don't understand villagers, they call them uneducated and old-fashioned.'

I listened to her reprimand, keeping my head down. The Rani Sahiba's rare loss of temper could not be taken lightly.

'So why do they want to coronate me? Nothing else entertaining happening in Dumraon?'

'They want to because the so-called government doesn't seem to care.'

I poured a glass of water and handed it to my mother.

'Ma, I have finished college and come back. Can you not shout at me within the first hour of meeting me?'

'Your actions deserve it, so what can I do?'

'Okay, sorry. I am sorry, Ma.'

She relented and we sat on the sofa again. I placed four more littis on my plate.

'There's dinner. Don't stuff yourself with these,' Ma said.

'Sorry,' I said, and put my plate back on the table.

'Anyway, it is just a two-hour-long ceremony—the rajyabhishek puja and lunch. What is the problem?'

'No problem at all. I'll do it.'

The fan in the room stopped. In seconds, sweat beads appeared on our foreheads. In minutes, mosquitoes hovered over us.

'What happened?' I said.

'Load-shedding. Go thank your government for this,' my mother said.

16

'How much longer, Pandit ji?' I said. My back hurt from sitting cross-legged on the floor for over two hours. Marriages get done faster than this. The village priest chanted holy mantras for my peaceful and successful rule. Whatever.

Around two hundred people from Dumraon and nearby villages had come to attend the ceremony. People sat on red plastic chairs. Giant pedestal fans recirculated the hot air.

I recognized a few important guests. MLA Vijay Ojha, a sixty-year-old man who had been in local politics for over forty years, sat in the front row. The district collector and the police inspector sat next to him. Local press reporters took pictures and hovered around them.

Finally, my mother presented the royal crown to Pandit ji; she had taken it out of our family safe. It was one of the few precious items we had left.

Pandit ji placed the two-kilo crown on my head. The crowd applauded. My mother burst into tears. She gave me a hug—an embarrassing public display of affection.

'Happy now?' I said, whispering in her ear.

'My rajkumar.' She hugged me even tighter.

I was sweating profusely in my velvet bandhgala suit. 'Rajkumar is melting in the heat. Can I change?' I said.

I came down from the stage. Reporters made me pose for photos. My mother introduced me to guests even as reporters took my pictures.

'Mubarak, Rajkumar sahib,' said a young man in his twenties. My mother introduced him as Akhtar Hussain, one of the two teachers in her school.

'Call me Madhav,' I said to Akhtar, shaking his hand. He seemed embarrassed at the suggestion.

'Madhav, meet Tej Lal, another teacher at our school, and Tarachand ji, the administrative officer,' my mother said.

I folded my hands to wish both men, each in their fifties. 'I will be joining the school too,' I said.

My mother's staff looked at her in surprise.

'I thought you went to a top college in Delhi,' Akhtar said.

'So?' I said.

'You can get a good job anywhere,' Akhtar said.

'This is not a good job?' I said. Everyone grinned.

MLA Ojha reached us. He had a thick moustache, upwardly mobile on either side.

'Congratulations, Rani Sahiba,' he said.

'Ojha ji, thank you so much for coming,' my mother said.

He folded his hands to take permission to leave.

'But what about lunch?'

'I have two other functions in Buxar. Please excuse me,' he said, hands still folded.

My mother looked at me. She wanted me to persuade him to stay.

'Ojha ji, stay a little while. We can eat together,' I said.

'No, Rajkumar ji. Besides, you won't be done soon. See, the line has built up.'

I turned around to find a queue of about fifty villagers waiting to seek my blessings. A few kids came up to me. They wanted to touch the sword attached to my waist. I guess if you look like a clown, you do attract some attention.

'If only voters loved their netas like they love you,' MLA Ojha said before he left.

One by one, I blessed the villagers.

'Is he a real prince? Like those in stories?' I overheard a young girl whisper to another.

'Of course he is,' her friend said.

'So where is his princess?' the young girl said.

I smiled. My princess had moved to another faraway kingdom.

'What time is school tomorrow, Ma?' I said.

'Seven in the morning. Think about work later. Enjoy being the ruler today,' she said.

It is no fun being a ruler when someone else still rules you.

◆

The Dumraon Royal School is a twenty-minute walk from our haveli. I accompanied my mother as we hiked through fields at 6.30 in the morning. 'There are three shifts, over two hundred students in each,' my mother said. '7 to 10.30, 10.30 to 2, and 2 to 5.30.'

We reached the grey-and-black school building. It seemed much older than the last time I'd seen it.

'Why is it black?' I said.

'Hasn't been painted in five years. Every year, the rains wreck the plaster even more.'

I wondered how Stephen's managed to keep its walls a perfect reddish-brown.

The first-shift kids had arrived. They played in the fields outside the school. We had two classrooms and a common staffroom. The staffroom had a long table with several chairs—the teachers used the room to rest in during breaks or to check notebooks.

'Why is it so dark?' I said.

'Power comes at eight,' my mother said.

The long table had a stack of files and books at three corners.

'Akhtar, Tej and I have a corner each. The empty one is yours,' my mother said.

She sat down on her end. She lit a candle and opened a file.

'These windows could be bigger,' I said.

My mother nodded without looking up. Akhtar, Tej and Tarachand arrived in the next five minutes. They folded their hands when they saw me.

'Please treat me as a new employee,' I said to them.

Amused, Akhtar and Tej collected their books for class. Tarachand stepped outside the staffroom. He rang the brass bell in the corridor. The teachers left for their classes. Tarachand came back and spoke to my mother.

'SMDC didn't send anyone,' he said.

'Oh no,' my mother said. 'He promised. The officer gave me his word, Tara ji.'

'I went to his house, Rani Sahiba. He said he tried. Hard to justify more funds,' Tarachand said.

'We want one toilet. How hard is it to justify funds for one toilet for seven hundred children?' my mother said.

'He said most schools in the area manage without one. Why is

Rani Sahiba fussing?'

'Ask him for half a toilet. Tell him to make one for the girls. One girls' toilet, Tara ji,' my mother said.

'Don't embarrass me, Rani Sahiba. I tried. We need money for so many other things too. We need to plaster the roofs, make more rooms and whitewash the building. SMDC said they have nothing.'

Noises came from the corridor. Kids had assembled outside.

'Make them sit, please,' my mother said.

Tarachand stepped out to manage the crowd. The children sat down at one end of the corridor. They faced a wall painted black.

My mother held her forehead with her right hand.

'You okay?' I said to her.

She nodded.

'What's SMDC?'

'The School Monitoring and Development Committee. A government body meant to help rural schools. They come, watch and leave. Nobody ever helps anyone.'

The lights came on. The fan above started to creak. The cool breeze felt wonderful on my sweaty skin. My mother leaned back in her chair and closed her eyes, enjoying the fan's breeze.

'Why are the children sitting in the corridor?' I said, disturbing her reverie.

'Huh? Oh, that is class I,' my mother said.

The morning shift had classes I to IV. Classes II, III and IV used the available classrooms. Class I used the corridor as their classroom.

I looked outside the staffroom. Kids sat on the floor, waiting for my mother.

'Help me with enrolment. Villagers don't like sending kids to school,' my mother said.

'But Ma, I want to teach as well,' I said.

'There's lots of other work. Tarachand ji is hopeless at paperwork.'

'Sounds boring.'

'It's important. I need someone to keep records and lobby with the authorities. I don't have the energy.'

I took a deep breath and nodded. Like the school, my mother was turning old and weak.

'Ma, can't we pay for some of these repairs?' I said.

My mother looked at me. I knew the answer from her expression.

'I try to give what I can. We hardly have money to repair the haveli. You were studying in Delhi, so I had that expense. Don't have much.'

I felt guilty. I wondered if I could have served my mother better by accepting that HSBC job. At least I could have sent her a cheque every month.

'We manage. Don't worry. I'm happy you're here,' my mother said, reading my mind.

'How?' I said.

'I take no salary. I pay the staff. If something breaks down I pay for it. Beyond that, it is difficult. The government is supposed to aid us. They don't.'

'What about what we earn from the fees?'

'It's nothing. The fee is five rupees a month. Even then, many students don't pay on time. If we are lucky, the fee covers the electricity bill.'

The noise levels in the corridor increased. A cacophony of conversation, laughter and screaming drowned our conversation.

'Look at them. Noisy monkeys. I better go,' my mother said. She walked out.

The difference between seventy kids on their own and seventy kids with a teacher can be immense. In an instant, the class fell silent.

I spent the rest of the morning reading all the files and documents related to the school. I quickly realized that running a school of seven hundred with a staff of four is no joke.

'Okay, start counting in English,' my mother shouted outside.

'One, two, three…' the kids chanted in unison. I didn't know whether these kids from the village would ever use their knowledge of English numerals. Still, watching them learn something felt good. It felt better than watching a movie at a Delhi multiplex. It felt better than the posh party at Riya's house.

'From now on, these kids are my life,' I told myself.

17

Six months later

'You promised, Sarpanch ji,' I said, using a hand fan to cool myself. I had come to his house a third time. Sarpanch Gopi, the man in charge of Aamva village, had assured me that every child in his village would come to school.

His wife brought us two glasses of lukewarm sattu, a roasted powder of pulses and lentils mixed in water. I wished it was a little cooler and less sweet, but drank it anyway.

The sixty-year-old sarpanch wore a greyish-white turban, matching his clothes.

'I thought they joined school. We sent eight children,' he said.

'They stopped coming after a week.'

'So what can I do, Rajkumar sahib? I tried.'

'You have to tell them to commit to it. School isn't like visiting the village fair. It takes years to get educated.'

'And what do they do with it?'

'Excuse me? It's almost free. Where is the problem?'

Gopi paused to look at me. He took out a beedi from his pajama pocket and lit it.

'Time. Their parents would rather the children help in the fields.'

'And what will they do when they grow up?'

'They will grow up only if they have food. They need to work in the fields for that.'

I fell silent. You can't win over villagers with an argument. You have to listen to what they have to say.

The sarpanch took a deep puff from his beedi.

'You studied in a big city?' he said.

'Yes. Why?'

'Big-city types never get it. Without knowing us they have all the answers for us.'

'I am from here. You know that, Sarpanch ji.'

'I know, Rajkumar ji. But what do these poor farmer's kids do with the A–B–C and 1-2-3 you teach them?'

'What do you mean?'

'A farmer sends his small child to school. Sounds great. But what does the school give him?'

'Education. What is he without education?'

'What will he do if, say, you make him an eighth-class-pass from Dumraon? Will he get a better job? More money? Nothing. It's a useless qualification. Here, he at least helps at home.'

'What is his future?' I said, confused about how to convince someone about something as basic as schooling.

'He has no future. Like his father, he will also work in the fields and try to survive. Schools are for rich people.'

I hung my head.

'Don't make the poor dream of having a future, Rajkumar ji. The schools you have don't help us get ahead in life. So we don't send our kids there. It's as simple as that. We are not village idiots who don't know better.'

I nodded. On the one hand I had to increase enrolments and, on the other hand, I couldn't fault his logic.

'Anything I can do to help you?' I asked as I stood up to leave. His own little grandkid lurked behind him, watching me with curiosity.

'Help us get water. Kids in the village walk two kilometres for it every day. If that ends, we will send them to school.'

◆

Every politician's office always has people waiting outside. On a per-capita basis, netas meet more people than anyone in any other profession on earth. MLA Ojha's home-cum-office was packed. Groups of villagers sat outside on the veranda, each with a set of complaints or demands. Pankaj, the MLA's secretary, offered to push me ahead in the queue. I declined. I had little interest in my entitlements as a fake prince.

The villagers waited silently. There is something about people with no hope for a better future in life. You can identify them from their expression. Most of all, it is in their eyes, which don't sparkle anymore. They aren't sad eyes. They are resigned eyes. The villagers had accepted that life would be what happened to them, not what they made of it. After all, this was rural Bihar. You can't decide one day to work hard and make it big in life. Nobody will let you. You have ramshackle schools that teach you how to read and write, but not help you make it in life. Even if you did educate yourself, you would find no jobs. What is the point of dreaming big? It is better to sit, wait and retire from life.

'What have you come here for?' I asked one of the village elders.

'Power. We get it one hour a day in our village, Bastipur. Not enough to pump water. We want to ask for two more hours.'

That's it. The man wanted three hours of power in twenty-four hours. And even for that he had to wait to meet his leaders with folded hands. *There must be millions of Indians like this*, I thought. A lot more than those who attend sushi parties on Aurangzeb Road, for instance.

I waved a bunch of flies away. Pankaj came up to me.

'Come, Ojha sir doesn't like it that you're waiting outside,' Pankaj said.

'I'm fine, really,' I said.

Ojha came out of his office. 'You're sitting on the floor?' he said, surprised.

'Like everyone else,' I said.

He looked around. 'Enough now, just come in, Madhav ji,' he said.

We sat in the MLA's living room. His wife brought me orange juice.

'You should have just walked in,' he said.

'I didn't want the villagers to think you give me preferential treatment,' I said.

'Now the villagers will say that I made the prince of Dumraon sit on the floor. Trust me, they care more about class than fairness. Anyway, what brings you here?'

'I need help for my school. And some hand pumps for the nearby villages.'

'Your school I can understand,' Ojha said as he raised his eyebrows just a little, 'but hand pumps for villages?'

'Yes. In Aamva.'

'You're turning into a social worker? Or entering politics?'

'None of those. The kids are not allowed to go to school. They have to walk two kilometres to fill water. More hand pumps in villages, more enrolment in my school.'

'Ah,' the MLA said as he finished his glass of orange juice. 'Thank God.'

He burst into laughter. I sat there, puzzled.

'If you join politics, my job is in danger,' he guffawed.

'Don't worry, I will not. Also, my school needs help.'

'I know. Your mother told me. It needs repairs worth lakhs. Unfortunately, it is not a government-run school.'

'But it is the only option for our kids.'

'You want something to eat? My wife made pakoras.'

I shook my head.

'If you could help with the school,' I said, as he interrupted me.

'Rajkumar ji…'

'Madhav. Please call me Madhav.'

'Okay, Madhav ji, see, my MLA funds are limited. I have to repair roads, fix power and install hand pumps. In fact, I have already run out.'

'How about the state education ministry?'

Ojha laughed. His laugh gave away the answer.

'It's Bihar. You should know,' he said.

'So you can't do anything?'

'You want a personal donation from me? I am a humble government servant,' he said.

'No, that is not what I came for. I felt the local government should support the only proper school in the area. Parents of these kids vote for you.'

'They do. However, they also have other, more important issues they want me to focus on.'

I stood up to leave.

'You sure you don't want to try the pakoras?'

◆

An angry Rani Sahiba is not a pretty sight. I sat at the dining table, eating pulao and raita for dinner.

She stood before me.

'Sit,' I said.

'Stand up,' she said, her voice calm; too calm, in fact.

I flicked the rice from my fingers and stood up.

'What happened?' I said.

'I'm allowing you to help out in the school. It doesn't mean you do whatever you want.'

'What did I do?' I said.

'You went to meet that arrogant MLA without telling me?'

'I thought he might help. We can't run the school without toilets forever.'

'Him? He wants the royal family to look bad.'

'Why?'

'How else will he look good?'

I kept quiet.

'Sit,' my mother said.

We both sat down, facing each other at the dining table. The huge dining-cum-living room was eerily silent as she spooned some rice on to her plate.

'What did he say, anyway?' she said.

'He said he had no money left from his fund.'

'Because he ate it all up,' my mother said. 'Sometimes I wish I had not declined the ticket.'

'What ticket?'

'His party had asked me to contest last time. Why do you think Ojha is so insecure about our family?'

'Contest elections? You didn't tell me.'

'Well,' my mother said, 'I wasn't interested. And did you have time in Delhi to listen to your mother?'

'I was studying, Ma.'

'Or playing basketball.'

The mention of basketball, without any warning, made me go blank.

'But you never really listened to me even when you called. Wonder what kept you so distracted there. No girl and all, no?'

I kept quiet.

'Was there?' she said and laughed. 'Can't imagine you having a girlfriend.'

'Pass me the raita,' I said.

'Say, no, if there was someone.'

I shook my head.

'What?'

'Nobody.'

'You sure? Why have you become all quiet?' my mother said.

'I miss the game. You mentioned basketball. I haven't played in a long time.'

'So go play. Go to Raj High School, people still play there.'

I nodded.

'In fact,' my mother said, 'you could even...'

She turned silent mid-sentence.

'Even what?'

'Nothing.'

'Say it.'

'Was going to say you could even teach the kids at school. But...'

'We don't have a court. Or the money for it,' I said, my voice irritated.

'So I didn't mention it. Anyway, you go play. It'll clear your head.'

'My head is fine.'

'See how you talk to your mother? If your head was fine, you wouldn't have gone to the MLA.'

'I just wanted to help.'

'Enough. Eat your food.'

My mother still treated me as if I was ten years old. The funny thing was, I let her.

18

I reached the Raj High School playground at 6 in the evening. I saw a few teenage students on court. We smiled as we acknowledged each other. I asked for the ball. A student passed it to me. I was touching the dusty and dotted-rubber texture of the ball after ages. I took a shot.

Chhaak. The soft sound of the ball going through the net without touching the ring told me I still had it in me.

A few students clapped.

'Where's St. Stephen's?' one boy said. He had noticed my college T-shirt.

I looked at the boy. He seemed clueless about my fancy college. I had been like him not too long ago. I told him about my alma mater.

'English college?' he said.

'Completely. That too high-class English,' I said and laughed.

'I will never make it.'

'I entered through the sports quota. Maybe you can too.'

I dribbled the ball. The thumping sound matched my heartbeat.

'I'm not that good,' he said.

I threw the ball at him. He caught it reflexively.

'Let's see. I'm Madhav, by the way.'

'Parth,' he said and dribbled the ball.

I tackled him as he ran across the court. He was good, but not experienced. It took me twenty seconds to take the ball back from him. I took a shot even though the ring was quite far. I missed. Parth collected the ball and took a shot. He scored. I high-fived him.

The last of the sunlight fell on the court. It cast long shadows of the already tall players. I stared at the darting shadows, unable to focus on the game.

'What?' Parth said. He had scored another basket.

'Nothing,' I said, blinking rapidly.

He passed me the ball. I caught it by habit, still lost in thought. I wondered if they had basketball courts in London. I was pretty sure they did. I wondered if she still played. And if she did, did she think of me?

'Shoot, bhaiya,' Parth said.

I threw the ball. It not only missed the basket, but also the entire frame. My laziest and worst shot ever.

Parth looked at me, shocked.

'What level did you play, bhaiya?' Parth said. His hopes of joining Stephen's went up. If someone as sloppy as me could get in through sports quota, so could he.

I smiled at him. I ran across to pick the ball. I took a shot. I missed again. I passed the ball back to Parth.

'I guess I'm not much of a player anymore,' I said.

'Should I call my other friends? We can play a game.'

I shook my head.

'I'll just bring down your level,' I said and left the court.

◆

'Why has the MLA called us? This can't be good,' my mother said.

'Let's find out. Why are you getting so stressed?'

My mother and I walked from our house to MLA Ojha's residence.

'Useless fellow,' Ma said.

'Shh, we're here,' I said as we entered the compound of Ojha's bungalow.

◆

A freshly shaved Ojha in a sparkling white kurta–pajama received us with folded hands.

'What an honour, Rani Sahiba,' he said, beaming.

'You ordered us to come. What choice do we have, Ojha ji?' my mother said.

'It was a humble request, Rani Sahiba,' Ojha said. We followed him to his huge living room and took our seats on red velvet sofas with huge gold embroidered flowers. His dutiful wife, her head covered, arrived with a tray of water and juice. My mother took the tray from her. Mrs Ojha touched my mother's feet.

'Bless you, Kusum,' my mother said. Kusum scurried back into the kitchen and brought back a tray of snacks comprising laddoos, kaju katli, bhujia and almonds.

'Please don't be formal,' my mother said.

Ojha sat on the sofa across us, a fixed grin on his face. 'Rajkumar ji came to me for assistance. I'm sorry but I explained my helplessness,' he said.

'We understand,' my mother said.

'Well, I have a proposal. You can help me. In return, maybe something can be done for the school.'

'Is it legal?' my mother said.

Ojha laughed hard. His plate shook in his hands.

'Nothing like that at all. In fact, a chance to make Dumraon and your school proud.'

Mother and I waited. Ojha put his plate down. 'Frankly, it's a big headache for me. I need your help as I'm stuck.'

'What's the matter?' my mother said.

'Have you heard of Bill Gates?'

'Bilgate? No. Is it a place?' my mother said.

'No, a person. Some videshi who makes computers or something.'

'Mr Bill Gates, chairman of Microsoft. They make computer software,' I said.

My mother and Ojha looked at me as if I were a genius.

'You know this person?' my mother said.

'The richest guy on earth,' I said.

'Yes, that's what I have heard. He has lots of money,' Ojha said.

'Sixty billion dollars,' I said.

'How much?' Ojha said.

'Two lakh forty thousand crore rupees,' I said.

Ojha's eyebrows went up an inch.

'What?' my mother said. 'So much? And how do you know all this?'

'Read it in a magazine. It's common knowledge, Ma,' I said.

'Hmm... Mr Ojha. You were saying?' my mother said.

'Well, this Gates is coming to India. To Bihar, in fact.'

'Has he gone mad? He makes so much money so he can come visit Bihar?' she said.

Ojha laughed. 'I don't know much, Rani Sahiba. He has some NGO. They are bringing him here.'

'Why?'

'Maybe he will see the interiors of Bihar and feel richer.'

My mother and Ojha laughed. Ojha left the room and came back with a letter. He handed it to me. The letter had come from the state ministry of rural welfare:

To all MLAs/District Collectors/DCPs,

The state ministry of rural welfare is pleased to inform that eminent entrepreneur and philanthropist Mr Bill Gates will be visiting Bihar along with delegates from the Gates Foundation from 15 April to 22 April 2009. The state government would like to extend its support to his team. In that regard, request your good offices to provide all cooperation as needed. Suggestions for places Mr Gates could visit or any events he could grace as chief guest on his week-long trip to Bihar are welcome and encouraged.

Please contact the relevant officials in the rural welfare ministry with any queries or suggestions.

Signed,

Bhanwar Lal

Minister for Rural Welfare

State Government of Bihar

The other side of the page carried the Hindi translation of the same letter.

'So how can we help you?' my mother said, after reading it herself.

'Rani Sahiba, if Bill Gates comes here, my constituency will be in the news. Will be good for Dumraon.'

'You will get press coverage. The minister will give you a pat on the back. Say that, Ojha ji,' my mother said.

He couldn't suppress a smile.

'Well, that too,' he said. 'But ultimately it is good for our town.'

My mother knew the political game. Ojha wanted a Lok Sabha ticket in the next election. He had to do things to get noticed.

'What exactly would you like us to do?' I said.

'Organize a school function. Invite him as the chief guest. Through me, of course. I'll ask the ministry to put the school visit on his agenda.'

'No, no, no…' Ma threw up her hands in the air.

'What, Rani Sahiba?' Ojha said.

'I can barely run the school. I don't have the resources to organize a function. Who will pay for the arrangements?'

'We will,' Ojha said promptly. 'I will pay for the function.'

'I thought you didn't have any funds,' I said.

The MLA looked at me.

'See, son, I am trying to help you. But there has to be something in it for me.'

'So you pay for the function. People come, attend and leave. What do we get in return?' I said.

'Your school's name will be in every paper,' he said.

'We don't need publicity, we need toilets,' I said.

'We will arrange some makeshift toilets for the day.'

'Exactly. You are only interested in that day. What about us after that?'

My mother stood up to leave.

'We will whitewash the school for you,' Ojha said.

I looked at my mother. Perhaps there was something here.

'Toilets?' I said.

'Over there,' Ojha said pointed to a door in the right corner.

'No, I don't want to use the toilet. I meant, what about the school toilets?'

'That's a big project. The school doesn't have plumbing. Everything needs to be done from scratch. Too expensive and too little time to do that.'

'That is what we need. Toilets, electricity and a new roof,' my mother said.

'For just one function I can't justify so much. I will whitewash the school, make all the arrangements for the function.'

'Sorry, MLA ji,' my mother said.

We walked out of the house. The MLA called me aside.

'Think about it,' he whispered in my ear. 'Rani Sahiba never trusts me. But you know how important this Gates is. A lot of important people will come.'

I walked up to my mother.

'Let's do it,' I said.

'Who'll do all the work?' she said.

'I will. Don't you want a whitewash?'

She looked at me.

'Please, Ma.'

She gave a brief nod.

'Okay?' I said.

'This is the first time I've seen a sparkle in your eye since you came back. So yes, okay.'

I gave Ojha a thumbs up.

19

I prepared a proposal for Ojha as per his directions. We proposed Bill Gates make a visit to a self-run, not-for-profit school. We would celebrate the annual day of the Dumraon Royal School with Mr Gates as chief guest. The MLA forwarded the proposal to the rural ministry.

'They have ninety requests,' Ojha said, 'and he can only visit ten places during his trip. So they will shortlist and let us know.'

'I didn't realize there would be so much competition,' I said, surprised.

'I'm going to Patna tomorrow. Come with me and I'll introduce you to the ministry people. You can persuade them.'

I accompanied the MLA in his lal-batti car on the three-hour ride to Patna. We reached the state government offices. I met Mr Shyam Kaushal, a middle-aged official in the rural welfare ministry, in his dusty office. He wore a grey safari suit that I think all government employees get free with their offer letters.

'Headache. This whole Gates trip is a headache,' he said and held his head.

He showed me the file of requests. Alongside, another fat file contained press requests for interviews, communication with the foundation and papers on various official government functions being planned.

'Why do we go crazy over these white guys visiting India?' Mr Kaushal said.

'Because of this white guy, my school will get a whitewash,' I said.

'Do you speak good English?' he said. 'Because they will call you many times.'

'I manage,' I said.

'Manage means what? When he comes, who will talk to him?'

'I will.'

'What will he see in your annual day? It's a Hindi-medium school. The entire programme will be in Hindi, right?'

I kept quiet.

'See.' He opened the file. 'There is this school in Patna that really wants him. They will do a skit in English for him. About the invention of computers and the role of Microsoft.'

I saw the request. It had come from the Delhi Public School in Patna.

'This is an English-medium school. He can find this anywhere. What's so Bihari about it?' I said.

'Well, it is convenient. We can take him to DPS straight from Patna airport.'

'Mr Kaushal, I think Mr Gates wants to see the real Bihar. The posh English school you will take him to means nothing.'

'So what to do?'

'Bring him to Dumraon Royal. Don't worry, we will do a dance or something without words.'

Mr Shyam Kaushal remained hesitant. Government employees are the lowest risk-takers on earth.

Finally, he shook his head. 'Something needs to be there in English. His team has told us. They want Mr Gates to engage with the event.'

'Okay, we'll do something in English.'

'What?'

'I'll figure it out,' I said.

A knock on the door startled us. MLA Ojha came in. Mr Kaushal stood up automatically. Government employees have a servile switch in their brains. It makes them grovel in the presence of netas.

'Listen to us poor Dumraon people at least once, Kaushal ji,' Ojha said.

Mr Kaushal folded his hands. 'Trying, Ojha sahib. Goras want to see the real Bihar but in English. I'm going crazy.'

Ojha slapped my back.

'Rajkumar ji went to the best English college in India. He will handle them well.'

I smiled. I did go to the best English college, but my English still, well, sucked.

◆

My cell phone rang in the middle of a maths class. The call came from an unknown number. The class III students looked at me. I held a chalk in one hand and the phone in the other. I cut the call and continued to teach.

'Twenty-three multiplied by twelve,' I wrote on the squeaky blackboard.

The phone rang again.

'Do this sum, I'll be right back,' I said and stepped out of class.

'Is this Mr Madhav Jha?' asked a female voice in an unfamiliar accent when I picked up the call.

'Yes,' I said.

'This is Samantha Myers from the Bill Gates Foundation, calling from New Delhi.'

'What?' I said. I tried to figure out her words despite the strange accent. 'Hello. Myself Madhav. What can I do for you?'

I kicked myself for saying 'myself Madhav'.

'I am part of Mr Gates's advance party. We would like to inspect your school before we decide our itinerary.'

She spoke so fast I couldn't understand most of what she said.

'Yes, Mr Bill Gates. Is he coming?'

I had not had any update since my visit to Patna a week ago.

'Well, I need to visit you first.'

◆

'Your school is...' Samantha paused as she hunted for the right word.

'Not in great condition?' I said.

I had taken her on a school tour.

The plaster was coming off the walls. The noise of kids repeating mathematical tables drowned out our conversation. Students peeped out of classroom windows. They stared at the alien creature with golden hair and white skin.

'No. I wanted to say quaint.'

'Quaint?' I said. I didn't understand the word.

'Different. Different in a charming sort of way.'

I failed to understand the charm of a school with leaky roofs and furniture that was falling apart. White people think differently, I guess.

We came to the staffroom. She greeted my mother and the other teachers. Tarachand ji brought us two cups of tea. Samantha noticed the damp walls.

'We will whitewash everything. The local government has assured us,' I said.

'Yeah, that is fine. Can we sit outside? I'd love to get some sun,' Samantha said.

We walked out, carrying a classroom chair each. We sat in the fields facing the school entrance. The February sun felt warm. It made Samantha's golden hair shine even more. She was pretty. Why had she left the comforts of her own country to roam dusty villages in India?

'This is gorgeous,' she said, looking at the rice crops sway in the air.

'Mr Gates will like it? We can arrange the annual-day function in the fields.'

'Oh, I'm sure he will.'

'We're a little short on funds. But we will do our best to put up a good show.'

'Sure. Are there enough toilets for the dignitaries?'

'Well,' I said, wondering what to say. In some ways, the entire field was available as a toilet.

'Western-style toilets, I meant.' Samantha laughed. 'Most of the delegation is from the US.'

'We will have temporary ones put up,' I said.

'You don't have them at the school?'

I looked at her. She seemed more curious than judgemental. I decided to be honest.

'We are a poor school. We don't have the money to do many things. We are doing this to get noticed so some government officials might help us.'

Samantha frowned.

'We will, however,' I said, 'do a good show. The local MLA is with us.'

'I believe you will. Since you mentioned lack of funds, would you like to be considered for our grants programme?' Samantha said.

'What's that?'

'Our foundation gives grants, or a sum of money, to deserving social projects. We had you as a tourist stop for Mr Gates, but you are doing social service, too.'

'Well, it is service for us. My mother has given her entire life to this school. Even I turned down job offers to come here.'

'Great. You can make a pitch for that, too.'

'Pitch?'

'The grants programme is highly competitive. We get a lot of wonderful proposals, but give funding to only a few.'

'What do I need to do?'

'Ideally, you need to submit a proposal and make a presentation to the selection panel. However, there's no panel meeting expected anytime in the near future.'

'Then?'

Samantha paused to think.

'Please, Miss Samantha, I really need money for my school. You have seen the condition it is in.'

Samantha finally spoke. 'Here's what I suggest. Make a good speech to the visiting delegation. Mr Gates himself will be present. If he and the delegation like what you say, they may grant you something on the spot.'

'Really?'

'If you can say something inspiring, a pitch that comes across as genuine, a small grant might be possible.'

'What's a small grant?'

'Twenty thousand dollars. Maybe more. But like I said, it may not work.'

I let out a huge breath. Eight lakhs could transform my school.

'A speech, eh?' I said.

'Yes, not too preachy, not salesy. Just from the heart.'

'How long?'

'Five to ten minutes. In English, of course.'

'What?' I said and jumped up from my chair. My sudden movement caused her to spill her tea.

'Sorry? Everything okay?' Samantha said.

I sat back down.

'English?'

'Yes. But we are speaking in English.'

'I can barely talk to you. Addressing a US delegation in English in front of an audience? I can't.'

'Well, we could have translators. But I'm afraid that just doesn't have the same effect.'

We finished tea. She called her driver. Kids continued to stare from the classroom windows at the white princess in her white Innova.

'My English is terrible,' I said to her. She got into the car.

'It's completely your choice.'

The driver started the car. I continued to stare into Samantha's grey eyes.

'So?' she said.

'I'll do it,' I said and inhaled deeply. 'I will make a speech in English.'

My heartbeat was louder than the car's engine.

'Nice. Look forward to it. See you in April,' she said coolly.

The car zoomed off. I stood still, wondering why on earth I had agreed to give a speech to the richest man on the planet.

20

'Speech?' my mother said. 'In English? To goras? Have you gone mad?'

'The state of the school has driven me mad.'

She sat up on her rickety chair, her eyebrows high. She rested her elbows on the table, her fingers entwined.

'Whatever it is, it is my school. If you don't like it, leave.'

'Don't be dramatic, Ma. I like it, so I'm doing all this.'

'First, I have no idea who this Gates is or what he does to make so much money. Next, he is coming to my school with a paltan. Now you have to give a speech.'

'He makes software.'

'Soft wear? Like soft clothes? So much money from that?'

'No, computer software. Like Windows.'

'Windows. Gates. What is he? A furniture dealer?'

'Forget it, Ma. I have to practise my English speech.'

'Good luck.'

She slid a stack of students' notebooks towards herself. She opened one and started to correct it.

'I want you to help me.'

She looked up.

'How? I don't speak English. Barely understand it.'

'Please let me know if I sound okay.'

I stood up straight. I pretended I had a mic in my hand.

'How will I know if you said it right?' Ma said.

'Imagine yourself in the audience. See if I come across as confident and intelligent.'

She giggled. I shushed her and began my speech. As I didn't know English well then, this is what I came up with.

'Good morning, Mr Bill Gates, Miss Samantha and guests. I, Madhav, welcoming you all to the Bihar. My school doing excellent coaching of children, farmer's children, poor children, small children...' I couldn't think of what to say next so I referred to various kinds of children. I continued, '...boy children, girl children, and many, many children.'

I heard my mother snigger.

'What?' I said.

'Who are all these children?'

I scratched my head.

'Anyway,' I continued. 'My school needing toilet as nobody able to toileting when toilet time coming.'

My mother burst out laughing.

'Now it's toilet,' she said.

I gave her a dirty look.

'Please go on,' she said, enjoying herself. I threw up my hands in the air.

'I'm useless. What have I taken on?' I went into panic mode. I was going to turn myself into a joke.

'Can you say no?' my mother said.

'I can. Maybe I should. Should I?'

My mother shrugged. I sat down next to her.

'I will tell them I can't do it. They can take me off the grants programme.'

'Quitting, eh?' she said.

'You laughed at me. Now you are calling me a quitter.'

'I only laughed at your current speech. You can learn to give a better one.'

'How?'

'How much time do you have?'

'Two months.'

'So learn English.'

'I didn't learn it properly in three years at St. Stephen's. How can I do it in two months?'

'We don't quit, Madhav. It's not in the Jha family's genes.'

'Meaning?'

'Meaning we may lose everything, but we don't quit. That's what your uncles did, at the gambling table or in business. Being bankrupt is okay, but quitting is not.'

'So what do I do?'

'You work that out. I have to take a class.'

My mother collected her notebooks and left.

Half an hour later, I stomped into her classroom. The students looked up at me.

'Don't barge in when class is on. Wait outside,' she said and shooed me out.

She came out when the period ended.

'I'm going for it,' I said.

'Good,' my mother said. 'But next time, knock.'

'I want to join English classes. In Patna.'

'Patna?'

'There's nothing good in Dumraon.'

'That's true. But how?'

'I'll commute. Weekdays here and Patna on the weekends. Is that okay?'

'Where will you stay in Patna?'

'I'll find some place.'

'We have relatives. Your chachi stays there. She is one weird woman, though.'

'I'll find a guest house. Let me look for good classes there.'

'Come here.' My mother gave me a tight hug.

'Just stay happy, all right?' she said. 'Do what you have to, but don't be a grumpy man like your father.'

'Thank you, Ma,' I said.

'Welcome, English boy.'

21

'Six thousand for three months.' He pushed a brochure towards me.

I had come to Patna's Pride English Learning Centre on Boring Road. M. Shaqif, the thin, almost malnourished owner of Patna's Pride, explained the various courses to me. He wore a purple shirt. Sunglasses hung out of his front pocket.

'We teaching for five years. Good English. Personality development, interview preparing, everything people learning here.'

I was no expert in English, but I could still tell there was something wrong with what he had said. One too many 'ings'.

'I have to give a speech. To an important audience.' I spoke in Hindi, to explain my situation better.

'No problem. Speech okay,' Shaqif said. 'What qualification you having?'

'Graduate.'

'Good. Local?'

'Delhi. St. Stephen's.'

The name didn't register. He nodded out of courtesy. He rummaged in a drawer, took out an admission form and handed it to me. I wondered if I should pay up or check out other classes. He sensed my hesitation.

'Sir, we will make you top-class. Multinational-company English.'

'I only have two months,' I said. 'I need fast results.'

'We arrange private classes for you. Extra five hundred per class.'

'Five hundred?'

'Okay, four hundred.'

I shook my head.

'Three hundred. Please. Good deal,' he said.

I filled up the form and paid him an advance for the first month. In addition, I signed up for private classes every Saturday and Sunday.

I left Patna's Pride and took an auto to a road outside the railway station, full of guest houses. I finally struck a weekends-only deal with a small hotel called Nest, provided I didn't ask for a receipt.

◆

Ten minutes into my first class at Patna Pride, I had a sinking feeling. This wouldn't work. I shared the classroom with fifteen other students, mostly around my age and all men. The teacher asked us to call him 'Verma sir'.

'Say "how",' Verma sir said, asking the class to repeat the word.

'How.' The response came in ten different accents. The word sounded like 'haw' or 'haau' or 'ho'.

'Are.You,'Verma sir said.'How are you?'

The class repeated the words with a Bihari twist.

'Confidence,' Verma sir said, 'is the secret. It is the key difference in coming across as high-class English or low class.You have to sound right, too.This is a foreign language. Not Bhojpuri. So the sounds are different.'

He turned to a student called Amit. 'Why are you here, Amit?'

'To learn English, sir,' Amit said.

'What kind of English?'

'Top-class English.With big vocabulary.'

'Relax,' Verma sir said.'Forget big vocabulary in my class.'

'Sir?' Amit said, confused.

Verma sir turned and addressed the whole class.

'Students, all you have to learn is simple, confident English. Don't be scared of people who use big words.These are elitists.They want to scare you with their big words and deny you an entry into the world of English. Don't fall into their trap. Okay?'

Everyone nodded, irrespective of whether they understood Mr Verma or not.

'Anyway, let's get back to "how are you",' he said.

Verma sir explained the 'au' sound in the word 'how' and that it did not exist in Hindi.

'Like cow. It is not ca-u. It is a mix of aa and o together.Try.'

The class struggled to utter the simple word. I bet the British would have struggled just as hard if they tried to speak Bhojpuri. If the Industrial Revolution had taken place here, there would be Indian ex-colonies around the world.White men would have had to learn Hindi to get a decent job. White teachers would tell white men how to say cow in Hindi with a perfect accent.

Verma sir interrupted my desi-invasion daydream.

'Yes, what is your name?'

'Madhav, Madhav Jha, sir.'

'Okay, Madhav, repeat after me: "I am fine, thank you".'

'I am fine, thank you,' I said.

'Good,' he said.

After three years at Stephen's, I wasn't that hopeless. I could repeat simple phrases. I wanted him to teach me how to give a speech. Meanwhile, he moved on and corrected another student.

'Faa-in. Not fane. Please open your mouth more.'

◆

I spent the weekend in Patna. Apart from attending the classes, I bought a book on confident public speaking from the Patna Railway Station. I ate puri-aloo from a platform stall. The book recommended practising English with random strangers, so one would feel less ashamed if one made a mistake.

'Excuse me, sir. Would you be kind enough to tell me if this is the platform for the Kolkata Rajdhani Express?'

I practised this sentence on the station platform ten times. In many cases, the passengers didn't understand me. I moved towards the AC compartments. Rich people usually know English.

'I'm not sure. I suggest you ask the TC,' said one bespectacled man.

'Was my English correct?' I said.

'Huh?' he looked at me, surprised.

I explained my attempts at English practice. He patted my back.

'You did fine,' he said.

'I'm trying,' I said. 'Your English is so good. What do you do?'

'I'm in software sales. I'm Sudhir.' He extended his hand.

'I'm Madhav,' I said.

'All the best, Madhav,' he said.

◆

Private classes seemed much better at Patna's Pride. I explained my situation to Verma sir.

'I see,' he said. He stroked his chin stubble. 'Not only do you have to learn correct English, you have to also learn to deliver a public speech.'

'Exactly, sir. I am so nervous.'

'But you do know some English. You graduated English-medium, right?'

I wanted to tell him I didn't just graduate English-medium, I graduated from a place where even the grass grows in English.

I switched to Hindi to explain myself. 'Sir, I can put a sentence together in English. But all my effort goes into remembering the right words. I can't think of what I'm saying.'

'I understand,' Verma sir said. 'When you don't know the language well, you are self-conscious. It shows in your confidence level. It affects your personality. Not good for job interviews.'

'Sir, this isn't just a job interview. This is about the future of my school and the students who study there.'

I showed Verma sir the book I had brought from the railway station.

He shook his head. 'No, not this. You don't learn how to become a confident English speaker from books found at a railway station. Else the whole country would be by now.'

'Please help me, sir,' I said.

Verma sir became silent.

'Why are you quiet?' I asked, worried his silence meant I was a hopeless case.

'Well,' he said. 'I'm wondering how to go about this.'

'Should I quit?' I said.

He shrugged. My heart sank.

'Give it a few weeks. We can decide then. Now stand up and speak your fears out loud.'

'Fears?'

'Yes, open up and face them. In English.'

I stood in front of the empty classroom. Verma sir took one of the student's seats.

'Hi, I am Madhav Jha, and I have a fear of speaking in English.'

'Good. And?'

'I have a fear that my school will not manage itself and close down.'

'Go on. One more fear.'

'I have a fear that I will never be able to get over someone I loved deeply.'

22

I returned to Dumraon after my Patna weekend and resumed duties at the school. I also coordinated with MLA Ojha's office for the whitewash.

Later in the week I sat with a paint contractor in the staffroom. My phone buzzed.

'Madhav? Hi, this is Samantha from the Foundation.'

'How are you, Samantha?' I said, pronouncing the words just right, as Verma sir would have liked.

'I am great. How are the preparations going?'

'We are working on it,' I said slowly.

'Super. Listen, two of my colleagues are in Patna later this week. I think you should meet them.'

I tried hard to understand Samantha's words, given their breakneck speed.

'Meet whom?'

'My seniors from the New York office. They have a say in grants. You should network with them.'

'Network?'

English is hard enough to decode, but when these Americans speak it, it is impossible.

'Get to know them. Can you come?'

'I am in Patna on weekends anyway.'

'How about Saturday then? We have field visits later, but you can meet us for breakfast.'

'Sure,' I said.

'We will be at the Chanakya Hotel. Eight o'clock?'

'Eight is fine.'

'See you on Saturday,' she said and hung up.

The paint contractor looked at me in awe. I had managed an entire conversation in English.

'What?' I said to him.

He shook his head and took out the shade card.

◆

I entered the Chanakya lobby at 7.47 a.m. I mention the exact time because it changed my life. A minute earlier or later and things would have been different. Samantha and her colleagues entered the hotel lobby at 7.51.

'This is Chris and that's Rachel,' Samantha said. I shook hands with the rich who wanted to help the poor.

'Breakfast?' Samantha said.

We entered the hotel coffee shop at 7.55. The breakfast buffet consisted of over twenty dishes. I loaded my plate with toast, porridge, fruit, paranthas, poha and idlis. I ordered a masala dosa at the live cooking counter.

'Madhav here runs a village school,' Samantha said. She nibbled at her jam and butter toast.

'You look really young,' Chris said, opening a bottle of mineral water.

'It's my mother's school. I help out,' I said.

I told them about the Dumraon Royal School.

'Seven hundred children, negligible fee, no state support. Amazing,' Chris said.

'I saw the school. The staff and owners are really dedicated. It's sad they don't have basic facilities or the funds to grow,' Samantha said.

My American friends ate little; the buffet was wasted on them.

I refilled my plate thrice. I wanted to eat enough so I didn't need food the entire day. We finished breakfast at 8.27 a.m.

'We better get going. Our project is in Mongor. Four hours away,' Samantha said.

'You mean Munger?' I said.

'Hey, sorry, I murder the names of places here,' Samantha giggled.

I have murdered English all my life, I wanted to say.

We stood up to leave. Samantha and Rachel collected their handbags. Chris called the driver.

I looked around. I wondered if I should have eaten some more.

That was when I spotted a tall girl, her back to me, at the other end of the coffee shop. Her long hair came down to her waist. She wore a mustard salwar-kameez. If she wasn't tall, I wouldn't have noticed her. If we had started breakfast a few minutes later, I would still be eating and wouldn't have noticed her. It had to be just that moment. At 8.29 a.m., when I stood up to leave, was exactly when she had stood up to leave as well. She picked some files from her table.

'Lovely meeting you, Madhav,' Chris said. He extended his hand.

I nodded, my eyes still on the girl, as I shook hands with him.

'All okay?' Chris said. He turned his head to see what had distracted me.

'Huh? Yeah, I am fine,' I said, my eyes still on the other end of the room.

She turned towards the exit. The waiter followed her to get a bill signed. She stopped and turned towards the waiter. I saw her face for half a second. Yes, it was her.

'Riya Somani,' I said.

'Who?' Chris said. Samantha and Rachel turned towards her, too.

Before any of us could react, Riya had left the restaurant.

'Is she someone famous?' Rachel said.

'Excuse me, I need to go,' I said. My fingers trembled as I shook Samantha's hand.

'Have a good trip to Munger,' I said.

'We'll see you soon in Dumraon,' Samantha said, her voice cheerful.

'Yeah,' I said absently. I walked towards the door. I wanted to run towards it but I didn't want to create a scene. I came to the lobby, but there was no sign of her.

Did I hallucinate? I asked myself. No, I had seen her. The walk, the gait, the face—there is only one Riya.

I rushed to the foyer and just about saw her leave in an Innova. She had sunglasses on. The car windows were rolled up.

'Can I help you, sir?' a young hotel staff member at the concierge desk asked me.

'The lady who left just now. You saw her? Mustard salwar-kameez?'

'Yes.'

'Where did she go?'

'We don't know, sir. It's a private taxi.'

'Will she be back?'

'Not sure, sir. Sorry. Is there a problem, sir?'

I shook my head. I walked back into the hotel, wondering what to do next.

I went to the coffee shop again and found the waiter.

'You just gave a bill to a lady.'

'Yes, sir.'

'She might be an old friend of mine. Can I see it?'

The waiter looked at me with suspicion.

'I was just here with the foreigners. We sat there,' I said, pointing to our table. If you are seen hanging out with white guys, people assume you are not a bad person.

The waiter went to the cash counter. He brought back the bill. I saw her signature. Yes, I had bumped into Riya Somani, after all.

'231,' the waiter said. 'She signed the bill to her room.'

'She is staying here?' I said.

'Of course,' the waiter said. He looked at me as if I was a certified idiot.

I heaved a sigh of relief. I came to the reception and enquired about a guest named Riya in 231.

'Yes, it is a company booking. She is here for a week.'

'When will she come back?'

'Can't say, sir. If you leave your name and number we can ask her to contact you.'

I wasn't sure if Riya would do that. If I had to meet her, I had no choice but to wait. I decided to skip my English classes. I sat in the lobby, my eyes fixed on the entrance.

I waited for twelve hours.

I didn't allow myself to use the bathroom lest I miss her again. I didn't eat food or drink water all day either. My eyes scanned every car arriving at the hotel.

At seven in the evening, Samantha, Chris and Rachel returned from their trip. Their faces had turned black with Bihar's dust. They looked exhausted.

'Madhav?' Samantha said, surprised.

'Oh, hi,' I said, pretending to be equally astonished. 'I came for another meeting.'

'At Chanakya itself?' Samantha said.

I nodded. Chris said he needed a shower or he would die. They left me in the lobby and went up to their rooms.

At 8.30 p.m., an Innova pulled into the front porch. Riya stepped out of it. My heart started to play hopscotch. A part of me wanted to run away. It shuddered at the thought of facing her. Another part had made me sit here without a break for twelve hours.

She didn't notice me. She went up to the reception.

'231, please,' she said. The receptionist turned towards the key rack.

I walked up to the reception. 'Excuse me, which way is the coffee shop?' I said. I had to make it seem like she saw me first. That's Riya. She had to find me. If I found her, she might just run away.

'Oh my God,' Riya said. 'Madhav Jha.'

'Riya... Riya Somani, right?' I said.

'Wow, you have difficulty recollecting my name, Madhav Jha!'

'Riya Somani,' I said, giving up all pretence of indifference. The receptionist seemed surprised at the happy coincidence right at her counter.

Riya took her keys and we stepped away from the counter.

'What are you doing here?' she said. 'Wow, I still can't get over it. Madhav Jha.'

'I am a Bihari. This is Patna. My hometown is not far away. I should ask you what you are doing here.'

'Work. My company sent me.'

'Work?'

'Yeah, you didn't think I could work?' Riya said.

'No, nothing like that. What kind of work? You moved to London, right?'

Riya looked around the hotel lobby.

'Let's talk properly,' she said. 'You had dinner?'

'No.'

'Hungry?'

I could have eaten the flowers in the lobby at this point.

'A little bit,' I said.

'Let's go to the coffee shop.'

'Okay, but can I use the toilet first?' I said.

◆

We entered the coffee shop. The waiter from the morning was still on duty. He gave me an all-knowing smile. I smiled back.

'You found madam,' he said. *Ass*, I thought.

'What?' Riya said.

'Nothing. Yes, for me and madam. Table for two, please. '

23

We sat at a corner table and had our first meal together in three years. The effect some people's mere presence can have on you is indescribable. Everything on offer in the rather ordinary evening buffet tasted divine. The salty tomato soup was the best I had ever had. The matar-paneer tasted like an award-winning chef had made it. The lights from the traffic jam visible outside the window looked like fireflies. I kept silent, worried I would say something stupid to upset her or, worse, make her run away.

'You've become so quiet,' she said.

'Nothing like that,' I said. I looked at her. She looked, if possible, even more stunning than she had been in college.

'So, tell me, what have you been up to?' she said.

Over the next ten minutes, I told her about my life since college.

'You run a school. And Bill Gates is visiting it,' she said. 'Wow.'

'He's visiting many places.'

'Come on, don't be modest. You are doing something so different from the rest of our batchmates.'

'I'm a misfit, I guess. Who leaves HSBC to come to Dumraon?' I said.

'Cool people,' Riya said. Our eyes met. I tried to read her, considering she had said so little about herself. I couldn't find anything too different, apart from a touch of maturity. I wanted to ask her about her past few years. However, I wouldn't push it.

'How's Rohan?' I said.

'You remember his name? So what was that "Riya, Riya Somani, right?" business in the lobby?'

I smiled. She had caught me red-handed.

'Rohan should be fine,' she said.

'Should be?'

'I don't know. He must be.'

'Rohan is your husband, right?'

She became quiet.

'You want anything sweet? They have kulfi and gulab jamun,'

I said, desperate to change the topic.

'We got divorced,' she said in a calm voice, as if she had expressed her sweet-dish preference.

I didn't have anything to say. Apart from shock, I felt a warm tingle at the back of my neck.

Had I just felt happy at what she said? I clenched my teeth. I didn't want my smile to leak out.

Oh my God, that is the best news I have heard in years, a cheerful voice spoke inside my head. Even my soul jumped about in excitement.

I tried to look as serious as possible.

'That's terrible,' I said at last.

She nodded.

'Sweet dish?' I said in a soft voice. Well, the occasion did deserve something sweet.

She shook her head. She looked upset, on the verge of tears. I wanted to touch her hand, but I restrained myself.

'What happened?' I said, my tone as genuine as possible.

'I don't want to talk about it.'

I nodded. *Typical Riya,* I thought.

'Can we talk about something else, please?' she said.

'Yeah, sure. What?'

'Anything?'

'You want kulfi?' I said.

'No, Madhav, I don't want kulfi. Or anything else to eat. Can you talk about something else, please?'

I thought I had talked about something else. *Doesn't the topic of kulfi count as something else? Well, who can argue with girls?*

'How long are you in Patna for?' I said.

'My job is here. I have to find a place to live, actually.'

'Really? Which company do you work for?'

'Nestlé. I am in sales, for their yogurt brand.'

'Ah,' I said.

'What?' she said.

'Nothing.'

'In case you're wondering what the hell I'm doing selling yogurt in Patna, well, it's hard for a college dropout to find a job, isn't it?

Especially when the dropout wants to work on her own and not with her rich dad?'

'I wasn't wondering about that at all,' I said. I really didn't care why she was in Patna; I was only delirious with joy she was in Patna.

'Anyway,' she said, 'when do you go back to Dumraon?'

'You remember Dumraon?' I said smilingly.

'How can I forget the only prince I have ever known and his kingdom?'

She picked up a spoon and took a bite of my kulfi. I thought she didn't want anything sweet.

Why do girls always do the opposite of what they say they want to do?

She took more bites of the kulfi and ended up eating more of it than me.

'Do you remember anything else, Riya?'

'Like what?'

'Us?'

She looked at me.

'Madhav…'

'Yes?'

'I've changed, Madhav,' she said. 'In college I was an immature, over-protected, idiotic eighteen-year-old with no clue about life.'

'We were all young back then,' I said, jumping to her defence.

'I am sorry, because I know I hurt you. The last two years have taught me a lot.'

Her unexpected apology startled me. I realized that I could be in love with this Riya even more than the previous one. 'What actually happened?'

'I'd rather not talk about it. At least, not now.'

I clucked impatiently.

'What?' she said.

'Nothing. This is so you. The freezing up. I do know you, Riya, even if it was in the past.'

'If you know me, why do you push?'

'Who pushed? I met you after years, so asked you. However, I have no right to anymore. So, sorry, madam.' I became silent.

'Don't be like that,' she said.

I looked away and spoke again. 'You shoved a wedding card in my hand and disappeared. I run into you after years and I shouldn't ask you what happened?'

'You should.'

'That is what I did.'

'Fine, I'm sorry. And I've already apologized for the past. Madhav, look at me.'

I turned my gaze back to her. I could only be mad at Riya for so long. She smiled. I maintained a stern expression.

'Would you like to be friends with me?' she said.

I hate it when she says that. What the fuck is that? Is it an invitation? Is it a consolation prize? Is it a peace treaty?

I remained silent.

'I live in Patna. You come here often. We could be friends. Would you like that?' she said.

That was another thing I hated. That I always let her decide when to be friends or when not to. I had no power to refuse her.

'Yes, I would,' I said.

'Great. I would like us to be good friends, too,' she said. 'However, I have one condition.'

I rolled my eyes. There is always a catch with Riya. *What is it going to be this time? Have no expectations?*

'Say it,' I said.

'Don't ask me the same question twice.'

'What?'

'Ask me things. I will reply if and when I can. If I don't, please don't ask me again.'

'Really?' I said.

'Yes. That is when it seems pushy.'

'Fine. I don't want to be pushy.'

'Whenever you are in Patna we can meet up. Maybe you can show me the city.'

'I am here this weekend.'

'Sunday is my day off. I have some apartments to look at, though.'

'Would you like me to come apartment-hunting with you?' I said.

She fell silent. I had become too familiar too soon.

'It's okay. We can meet another time,' I said quickly.

'No, come. You are right. They will quote crazy rates to me otherwise.'

'I wasn't going to ask twice,' I said and she laughed.

'What time should I fix to meet with the broker?' she said.

'I have a morning class until eleven and then I'm free until four-thirty,' I said.

'Class?' she said.

'I'd rather not talk about it right now.'

She raised an eyebrow.

'Really?'

'Don't ask the same question twice. Applies both ways, right?'

I heard her laugh again, the most beautiful sound in the world.

24

'Oh, I love this place,' she said. 'Look at the balcony.'

'Stop it. If you praise it so much, he will never give us a good price,' I said.

We were in an apartment close to Dak Bungalow Road in Indiranagar, an upscale and relatively quiet neighbourhood in noisy Patna.

After viewing many apartments smaller than the servant quarters of 100, Aurangzeb Road, we had finally stumbled upon the right one. It was a colonial apartment building with twelve-foot high ceilings. It had old teak windows and doors. Both the bedrooms had a sunny balcony facing a park. There was a spacious kitchen with a loft for storage. I knew Riya would take this place.

'Shhh,' she said and placed a finger on her lips.

'Twenty thousand,' the broker said, probably sensing our keenness.

'So much? Have you had bhaang?' I said.

'It is the safest area in Patna. Madam is staying alone. And look at the balconies,' the broker said.

'True, it is lovely,' Riya said dreamily.

I glared at her. She placed a hand on her mouth, as if to say 'oops'.

'Fifteen,' I said.

'This is a gora flat, sir. Foreigners like these old places. I am showing it to a firangi couple later today,' the broker said.

'We will take it. Done. Twenty,' Riya said.

I shrugged at Riya. She smiled at me. Rich kids think money grows like the rice in the fields of Dumraon.

◆

'This is gorgeous,' Riya said. She took out her mobile phone and started to take pictures.

We had come to Gol Ghar, a giant round planetarium-shaped dome located opposite Gandhi Maidan. It had been built in 1784 as a granary when the British wanted a place to store grain to be used in times of famine. I bought the two-rupee ticket for both of us.

'You could have bargained. He would have agreed for eighteen thousand,' I said.

'I couldn't let go of the place. I'm going to live there. It's important,' she said. She clicked a picture of the bronze plaque, which read:

For perpetual prevention of famine in this province
This Granary
Completed on 20th July 1786

We climbed the steps that took us to the top of the dome. We saw wide green fields on one side and the clamour of the city on the other.

The dome walls were covered with paan stains, and couples' names had been etched on the surface. Losers who think little before destroying a city's heritage do this sort of stuff. There's a reason why people say we Biharis are uncouth. Some people in my community work hard to earn us that tag.

'If they clean this place up, it will be awesome,' Riya said.

'Yeah, the authorities don't care,' I said.

'It's not just the authorities. If the people cared, the authorities would care too,' Riya said.

I nodded. Empty cigarette packets and peanut shells lay strewn all over the steps and on the floor.

'This could be a really cool IMAX theatre.'

'What's that?'

She told me about IMAX theatres in London; they had screens four times the normal size.

I adjusted the heavy rucksack on my shoulder.

'Books?' she said.

I nodded. Her yellow-and-white dupatta fluttered in the breeze.

'You want to know what classes I'm taking?' I said.

'I can't ask you again,' she said and smiled.

'English. Spoken English.'

'Oh,' she said. 'Do you really need them?'

'Yes, on an urgent basis,' I said.

We walked down the Gol Ghar steps. I told her how the Gates Foundation people would arrive in six weeks and I had to deliver a speech.

'No speech, no grant, eh?' she said.

I nodded and hailed an auto. 'Maurya Complex,' I said to the driver.

◆

Maurya Complex is a grey box-shaped building with retail stores on the ground level and offices on the higher floors. While the building has no character, its compound area has some of the most popular street food stalls of Patna.

'Tried litti-chokha before?' I said.

'What's that?' she said.

I pointed to a stall where fresh littis were being made over red-hot charcoal. The cook took a ball of dough and stuffed it with spiced chickpea powder. Flattening the ball with his fingers, he roasted the litti over the coals. Once done, he gave the litti a quick dip in desi ghee. He gave us the littis in a plate with salad, chutney and chokha.

'What is chokha?' Riya said.

The stall-owner explained how chokha is made with tomatoes, eggplant and potatoes all mashed together and cooked with green chillies, salt and other spices.

Riya took a bite. 'This is unbelievable.'

Her expression made the stall-owner's chest swell with pride.

'Like it?' I laughed, knowing the answer.

'Why don't they have this in Delhi? All over India? The world?' Riya said.

'Bihari things are not considered cool.'

'Why?' she said, her mouth full.

'It's a poor state. Nobody wants our things, or us. Not yet, at least.'

'From now on I'm eating this every day.'

We finished our meal. I passed her tissues to wipe her hands.

'My mother makes even better litti-chokha,' I said.

'You make this at home?' Riya said.

'All the time. You should come sometime,' I said.

She kept quiet. I sensed her hesitation. We stepped out of the Maurya Complex.

'You don't have to come. I will bring some home-made litti-chokha for you,' I said.

'No, I would love to visit Dumraon. I want to meet your mother, too. I've heard so much about her.'

We found an auto outside Maurya Complex. 'Chanakya Hotel for madam first. After that, Boring Road,' I told the driver.

'What did you say? Boring?' Riya giggled.

'What? Yes, my classes are on Boring Road.'

'The name says it all.'

I laughed.

'They aren't bad. Just tough to learn English in such a short time.'

'The challenge is, you have to focus on three things at the same time: English, public speaking and, the most important, the actual content of the speech,' she said.

I looked at her. She had nailed the problem on its head.

The auto moved through the bustling traffic. I have no idea why everyone in Patna loves honking so much.

We sat in silence for a few minutes.

'Madhav,' Riya said.

'Yeah?' I said.

'Nothing.'

'Say it, Riya.'

'Would you like me to help you with English?'

I didn't reply at once.

'I'm sorry. It's okay. I won't ask twice.'

The auto reached Chanakya Hotel. As she stepped off, she held my hand for a second.

'I'm sorry. I didn't mean to imply my English is superior to yours or anything like that.'

'When can we start?' I said.

25

'Here's the plan,' she said. She slid an A4 sheet towards me. We were in Takshila Restaurant at the Chanakya Hotel for dinner. We were meeting a week later, after I had spent Monday to Friday in Dumraon. The waiter arrived to take our order. She ordered plain yellow daal and phulkas.

'I miss home food,' she said.

I missed you, I wanted to say but didn't. The five days in Dumraon had felt like five life sentences.

'Sure, I like yellow daal,' I said.

I picked up the A4 sheet. It read:

Action Plan: Operation Gates

Objective: Ten-minute speech in fluent English to a live American audience.

10 minutes = approximately 600 words.

Focus Areas:

1. Delivery: confidence, style, accent, flow, pauses, eye contact.
2. Content: rational points, emotional moments, call for aid.

I looked up at Riya. 'You typed all this?'

'No, little elves did at midnight,' she said. 'Go on, read the whole sheet.'

I turned to the sheet again.

Top Ten Tools:

1. YouTube videos of famous speeches.
2. Watching English movies with subtitles.
3. English-only days—no Hindi conversation allowed.
4. Working on speech content in Hindi first.
5. Recording an English voice diary on the phone through the day.
6. Thinking in English.
7. Watching television news debates in English.

8. Calling call centres and choosing the English option.
9. Reading out English advertisements on street hoardings.
10. Reading simple English novels.

I whistled.

'It's a different approach,' she said. She walked me through the ten steps and spoke non-stop for a few minutes, explaining each step.

'And last, reading simple English novels, like, the one by that writer, what's his name, Chetan Bhagat,' she said, ending her monologue.

I watched her face, pretty as always. *Do not fall for her again,* I screamed in my head.

'So, let us start. Talk to me in English.'

I switched to English. The English I knew at that time, that is.

'I am...very...thankful...for your making the list...for learning the English,' I said.

'Thank you for making this list of steps to learn English,' Riya said. She spoke in a calm voice, without sarcasm or judgement.

'Yes, same thing only.'

'So instead of "same thing only", say "I meant the same",' Riya said. 'I will correct you sometimes. It is not that I don't understand you. I just want to make sure you say it right.'

'Thanks,' I said.

'Now that one word was correct.'

I laughed.

She made me talk to the waiter in English. I did fine, since the waiter's English was worse than mine. She didn't correct me when the waiter was around anyway.

'And sweet...later,' I said as he left us.

'We will order the sweet dish later,' Riya said, 'or, dessert instead of sweet dish.'

'Desert? Like Rajasthan desert?' I said.

'D.E.S.S.E.R.T. Different word, same sound.'

'I hate that about English. Hindi doesn't have that problem.'

'Hindi is incredible. We speak it like we write it. There's no need to learn pronunciation separately,' Riya said.

'So why doesn't everyone speak Hindi?' I said.

'Because we are not...' Riya said and paused. 'Oh my God, you asked that question correctly.'

'What?'

'You said, "So why doesn't everyone speak Hindi?" in perfect English. When you say something without being self-conscious, you say it correctly.'

I tried to look modest.

'We will get there, Madhav,' she said. She patted the back of my hand on the table.

I wondered if we would ever get there as a couple.

Don't fall in love with her again, a voice within me warned.

You never fell out of love with her, another voice countered with an evil laugh.

◆

'Dolphins? In Patna?' Riya said.

'Yes, there are river dolphins in the Ganga. If you're lucky, you might spot them,' I said.

I had brought Riya to the Ganga ghat near Patna College off Ashok Rajpath on a Sunday evening. For twenty rupees a head, boatmen took you to the sandy beach on the opposite bank. She held my hand to keep her balance as we tiptoed on the wooden plank towards the boat.

She slipped a little and clasped my hand tighter. I wished the shaky wooden plank would never end.

We sat in the boat. The diesel engine purred into action, making conversation impossible. The sun had started to set. It turned the sky, the river and Riya's face the colour of fire.

On the other side, we stepped on to the sand and walked to the tea stalls. We sat inside one of the many gazebo-styled bamboo huts meant for tea-stall customers.

'It's beautiful,' Riya breathed.

'All we have for peace in this city,' I said.

We sat in silence and watched the ripples of water, my hand inches from hers. I wondered if she would be okay if I held it. She had held mine on the plank, after all. But I guess it was okay on the plank, because she needed to hold it. Now, it would mean something else. At least that is how girls think. Still, I decided to try my luck. I inched my hand playfully towards hers. She sensed it, and moved her hand away.

How do girls do this? Do they have antennae, like insects do? Or are they thinking of the same thing themselves? How else are they able to react so well so fast?

'You've started working on the speech?' Riya said, shaking me from my thoughts.

'Sort of,' I said.

I took out sheets of paper from my pocket. I had scribbled notes in Hindi on the key points I needed to address. I handed them to her.

'The school needs toilets, chairs, blackboards...' she read out. She turned to me. 'Madhav, you need to do more. This is just a list of things you want.'

'I'm still working on it.'

'He is Bill Gates. People ask him for things wherever he goes. The idea is to not ask for anything and yet earn a grant.'

'Not ask?'

'Yes. Never ask. It comes across as needy.'

I looked at her. *Did she leave me because of the same reason?* 'I do that sometimes. I come across as needy,' I said in a small voice.

She understood my context. She didn't admit it, of course. She simply paused before she spoke again. 'These goras are different. You have to come across as happy and confident. Not desperate.'

'Read the rest. I talk about other things, how the school was created and more.'

She patted my shoulder.

'You are doing fine. Don't worry. We will do this together. I've lived in London and met many Americans there. I know how these goras think.'

'How was London?' I said, barely able to make out her features in the dying light.

In classic Riya style, she stayed silent.

'It's okay. I won't ask again. Should we go back?'

She nodded. We reached the pier. The plank to the boat felt even more precarious in the darkness. She held my arm again. I don't know if I imagined it, but it felt tighter than earlier. She seemed a little more vulnerable. She came across as a little more, if I dare say the word she hated, needy.

We sat as far away as possible from the other passengers and the noisy diesel engine.

'London was nice in parts,' she said.

I wanted to ask which parts were nice and which parts weren't, but I didn't. *The more you ask, the more she clams up*, I thought. I looked at her. She smiled, but it did not reach her eyes. I could read her every expression, even in the darkness.

'Would you like to hold my hand?' I said.

'Why?' she said.

'The boat is moving,' I said. Lame answer. But how else does one answer such a stupid question?

'So?'

'Nothing,' I said and looked ahead. The whirr of the engine filled the awkward silence. Halfway through our journey, temple bells began to ring in the distance. I felt something near my hand. She placed her fingers on top of mine. I guess men have an antenna about these things, too.

I didn't turn towards her. I knew her. If I made eye contact now, she would withdraw.

'I am happier here than in London,' she said. I hadn't asked her to compare the two places.

'When are you coming home?' I said, still looking ahead but choosing my words with care, afraid she would withdraw.

'Soon. Let me move into mine first,' she said.

'I'm staying back tomorrow, to help you move in.'

'You don't have to. I hardly have any luggage.'

'Exactly. You need to buy things. The shopkeepers will rip you off. I'll come with you, okay?'

'Thanks,' she said. I guess that meant yes.

We reached the ghats. I clasped her hand and held it until we got off the plank on to firm ground. The old me would have asked her if holding hands meant something. But the old me had screwed up big time in the past. So I decided to 'play it cool'.

We took an auto back from the ghats. I talked about the furniture market near Nala Road, places to buy mattresses and the cheapest vegetable markets. Of course, these stupid topics meant nothing compared to the monumental development of her sliding two fingers on top of mine.

We reached her hotel. She stepped off the auto.

'Eleven tomorrow?' I said.

'Yes, thank you so much. And I loved the river-ride today.'

'Which part?' I asked and kicked myself mentally. Did I come across as fishing? Did it set off the 'desperate' alarm?

'Everything,' she said.

Miss Diplomatic Somani is not that easy a nut to crack, after all.

26

'I am officially, completely, exhausted,' Riya said. She wore a pink kurti and dark blue tights. Her face had turned pink to match her kurti.

She plonked herself on the four mattresses we had dragged into her apartment.

'Remove the plastic covers at least,' I said.

She ignored me. She lay down on the mattresses and did side leg twists like we used to do on court.

'Cut the drama,' I said.

'Do we have to do everything today?' she said.

We had made four trips to the market, one each to buy groceries, electrical appliances, utensils and mattresses.

'Why do you need four mattresses?' I had asked her in the shop.

'Two for the bedrooms, and two will become a diwan in the living room. I don't have a sofa.'

'Let's get a sofa,' I had said. She refused. She wanted a 'casual-chic' look. I guess it means not rich-looking but still classy.

'Get up,' I said and pulled her up by her hand.

'Thanks,' she said. 'Thanks for everything today.'

'Mention not,' I said.

'Please don't mention it,' she said.

'What?'

'Sorry, correcting you.'

I laughed.

'I thought we only learnt English on weekends?' I said.

'No, sir. We practise it all the time,' she said.

I looked at my watch. 'It's nine. I better leave.'

'What about dinner?'

'I'll get something from outside,' I said in slow but correct English.

'Why? We have stocked up. We have a hot plate. Would you like some Maggi?' she said.

It took us a while to unpack and set up everything. She inaugurated her hot plate and utensils. An hour later, we ate Maggi noodles in new stainless steel bowls from which the stickers wouldn't come off.

I slurped the noodles from my spoon. At one point, she removed a noodle from my chin. I wanted to spill noodles all over my face.

We finished dinner and cleaned up the kitchen.

At ten, I decided to leave.

'You will get an auto?' she said.

'I can walk to the bus stand,' I said. 'There is a bus to Dumraon at eleven.'

'Maybe I'll come with you next week. Let me settle in.'

'You'll be okay alone?' I said.

'Yeah,' she said, her voice heavy, or perhaps just tired.

'Sure?' I said.

'I look forward to being alone, Madhav,' she said.

◆

'You sure your mother will be okay with me staying over?'

'Of course. It's a long way to go back the same day,' I said.

We were riding in her company's Innova, which made the journey a lot faster than the bus I usually took. The roads of Bihar are, well, for the adventurous, to say the least.

'Ouch,' Riya said as her head bumped against the car roof.

'That bump is a sign we are close,' I said.

◆

I showed Riya the guestroom.

'These rooms are massive. You really are a prince.'

'Everything is falling apart,' I said.

I took her to my room. She noticed the basketball posters on my wall. I sat on my bed, she took the chair opposite me. It reminded me of us in Rudra, years ago.

'You still play?' she said.

I shook my head.

'Me neither,' she said.

'Want to? This evening?'

'Work first. You have to watch *The Godfather* on my laptop.'

'I did,' I said.

'You saw the first part. Now see part two with subtitles.'

I made a face, which didn't impress her much. She wore a fitted white T-shirt and black tights. Although fully covered, the snug outfit highlighted her curves. I couldn't believe Riya was in my room in Dumraon.

I wanted to kiss her. I thought about how mind-blowing that would be after so many years.

'What are you thinking? Like, now?' She snapped her fingers.

Her question made me freeze.

'Huh? Nothing. Lunch. Should we have lunch?'

'Did you think of that in English or Hindi?'

I tried to remember. Well, I had not thought about lunch at all. I had thought about kissing her. And you don't think that in any particular language.

'See, Madhav, the so-called fluent English speakers, they think in English. Not all the time, but a fair amount. Like, when you make a decision in your head, do you make it in English or Hindi?'

'Hindi, of course,' I said.

'That's the issue here. If you want to speak English well, it has to start in the head.'

She knocked the side of my head. The contact made me feel a bit drunk. I guess guys are born with this defect. Once they like a girl, even an accidental touch can be intoxicating.

'I'm trying,' I said.

'Good. You have Internet here?'

I shook my head.

'I wanted to show you some speeches,' she said.

'There is a cyber café nearby.'

'Let's go, I will get to see Dumraon.'

♦

There isn't much to see in Dumraon. Yet, she found everything exotic.

'Such cute roads,' she said, as we walked along the narrow chicken-neck path outside my house.

'You should see them in the monsoon. Not so cute then,' I said.

We came to the Shakti Cyber Café. A bunch of local guys sat before dusty computers. They pretended to look at news websites, even though they were probably downloading porn from other open tabs.

'Steve Jobs's "Stay Hungry. Stay Foolish",' she said as she opened YouTube.

Hungry for you, foolish for you, I thought.

'Oh,' I said.

'What?' she said as the video took time to load.

'I thought of something in English.'

'Excellent. What?'

I quickly shook my head and watched the video.

'You want subtitles?' Riya said. It was magical how she could sense what I wanted even before I thought of it.

I nodded. She had already picked a video with subtitles.

Steve Jobs had founded Apple Computers. He had competed with Bill Gates of Microsoft, the man who I had to give a speech to. It was a perfect situation in which to use a word I had learnt in English classes—ironic.

Steve, a thin, balding white guy in graduation robes, stood on a podium at Stanford University. I listened to the speech and read the subtitles.

'I never graduated from college. Truth be told, this is the closest I've ever gotten to a college graduation. Today, I want to tell you three stories from my life. That's it. No big deal. Just three stories.'

I was immediately hooked. I didn't know this guy but I liked him in seconds.

He spoke about how he was born to an unwed mother who had put him up for adoption. A CEO of a major global company speaking so openly about his past stunned me. He talked about dropping out of college to save his adoptive parents' money, and then sleeping on dorm floors and attending the classes he liked.

'I returned Coke bottles for the five-cent deposits to buy food with, and I would walk the seven miles across town

every Sunday night to get one good meal a week at the Hare
Krishna temple. I loved it.'

He had said nothing about his achievements yet. Still, you felt his
greatness.

'And most important, have the courage to follow your heart
and intuition.'

'Intuition?' I said.

'Gut instinct, what you feel from the heart,' Riya said.

Did I have the courage to follow my heart? Did I have the courage to
propose to Riya again?

Finally, Steve ended his speech.

'Stay Hungry. Stay Foolish. And I have always wished that
for myself. And now, as you graduate to begin anew, I wish
that for you.'

The crowd in the video applauded. I joined in. The cyber café's owner
turned to watch the whacko customer who clapped after YouTube
videos.

'Can I see it again?' I said.

'Sure. I will check my mail on another computer.'

I watched the speech three more times. I repeated some of the
lines as practice. I stood up after an hour.

I saw Riya in the adjacent cubicle, her mail open on the screen.
She looked grave.

'Should we go have lunch?' I said. I guess staying hungry isn't so
easy after all.

I glanced at her monitor. I just about managed to read the subject
line: 'Dad'.

She pressed 'send'. The screen disappeared. She logged out and
stood up.

We walked back to the haveli in silence.

27

Savitri tai served us daal and subzi with chapatis.

'Litti-chokha is for dinner, when Ma arrives,' I said.

'Sounds great,' Riya said with no noticeable enthusiasm.

'Everything okay?' I said.

'Dad's been unwell for a while.'

I did count. This was the first time she had shared something substantial with me.

'What happened?'

'He's a heart patient. The last by-pass didn't go well. It's not looking good.'

'Will you need to go to Delhi?'

'Probably. I don't know. They hide things from me,' she said. I guess hiding things from one another is a Somani family tradition.

She was looking down at her food, her spoon circling the daal. Perhaps it was Jobs's speech that gave me the courage to stand up and move to her side. I put my arm around her shoulders.

She stood up and hugged me back, though not too tightly.

'I'm sure he'll be fine. The best doctors in Delhi must be looking after him,' I said.

She nodded and sat back down.

'Sorry,' she said. 'I'm such a bother.'

'It's not a bother, Riya. It's okay to be down now and then. And to talk about it.'

'No, it's not,' she whispered, more to herself than to me.

We finished our meal. She picked up the plates.

'Where's the kitchen?' she said.

I pointed towards it. I tried to imagine her living in my house forever. She would never adjust to living in Dumraon, of course. My crumbling haveli could never be her 100, Aurangzeb Road.

I went to the kitchen and found her washing dishes.

'What are you doing?' I said, surprised.

'Relax, I do this in Patna, too,' she said.

'My mother should see this.'

'Why?' she said.

'Nothing,' I said.

◆

'Is she here?' my mother said.

'Yes,' I said.

I met my mother in the courtyard as she came back from school. I took her bag filled with notebooks. We walked into the house.

'Where is she?'

'In the guestroom.'

'Girls are also strange these days. Go live in whichever boy's house.'

'What are you saying, Ma? She is a friend from college. I invited her over.'

'Do her parents know?'

'I don't know.'

My mother shook her head.

'Be nice, Ma,' I said.

'You like her?'

'What kind of a question is that? You get people you dislike home?'

'Answer straight.'

'I need to bathe.'

◆

The water in the bathroom tap was a mere trickle. It took me forty-five minutes to fill a bucket and bathe. I changed into shorts and a T-shirt and came down to the living room. Riya and my mother were already there.

'You met already?' I said.

'Hi,' Riya said. 'I was just chatting with aunty.'

'You played basketball with her?' my mother said, sounding betrayed.

'Sometimes.'

My mother didn't respond. I felt guilty. I needed to give a longer answer.

'Well, she was in the team too. Girls' team,' I said.

'You never mentioned her. You used to talk about basketball so much,' my mother said.

'I didn't?' I said, pretending to be surprised.

'No,' my mother said.

'We only played in the first year,' I said.

'Why?' my mother said.

I paused to think. 'Our groups changed,' I said.

Riya and I looked at each other. Savitri tai brought nimbu paani for all of us.

My mother turned to Riya.

'So how long were you married for?'

My mouth fell open. How did my mother know? Riya sensed my shock.

'We were chatting earlier,' she said.

About your divorce? I thought. She never spoke about it with me.

'A year and a half,' Riya said.

'Kids?' my mother said.

What the hell? What is Ma talking about?

Riya shook her head.

'Why did you get married so early?' my mother said. She obviously had no filter in her head on what to ask or not. Of course, it was a question I wanted to ask Riya too.

To my surprise, Riya didn't filter her responses either.

'I was stupid. They were family friends. Everyone thought it was a good idea. But mostly, I did it because I was stupid.'

'Where are your parents?'

'Delhi.'

'You're a Punjabi?' my mother said, like all grown-up Indians do. They just have to know your community.

'Marwari. I'm Riya Somani.'

'Ah,' my mother said. 'They let you come to Bihar and work?'

'They don't let me do things. I wanted to. I can decide for myself,' Riya said, her feminist feathers beginning to flutter.

'You can?' my mother said. I sensed a tinge of sarcasm in her voice. Riya did too.

'I mean, those decisions don't always work out so well. But I do like to make my own decisions,' she said.

'They have a big business in Delhi, Ma,' I said. 'Infrastructure.'

'Marwaris are a rich community,' my mother said. 'Why are you working?'

'I want to be independent,' Riya said.

I realized this whole conversation was not flowing like the river of milk and honey I had hoped it would.

'Riya loves litti-chokha. In fact, I called her home for that,' I said.

My mother's frown vanished at the mention of her favourite cuisine.

'Really?' she said. 'When did you have it?'

'Here in Bihar. Madhav takes me to Maurya Complex in Patna all the time.'

'All the time?' my mother said, one eyebrow raised.

'Well, a few times,' I said, my tone guilt-ridden again. 'Twice or thrice. Classes keep me so busy, I don't get the time.'

Ma took a big sip of her nimbu paani.

'I thought you go there to study,' she said. 'Is the speech ready?'

'Going on. Riya is helping me,' I said.

'Is she?' my mother said. I wished I had told her more about Riya, but I could never gather the courage. I decided the only way forward was to change the topic.

'Should I ask Savitri tai to lay the table?' I said.

'I can do that,' Riya said.

My mother looked at her.

'If it's okay? I know the kitchen. I can help Savitri tai.'

My mother did not respond. Riya took it as assent and left. 'Now I see why you go to Patna,' Ma said.

'It's not what you think. Riya is just a friend. An old classmate,' I said.

'How come she's already married and divorced?'

'That surprised me too. I ran into her in Patna by chance.'

'And she latched on to you,' Ma said.

'Not true. I can't study English all the time, Ma. I need friends there. Besides, she helps me practise. Her English is excellent. She is from a high-class society.'

'I can see the class,' my mother said.

'I don't know the details of her divorce. Her father is sick. Be nice to her.'

'I am nice. She is staying in my house. What else do you want me to do?'

I rolled my eyes.

'Why is she wearing such tight pants?' she said next.

'I have no idea, Ma,' I said, my voice loud. 'I don't know why she got married or divorced or wears tight pants. Can you let her be?'

'You are shouting at your mother for her?'

My mother looked away from me. It was Rani Sahiba's classic sulky face.

'I'm not shouting,' I said, my voice still too loud to classify it as anything else. My mother looked away.

I realized I needed her cooperation to have a peaceful dinner.

'Sorry,' I said.

Ma sniffed.

En route to the dining room with a stack of plates, Riya smiled at me. I smiled back.

'I said sorry, Ma,' I said after Riya went back to the kitchen.

My mother glared at me.

'I've suffered enough in life. Don't add to it,' she said.

'I'm not,' I said. 'By the way, have you heard of Steve Jobs?'

I explained how watching speeches on YouTube had helped me, as had many of Riya's unconventional techniques.

'I have to think in English, Ma. Like high-class people. Their English sounds different, no?'

'We are not low class either,' my mother said.

'Dinner's served,' Riya said, clapping her hands in the dining room.

We had a peaceful dinner, with no major retorts, taunts or sarcasm. When two women don't share the right vibe, a peaceful hour together is a minor miracle.

'I ate too much,' Riya said and held her stomach. 'This was one of the best meals I have ever had.'

'We eat like this every day,' my mother said, and stood up and left the table.

28

'I have a confession to make,' Riya said. We were sitting on a jute charpoy on the haveli's roof, looking up at the millions of stars you could never see in the Delhi night sky. 'What you said about Bihar and its simplicity in college had something to do with me accepting the Patna offer.'

'Really?' I said. 'And that you hoped to run into me?'

'Yeah, right.' She laughed, so I couldn't tell if she was being sarcastic.

'Don't worry about my mother,' I said.

'I'm not. Why should I be worried?' she said and smiled at me. 'All mothers are the same, I guess.'

'Meaning?'

'Nothing. She's Rani Sahiba. Literally, the queen of her castle. She is entitled to say whatever she wants.'

'She's not bad at heart,' I said.

'I know. Did she mention me? When I went to the kitchen?'

'Not really. Why?'

'My clothes. My divorce. Anything?'

'Nothing important,' I said, thinking of little else but how to casually hold her hand. When I did gather the courage to do it, I lunged forward suddenly and grabbed her hand. It was not a subtle move.

'Careful,' she said.

'What?'

'My left wrist. It's a little tender.'

'How come?'

'An old injury.'

'Basketball?'

She gave a hesitant, non-committal nod. I released her left hand and held her right.

'Your mother is downstairs,' she said.

I took her words as encouragement. She had not said that holding her hand was wrong, she only mentioned my mother.

'She's asleep,' I said.

I entwined my fingers with hers. She didn't protest.

I turned my face towards hers. She freed her hand and slid a few inches away.

'Hey, you want to do speech rehearsals here? It's a good place to do it,' she said. It is unique, the grace with which girls can deflect situations and topics.

'Not now, I'm tired,' I said.

'Should we go downstairs then?' Riya said, all innocence.

I looked into her eyes. She understood that look. We had shared it years ago in college.

I leaned forward, my lips an inch from hers.

'No, Madhav, no,' she said and gently placed her hand on my chest. However, she didn't push me away. Her fingers were directly over my heart. I leaned back a bit.

'Why not?' I said.

'We agreed to be just friends. No more.'

'Why not?'

'Don't ask the same question twice.'

'I can try twice.'

I leaned over again. This time, she pushed me back.

'Don't do this. Please.'

Her eyes were wet. I withdrew.

'Can we at least talk?' I said. Losers get words from girls; winners get kisses.

'We are talking.'

'Are you worried about your dad?'

'Among other things.'

'Which you won't share with me.'

'Madhav, you are a nice guy. An amazing guy, okay?'

'If you say so,' I said.

'But.'

'There's always a "but".'

'Can we please not do all this other stuff?'

'Not now,' I agreed. 'But maybe later?'

'Madhav,' she said, 'I don't want to get your hopes up. So no "maybe later".'

'Why? Because of what I did in college?'

'Are you crazy? Do you really think I will hold on to something from years ago?'

'So what is it? I'm not good enough for you?' I said.

She smiled at me.

'What?' I said.

'I just said you are an amazing guy.'

'Give us a shot, Riya,' I said.

'A shot? Wow. Someone knows English slang.'

'A chance. Whatever. Anyway, let it be. Okay, fine, friends.'

I realized I had blown my moment. A failed attempt at kissing has to be aborted, not converted into an argument.

We stayed silent for a minute.

'My father is dying,' she said. 'And I don't know what to feel.'

'He is your father.'

'Yes, I hope he makes it.'

'I can't live without you, Riya,' I said, or rather, blurted out.

She turned to me.

'Not again.'

'Sorry,' I said.

I turned the other way. Girls have no idea how much it hurts when our love is rejected. Yet, men are expected to keep trying and take hits all the time.

She held my hand. I pulled it away. Be a man, they say. Well, it sucks to be a man sometimes.

'Stop sulking, Your Majesty,' she said.

'One kiss,' I said.

'What?'

'Just one kiss. After that I promise we will be friends. Just friends.'

'How does that work?'

'I don't know. I can't get that one kiss out of my head. I need to know I mean something to you. I understand your situation—the divorce, your dad and your job. I won't expect anything. I will let you be. I will be a friend and value you as one. But just one kiss.'

She applauded.

'What?'

'You said that entire thing in English. Oh my God, Madhav.'

For a moment I forgot about the kiss. I reflected upon my achievement.

'I really did,' I said, surprised.

'Awesome,' she said.

I returned to reality.

'So, yes, one kiss.'

'But…'

'Shh…' I said and kept my hand on her mouth. I came forward and kissed my fingers placed on her lips. Her eyes blinked in surprise.

I removed my fingers. My lips landed on hers. We had kissed exactly three years, four months and eleven days ago. She put her arms around me as if to keep her balance. The kiss was light at first, and then picked up intensity. Frogs croaked, crickets chirped and the breeze soared as Dumraon's night sky witnessed Bihar's, if not the world's, best kiss ever.

She buried her face in my shoulder. More than kisses, I could tell she wanted to be held, as if she had not hugged anyone in a really long time.

I held her tighter, landing kisses wherever I could, on her face, neck, lips. After a minute, or maybe an hour, she stirred.

'That lasted a while,' she said.

'Still counts as one kiss. Was it nice?' I said.

'Madhav.'

'What?'

'You said one kiss. Not one kiss, then an in-depth discussion on the quality of the kiss, or what did the kiss mean, or can we do this again or let's get carried away. I did it for you. So you know you mean something. But please don't discuss, mention or bring this up ever again.'

I looked at her, shocked. How can you brush aside the most incredible kiss in the state, possibly the world, without even a basic review? But I said, 'Fine.'

'Sit up,' she said. She sat cross-legged on the charpoy. I faced her, but I moved far enough so she wouldn't feel I could strike again.

She smiled at me.

'What?'

'It was nice,' she said.

'What was?'

'What we just did.'

'We sat up cross-legged. That was nice?' I said.

'Yes,' she said and laughed. 'It was wonderful how we sat up. Wow. You sit pretty well.'

'We have sat before.'

'This was a different league. Guess maturity makes a man better,' she said, 'at...sitting.'

We laughed. I wanted to touch her, if only to touch my fingertips to hers, but didn't. I couldn't believe we had kissed again. We chatted about old classmates of ours. We had lost touch with most of them, but tried to update each other with our limited information.

Twenty minutes later, she coughed. Once, twice and then five more times.

'You okay?'

'Yeah, it is a little cold,' she said and went into a coughing fit.

'I'll get water.'

I ran downstairs to my room. I came back with a bottle of water. She lay down on the charpoy, right hand on her forehead.

'You're not well, Riya?' I said.

She coughed again, sat up and had some water.

I touched her forehead.

'You don't have fever,' I said.

'I'm exhausted, I guess.'

'Did I stress you out?' I said. I felt guilty about kissing her.

'No. I should just go rest.'

She had a coughing fit again, this time more violent.

I helped her stand up and escorted her to the guestroom.

'Will you be okay? You want someone here?' I said.

She smiled.

'Nice try, sir. But I will be just fine,' she said.

'I didn't mean that. I could wake up Ma.'

'No, no, please. I need sleep, that's all. We are going to the school tomorrow, right?'

'If you're feeling better.'

'I'll be okay. Goodnight, Madhav,' she said.

'Goodnight, Riya,' I said, not wanting to leave.

'Thanks for taking care of me,' she said, her voice sleepy.

She shut the door. I came back to my room. As I lay in my bed, I touched my lips. I thought about our magnificent lip-lock under the stars.

'I love you, Riya Somani,' I whispered before I drifted off to sleep.

29

'So this is the famous Dumraon Royal School,' Riya said, her eyes widening at the sight of hundreds of kids buzzing around like bees.

'Nothing royal about it,' I said.

'Well, I hear a prince runs it,' she said.

She smiled at me. I gave her an all-knowing, what-happened-last-night look. Of course, not much had happened. But a kiss is a kiss is a kiss.

'We decided never to talk about it,' she said.

'I didn't say anything.'

'Tell your eyes to be quiet then. They talk too much.'

I laughed. 'How's your cough?'

'Better,' she said.

We reached school at nine, two hours after Ma. Riya had slept in. Since she did not know the way, I had to wait for her. She had donned a skirt and top first, but I had asked her to change into a salwar-kameez instead. Not that the kids would care but the principal, or Rani Sahiba, would. She had to approve of the dress code. So Riya switched to a plain white chikan salwar-kameez.

We entered the staffroom.

'You finally made it. Welcome,' my mother said. I ignored her sarcasm. Riya and I greeted her, but Ma only nodded, without looking up from her notebooks.

I introduced Riya to the staff.

Tarachand ji duly rang the bell. My mother stood up.

'Where are you going, Ma? It is my period.'

'Are you working today?' she said.

'Yes, of course.'

'Good, because I have a hundred books to correct.'

She sat down again.

'Is it okay if Riya waits here?' I said.

'Oh, I could walk around,' Riya said.

'It's fine,' my mother said.

'Or I could help with the books?' Riya said.

My mother looked up and lowered her reading glasses.

'Help?'

'I can correct some notebooks. Should I take a pile?'

In a slow movement, Ma pushed a pile towards her.

I smiled. Rani Sahiba's heart could melt. I imagined the three of us at school every day, after it had received the Gates grant. If you are imagining it, might as well dream of the perfect scenario, so I thought of Riya, my mother and me, laughing and correcting notebooks. I thought of Riya and me teaching the school kids basketball.

'Madhav?' my mother interrupted my daydream.

'Huh?'

'Class?'

'I was just leaving,' I said.

◆

'Who is that didi?' a little girl in class III asked me.

I taught classes III, IV and V simultaneously. Since we didn't have enough teachers or classrooms, we had come up with a new system. I divided the blackboard into three parts.

Each class had a third of the blackboard. I would teach a concept to one class and give them a problem. While they solved it, I moved on to the next class. It wasn't the best way to teach, but the kids adapted to it.

'She's my classmate from Delhi. Same as you have classmates here,' I said.

'She's so pretty,' another class III girl called Shabnam said. 'Are all Delhi girls so pretty?'

I smiled.

'Just like all Dumraon girls are pretty.'

'Are all Delhi girls so tall?' Shabnam said.

'No. Only those who can write the nine-times table.' The girls giggled and got on with their classwork.

I moved to class IV and then to class V. Forty minutes into the class, I sat down for a break. I had finally managed to keep all three classes busy with their respective work.

'Madhav sir,' a ponytailed girl next to Shabnam said.

'What?'

'Bring your friend to class.'

'Why?'

'Please.'

'No. This is study time.'

A couple of other girls followed and started the 'please' routine. Soon, the whole class chanted 'please, please, please' to me. I had taught them about manners just the previous week. Now they were using them against me.

'Fine, I will get her,' I said, 'provided you stay absolutely quiet and work.'

Everyone nodded and placed their fingers on their lips. I left the classroom. The class burst into noise as soon as I stepped out.

My mother and Riya sat in silence, each busy with their stack of notebooks.

'Riya, the students want to meet you.'

'Me? Why?' Riya looked up, surprised.

'Just curious, I guess.'

Riya looked at my mother. Ma didn't react. I pulled Riya's arm.

'Come, no,' I said.

Riya and I stepped out of the staffroom.

'How is it going with Ma?' I said.

'Why do you ask?'

'She is sweet, no? Comes across as strict, but is a big softie.'

'Why are you telling me this, Madhav?' Riya said.

'Just.'

We reached the class. The students broke into applause.

'Hi, I am Riya,' she said. She knelt down to be on their level.

'You are so pretty,' Shabnam said shyly.

Riya tweaked Shabnam's nose. 'So are you,' she said.

Shabnam blushed.

Riya spoke to the girl next to Shabnam. 'What do you want to be when you grow up?'

The girl buried her face in Shabnam's lap.

Riya laughed. She repeated the question to another girl.

'Mother. I want to be a mother,' the girl responded.

'And?' Riya said.

'And what?' the girl said.

'Doctor? Engineer? Dancer?'

The little girl thought for a while.

'Teacher,' she said.

'Nice,' Riya said and patted her back.

Riya and I came back to the staffroom. My mother and the other teachers had class. Only Riya and I remained in the staffroom. We sat at the long table. She coughed again.

I said, 'You really don't sound okay.'

'I was fine. I don't know,' Riya said. She went into another coughing fit.

'Let's find a doctor,' I said.

'I'll see a doctor in Patna.'

Riya excused herself and stepped outside. She looked around.

'There's no toilet. Kids go in the corner there. Or in the fields outside,' I said, coming up behind her.

Riya walked out to the fields, still coughing. I saw her body shake from a distance. I ran up to her. She turned and smiled at me.

'I'm fine. I just need to properly cough it out.'

'Spit out the phlegm.'

'Sorry, I'm being gross.'

'As if,' I scoffed.

'I should head back,' she said.

'Alone? Let me come and drop you.'

Riya laughed. She patted my shoulder.

'You are so sweet. There is no need. It's just an allergy.'

'I should come with you,' I said.

She held my shoulders and flipped me around.

'You have classes. Now go back in, mister, before all your little girls come looking for you.'

30

'Louder, Madhav. You're speaking like a mouse,' Riya shouted, in contrast to my meek voice.

She was grouchy, perhaps because I had made six mistakes in my last rehearsal. She stood before me and stomped her feet. She wore an oversized purple T-shirt and Bermuda shorts. *Purple suits her*, I thought; everything suits her.

'You realize your speech is the day after tomorrow?' she said.

'You're making me tense,' I said.

'Fine.' She threw her hands up in frustration. 'Tense is not good. I'm calm. You're calm,' she said, trying to swing my mood.

'I'm screwing this up,' I said. I sat down on her double-mattress diwan.

I had come to her house on Sunday evening for a final rehearsal. Gates was arriving on Tuesday. I had to leave for Dumraon tomorrow.

'It's looking staged. They will see that I'm no good at this,' I said.

'Relax, Madhav. I'm sorry I shouted.'

She sat next to me and held my hand. She coughed again.

It was my turn to shout. 'Who is this stupid doctor who can't treat your cough?'

'I don't know. It's an allergy. Something in the air. Can't figure out what's making it flare up.'

'What is the doctor in Delhi saying now?'

Riya had gone to Delhi last month, after her family asked her to come meet her father one last time. He had passed away while she was there. She had spent two weeks in Delhi, attending the funeral and various last-rites ceremonies. During that trip, she had also met a senior specialist for her cough.

'Same. Find the allergen. You think I'm allergic to you?' She winked at me, indicating that she felt better. I smacked her with a red cushion.

'Everything okay at home, Riya?'

Riya had not reacted much to her father's death. She had come back from Delhi and hugged me as if she would never let go. She mumbled something about forgiveness. I didn't pry. She would only tell me what she wanted to tell me and when she decided to.

'Yeah. My brothers are taking care of the business and my mother sounded normal the last time I spoke to her.' Then she was all brisk and business-like, clapping her hands to bring me back to the present.

'And now we have Madhav Jha, from Dumraon Royal School.'

I stood in the centre of her living room.

'Respected Mr Gates, Ms Myers, other members of the Gates Foundation delegation, MLA Ojha, eminent people from Dumraon, students and staff of the Dumraon Royal School…'

'You know what?' Riya interrupted me.

'What?'

'Your greeting, it's too long. Let's cut it.'

'Riya, you're changing the script at this stage?'

'Minor change.'

We fine-tuned the words in my notes. I began again. She didn't interrupt me. I spoke for ten minutes.

'And that, my friends, is all I have to say. Thank you,' I said.

Riya clapped.

'How many mistakes?' I said.

'Five.'

'Five?'

'Yeah, but minor ones. They don't really change the meaning of the sentences.'

'You are just saying it to make me less tense, right?'

Riya smiled. 'Let's eat dinner. No point over-rehearsing. We are all set. Relax,' she said.

'Really?'

'Yes. I made some daal, but chapatis will take time. Should I just make some rice? Daal-chawal?'

'Sure,' I said. 'I'll help you.'

We went to her kitchen. She cooked dinner and I made a salad of tomatoes and cucumber with salt, pepper and lemon juice. I set the table while she cooked the food.

We sat down to eat, facing each other at the dining table.

'When will you arrive in Dumraon?' I said as I mixed the daal and rice.

'You won't freak out if I'm there, no?'

'Are you stupid? Just come with me tomorrow morning.'

'No, no. I can't. Too much work,' she said.

'So when?' I said.

'Tuesday morning with the Foundation people. You've told them about me, right?'

'Yes,' I said. I had already given Riya Samantha's number. Riya's car would follow the Foundation's contingent. They would all come together.

'The salad is nice,' she said.

'It's nothing. So simple,' I said.

'Simple and nice. I like it. I like simple and nice, Madhav.'

Is that how she sees me too—simple and nice? Or am I too simple and too nice?

◆

Post dinner, we cleaned up the kitchen and washed the dishes. We came back to the living room. Riya reclined on the diwan. 'I'm so tired.'

I checked the time. It was ten.

'I better leave,' I said.

Riya coughed again. I got her a glass of warm water.

'After this speech, your treatment is our first priority. We need to find that allergen or whatever,' I said.

'I'm fine. See, it's gone now,' she said.

She shut her eyes and patted the mattress, signalling for me to sit next to her. She then put her head on my lap and turned on her side towards me, her eyes closed, by all accounts fast asleep.

'You want to sleep here?'

No answer.

I got a sheet and pillow from her bedroom. I placed the pillow under her head and the sheet over her.

She smiled in gratitude, like a happy baby.

'I'm going,' I mouthed silently against her temple.

She shook her head.

What? I wondered to myself. *What does she want?*

She held on to me when I tried to move.

'I'll stay?' I said.

She didn't react. This is what girls do. At crucial moments, they won't give you a straight answer. What's a guy to do?

'I'll stay for a bit?' I said.

She nodded.

Thank God for some guidance.

'Okay, I'm tired too. If I stay, I need to lie down as well.'

She moved aside, eyes still shut, making space for me. I was shocked. Riya actually wanted me to lie down with her.

I slid in next to her, as quietly as possible, lest she woke up fully and came to her senses.

'Sleeping?' I said, giving her an awkward cuddle.

She nodded. Girl nonsense, again. I grinned. How could she respond if she was asleep?

'Me too,' I said. I think it is acceptable, almost necessary, for men and women to lie to one another.

She turned on her side and placed her arm around me. She also curled up a little, so her chest would not come too close to mine. Only her arms and knees touched me.

Girls are really good at such stuff. Even in sleep, they can contort themselves to maintain the boundaries of appropriate physical contact.

I shut my eyes. Of course, I could not, just *could not* sleep. I wanted to hold her close. I wanted to kiss her. Restless, I placed an arm around her. I think girls actually believe guys can casually place their arms around them with no other idea in their heads.

I didn't have courage to do anything else. *Maybe she is getting comfortable with me*, my mind told me. *Why rush it? Chill, Madhav, chill.*

The same mind came up with a different theory a few seconds later. *What if she wants you to do something? She's created the setting. Now if you don't act, she will probably think you are a wimp. Do something, Madhav. Don't just chill.*

The stress of two conflicting ideas in my head made me restless. Riya's smooth arm on me made things worse. I tossed and turned.

Meanwhile, she slept.

Two hours later, Riya opened her eyes. I had involuntarily poked her shoulder. I had pins and needles everywhere from trying not to move.

'What is it?' she said sleepily.

'You're awake?' I said, all sparkly voiced.

'You woke me up,' she said.

'Sorry,' I said and patted her shoulder. 'Go back to sleep.'

'Are you tense?'

A shiver went down my spine. *How did she know?* God has given too many senses to women.

'A little bit.'

'Don't worry. You will perform fine.'

'Huh? What?' I said. *What is she talking about?* Then it struck me.

'Oh, yes. I've done my best. The rest is up to Mr Gates.'

'Exactly. Now sleep,' she said and closed her eyes again.

'Riya.'

'Hmm?'

'I want to say something, Riya.'

'Shh,' she said, eyes still shut. She placed a finger on my lips.

'Say it to Bill Gates first,' she said and drifted back to sleep.

◆

'Thirty minutes? Our programme lasts an hour,' I said, my voice indignant.

Samantha had called me on Monday morning, a day before Gates's visit.

'I'm sorry, Madhav. It's a really tight schedule for Mr Gates. Maybe you can cut down on a few things.'

'But the kids have been preparing for months.'

'My apologies. Trust me, we have actually cancelled a few places. But there's no question of cancelling your school.'

'Fine. What time?'

'10.30 sharp. See you.'

I went with Tarachand ji to inspect the empty field being converted into a parking lot. From a distance, I could hear the sound of students practising the welcome song.

We had stopped classes for a week to focus on the annual day. Students had planned the cultural programme, scrubbed the floors and walls of the school, drawn new charts and made props for the stage. I went to the staffroom and told my mother about the shortened length of the visit.

She said, 'It was a stupid idea to call these moody goras to school. We've been going mad for the past few weeks for them, and now see.'

31

At 10.15 on Tuesday morning, my phone rang.

'We are entering Dumraon. Ten more minutes,' Samantha said.

I rushed to the school entrance. Twenty kids assigned to be the welcome party formed two lines facing each other. Each held a plate with rose petals to be showered on the guests. A girl from class V would apply the tika.

Parents had already arrived. Over a thousand guests sat on red plastic chairs under the tent set up for the occasion. Dignitaries and special invitees sat in the front VIP rows.

The fleet of eight cars became visible. The kids in the welcome team squealed in excitement. They started to throw flower petals at each other.

'Stop it,' I said to them.

Mr Gates stepped out of his car. Media persons surrounded him, taking pictures non-stop. A team of ten Americans, including Samantha, and five Indians from the Foundation, stood behind Mr Gates.

'Hi,' Riya's voice startled me. I turned to face her. She wore a baby-pink saree with little silver dots all over. She resembled the rose petals on the kids' plates.

'Saree?' I said.

She spread her arms. Just seeing her lean body, subtle curves and the pink chiffon fabric draped around her, made me feel richer than the richest man in the world who waited for me.

'How do I look?' she said.

'Like Miss India,' I said. She laughed.

'Now attend to your guests. I'll find a place inside.'

'But Riya…'

'Shh… Focus on them. All the best.'

She gave me a quick hug and hurried inside.

'Mr Gates, this is Madhav, one of the founders of the school, from the royal family,' Samantha said. 'Madhav, Mr Gates.'

I shook hands with the richest man in the world. They say Mr

Gates is so rich, he would not pick up a hundred dollars lying on the road. He makes more money than that in the time it takes to pick up the hundred-dollar bill. He shook hands with me for about five seconds. I wondered how many thousands of dollars he could have earned in that time.

'Good to see you, Madhav,' Mr Gates said. He spoke like an old friend. Students threw petals on him. Samantha made urgent motions that we start the function soon.

A mini-stampede occurred on stage. The welcome-song kids bumped into the dance kids, both sets unprepared for the merger of their programmes. The welcome song, a Saraswati Vandana, had not even ended when Bollywood music took over. The mash-up sounded odd but the audience clapped energetically.

I sat next to my mother on a sofa in the front row. My eyes hunted for Riya; she sat ten seats away on my left. I gestured for her to come sit next to me. She smiled and declined from a distance.

The dance ended with kids dancing to Salman Khan's hit number 'O, O Jaane Jaana'. My mother went up on stage and the music faded. She spoke in Hindi. 'Thank you, children. Can we have a big round of applause for the children, please?'

The crowd clapped hard.

'Let's also welcome Mr Gates and his team, who have come all the way from America,' she said. The crowd responded with loud cheers and more applause. Mr Gates turned around in his seat and waved.

'And now, I understand we have little time. So can I invite Prince Madhav Jha to give the welcome speech?'

The crowd cheered. My heart started to beat fast. I stood up and walked to the stage, passing Riya, who gave me a thumbs-up. I sprinted up to the stage.

◆

I scanned the crowd of over a thousand people from left to right, right to left. The crowd had stopped clapping and were now waiting for me to speak.

I took the mic in my hand. It slipped a little in my palm, which was sweaty with nervousness.

Not a word came out of me. Nothing. I saw the sea of people. Even though I had practised the speech a million times, I couldn't say a thing.

People were beginning to look a little puzzled. Was it a mic problem? they wondered.

I saw Riya in her pink saree in a corner of the front row, her eyes on me. Slowly, she stood up. I felt anxious. What would the crowd think? However, she simply changed her place to come sit right in front of me. I lip-read her.

'One line at a time, go slow,' she mouthed. Her presence kick-started something within me. I blurted out:

'Distinguished guests of the Bill Gates Foundation, respected dignitaries, my dear students and parents, welcome to the Dumraon Royal School.'

The crowd cheered. Most did not understand English, but the mention of Dumraon was enough to set them off. The Foundation delegates looked at me with attention.

Okay, I can do this, I told myself. *Just like at the rehearsals with Riya. Just imagine only she is here.*

I gazed at Riya. She gave me a nod and smiled. Encouraged, I continued:

'Mr Bill Gates is here with us today. He is the richest man in the world. I am sure he is sick of being told that all the time.'

From a distance, I noticed Bill Gates smile. *He is listening to me,* I thought.

'Sir, you know that rich in terms of money is not enough to have the richest life. That is why you are here. In my Bihar, which, even though we love it, is one of the most backward places on the planet.'

Riya was nodding after every line.

'And in this backward Bihar is this extraordinary school. This school with seven hundred kids, three teachers, negligible fees, no proper classrooms, no toilets, no real government support and yet, a lot of riches.'

Riya gave me two thumbs-ups. *Okay, no mistakes so far.*

'The real riches here are the kids. I am supposed to teach them. However, they have taught me so much. We grown-ups complain about what is lacking in this school. But these kids, they never complain. Come to our school at any time and you will hear only one thing from them—laughter.'

The front row, the people who understood me, broke into applause. The subsequent rows followed a minute later, if only to show that they understood as well.

'If you ask these kids, they will say this is the best school in the world. They love their friends. They love whatever they get to learn here. However, I know this school can give them more. I know kids deserving more only.'

Riya frowned. *Damn, I've made a mistake. It should be 'I know the kids deserve more'.*

I was panic-stricken. Riya gestured for me to breathe. I inhaled deeply and exhaled slowly. Composed, I continued, 'I know the kids deserve more. Because I have seen the value a good education can add. It is not just to get you a job. It is not just about knowledge and the new things you learn either. A good education gives you self-confidence.'

I paused to consult my notes. I looked up and spoke again.

'Today, I speak to you in English. I didn't know this language well. I was scared and ashamed. People made fun of me. I spent my whole college life with a complex. I don't want that to happen to these kids. I don't want anyone to tell them they are not good enough.'

People clapped. I don't know if they understood me, or if they had just connected with the emotion in my voice.

'For that I need resources. I need good teachers. However, good teachers won't come to a school without basic facilities. Students can't be taught without proper classrooms. You can't have a real school without toilets.'

Riya's eyes stayed on me. They kept me going.

'I don't want to beg from our government. I don't want to beg from anyone, actually. Money is not my thing. I left a job at a multinational bank to be here. But sadly, you need some money to do even good things in life.'

Riya signalled for me to sign off; the speech ended around here. However, I continued to speak, unrehearsed and impromptu.

'Mr Gates, people must tell you that you are a lucky man to

have so much money. It might irritate you also, since what you have achieved is not just because of luck. It is because of your creativity, vision and hard work. You deserve it. However, let me tell you one place where luck helped you.'

Riya looked at me, shocked. *When had I come up with all this*, she seemed to be wondering.

I continued, 'Where you are truly lucky is that you were born in America. To be born in a country where everyone gets a chance. One of my kids may have it in him to open a global company like yours, but he won't get a chance. Mr Gates, you were lucky to get that chance. Today, we don't run the school in the hope of aid or recognition. All we are trying to do here is ensure that every kid in our school gets that chance. Thank you.'

Thunderous applause. Some in the crowd, including Riya and Mr Gates, stood up. Soon, the rest of the crowd followed. I received a standing ovation. I couldn't believe I had delivered the speech I had obsessed over for months. I couldn't believe I had conquered one of my biggest demons—English. I folded my hands and left the stage.

I walked back to my seat. My mother turned to me.

'You learnt so much English?' she whispered.

'She taught me.' I pointed to Riya.

My mother and Riya smiled politely at each other.

Students took over the stage again. They did a dance-drama about Lord Krishna, the naughty boy who stole butter. The shortest student in class II, a little girl called Karuna, played Krishna. She wore a headband with a peacock feather stuck in it. After it was over, my mother went up on stage and thanked the participating students.

Samantha from the Gates Foundation came up to me.

'Bill needs to leave. Otherwise we will be late,' she whispered in my ear, her voice rushed.

'Won't he give a speech?' I said.

'He never does.'

My heart sank. I wanted to ask her how the speech went but Samantha seemed too stressed out to notice or care.

'I would like to call Mr Bill Gates on the stage to say a few words,' my mother said. Mr Gates smiled and folded his hands, however, asking to be excused.

I ran back up on stage. My mother seemed surprised. I took the mic from her. 'Mr Gates needs to leave. If it's okay, I would like to call him on stage to accept a small gift from us,' I said.

Mr Gates obliged. He came on stage, along with two members of his Foundation. A class V girl arrived with the gift. It was a small hand-painted clay pot. Several students had drawn flowers on it. In the pot was a flowering plant.

'It's beautiful,' Mr Gates said as he accepted the gift.

I smiled at him.

'Nice speech,' he said.

'Thank you, sir,' I said. I shook hands with the other two delegates on stage. One was Phil and the other was Roger, a young assistant to Mr Gates.

'Phil, do you want to?' Mr Gates said.

'Yeah, sure,' Phil said.

Want to what? I wondered.

32

'May I have the mic?' Phil said. I passed the mic to him.

'Namaste,' Phil addressed the audience. That one word in Hindi made the audience swoon in ecstasy. This is how we Indians are. If white guys speak even a tiny bit of Hindi, we love them.

'Kaise hain?' Phil said. The crowd roared in excitement.

'We loved the show. Congratulations to all students, mubarak,' he said. Applause rent the air.

'We found the students here extremely talented. We feel they deserve to have more opportunities to learn. We have decided to give the school a dozen computers, with all our software preloaded.'

The crowd clapped. I did too, wondering what we would do with computers without electricity. Maybe they will come with computer tables, I thought. We could use the tables. Phil continued, 'Of course, computers alone will not be enough in a school that needs infrastructure. Thus, the Gates Foundation would like to give the school a one-time grant of fifty thousand dollars and, subject to inspection, a grant of ten thousand dollars a year for the next five years.'

My head felt light. I saw the activity around me in a haze. Riya jumped. Really, she stood up and jumped. Everything else was a blur. The media sprang into action. Reporters barged ahead of the front row to take pictures. My mother couldn't contain her excitement. She came on the podium and translated the announcement in Hindi, and converted the amounts to rupees.

'Twenty lakh rupees now, and four lakhs a year for the next five years. We will now make this one of the best schools in Bihar,' my mother said. The crowd stood up and continued to clap. MLA Ojha inserted his face in front of as many cameras as possible.

My mother gave me a hug. Samantha came up to me and whispered in my ear, 'Congratulations, Madhav, you did it. We will talk later, okay? I need to rush. I'll call you.'

'Yes, thank you, Samantha. Thank you so much.'

'Here's my card,' Phil said as he slipped one in my hand. 'Your work has impressed us. I know St. Stephen's. To give up a career and come here is admirable.'

I wanted Riya to hear this too. I looked for her but she was nowhere in sight.

Crowds of villagers filled the stage. Security personnel escorted the Gates Foundation delegation out of the venue to their cars.

'Thank you, Rajkumar sahib,' a villager tried to touch my feet.

'You are our hero,' said another.

I wanted to bring Riya on stage. But the crowd wouldn't let me get past them. The crowd lifted me. I was thankful; at least it would be easier to spot Riya from someone's shoulder.

'Rajkumar Madhav,' said one.

'Zindabad!' the others shouted in response.

I saw her empty seat. *Where did she go?* I wondered. The crowd bobbed me up and down.

I looked around frantically. There was no sign of her. The media wanted quotes. I remember saying this was a fantastic outcome that would change the future of thousands of students of Dumraon.

'Are you happy?' one reporter asked me.

'Uh? Yes,' I said. I was happy. I mean, I should be happy, I told myself. *Where the hell was Riya?*

My mother came to me. The media turned to her.

'Ma, have you seen Riya?' I said.

'Who?'

'My friend. She was sitting in the front row. Where did she go?'

My mother shook her head. She turned to the reporters.

I extracted myself from the crowd on stage. MLA Ojha came up to me.

'Congratulations, Rajkumar ji. Lot of money, eh?'

'Thanks, Ojha ji. Thank you for the opportunity.'

'It's okay. Now are we sharing it or what?' he said.

I looked at him and his slimy eyes. He saw my shocked expression. He burst into laughter. 'Joking, Rajkumar ji. Always so serious. Of course, it is all for the school.'

I smiled and excused myself. The crowd thinned in about twenty minutes. Most of the parents and students had left. I asked the school staff if they had seen Riya.

'She was in the front row. We saw her stand up when the white man announced the money,' Tarachand ji said.

I went to the makeshift parking area. No cars. The delegation had left long back. I couldn't find Riya's car either.

I called Riya. Nobody picked up. I tried again, thrice. No response. I called Riya's driver.

'I am on leave. Madam must have taken another driver,' he said. I hung up.

I wondered what to do next. *Where could she have gone? Did she get an urgent call from home? Office? Where could she be?*

'Madhav sir,' a girl's voice interrupted my chain of thought.

It was Shabnam, my student from class III. She wore a dhoti and a kurta, having played a villager in the Krishna skit. Her parents stood behind her.

I folded my hands to wish them. They thanked me for a great function.

'Madhav sir, didi left something for you.' Shabnam handed me a brown envelope. 'Riya didi said to give this to you after the function. She left while you were on stage.'

'Did she tell you where she was going?'

Shabnam shook her head.

'Did she go in a car?'

Shabnam nodded and left with her parents. I tore open the envelope.

'Where are you?' my mother shouted from a distance.

'Here only,' I said. I slipped the envelope into my pocket.

'Many people are coming home for lunch to celebrate. Come, let's go.'

33

Our VIP guests had come to the haveli for lunch.

'What a son you have,' Kanta aunty, one of my mother's childhood friends, said.

'He deserves to be king. He is our asli rajkumar,' said Bela chachi, a third cousin of my mother.

I thanked my aunts for their compliments.

'Ma, I need to go upstairs to my room.'

'Why? What about your lunch?'

'I'm tired. I'll have it later.'

I ran upstairs and shut the door to my room. I took out the envelope again. Inside was a computer printout of a letter.

Dear Madhav,

I want you to remain calm when you read this. And, if possible, be calm afterwards too. I am writing this letter to tell you something important. I am leaving Patna.

I am not well, Madhav. I think you noticed my cough over the past month. It is not an allergy. Lung carcinoma is what the oncologist said. Lung cancer. I don't know how. You know I don't smoke. But sometimes it happens to non-smokers. And I had to be one of them.

I don't know why many things happened in my life, actually, so maybe this is all part of the crazy plan God has for me. Marriage, divorce and disease, all within a span of three years.

The funny thing is, you came into my life at various stages too. Perhaps we were not meant to be. I must thank you for accepting me as a friend again, Madhav. I was so lost. I made mistakes, I held so much back from you and yet you cared for me. I know you wanted more, but I'm sorry I was unable to give it to you. The first time, it wasn't the right time. The second time, well, I have no time.

I couldn't have asked for a better two months than those I spent in Patna. To be able to help you prepare for your speech was a wonderful and special time. The best part was that despite the challenge, you never quit.

I asked you to stay back last night. I had no right to. I just felt greedy and selfish. I wanted more of your caring, while knowing I couldn't give you anything in return.

I know what I mean to you, and if I ask you to care without being able to reciprocate myself, you will. Hence, I decided to go. I won't make it harder for you than it needs to be.

I'm not one for details. Suffice to say, I have a little over three months left. The last month is supposed to be horrible. I will skip the gory parts. But trust me, you don't want to know.

You have something meaningful going on in your life. Your school is beautiful. And if Bill Gates does what I think he will, you will be able to make it even better. If that happens, I don't want to be here diverting your attention. I have seen your love, I don't want to see your pity. I am a basketball girl. That is how I want to stay in your mind forever. Your basketball girl.

I shall leave you with your school and your mother. Meanwhile, in what little time I have, I plan to travel everywhere I can. In the last month, I will find a corner for myself in this world where I don't bother anyone. Then I will go. You know what? On my last day, I will think of you.

A good thing has come of my decision to leave here. I feel free enough to tell you everything. I don't have to hold back or say the right thing anymore. For instance, it isn't just you who had a sleepless night at my place. I never slept either. I thought of how hard it was going to be to leave you. Funny, I've never felt that way about leaving this world. But leaving you, yes, that is difficult.

So, no crying. No looking for me. No being a Devdas. You are such a good-looking and caring guy, you'll find a lovely girl. Someone who isn't a mess like me. Someone who will love you like you deserve to be loved.

I can't wait for tomorrow. You will rock the stage.

I want to end this letter by saying something I wanted to say to at least someone in this lifetime. So, here goes:

I love you, Madhav Jha. I absolutely, completely love you. And will do so to my last day.

Bye, Madhav. Take care.

Riya

My eyes welled up. Tears rolled down my cheeks. My limbs felt weak. I struggled to stand. The letter fell from my hands. I picked it up and read it again. Memories of me sitting in Riya's car came to me. Images flashed in my head—her fancy wedding-card box, the glucose biscuits and her driving off. She had disappeared to get married then. She had disappeared to die now. In both cases, she had taken, to use a tough English word, *unilateral* decisions.

I called her number again. This time it was switched off. Perhaps she was driving back to Patna and passing through a no-network area. Or maybe she had thrown away her SIM card.

I went numb, like someone had hit me on the head with a hammer. Nothing mattered to me. The guests at home, the Gates Foundation grant, nothing. Riya had lung cancer, and she hadn't even mentioned it. How could she do this to me?

'Patna, go to Patna,' I told myself. She would go home first, obviously.

I ran downstairs to the living room. A crowd was gathered there.

'Congratulations, Madhav bhai. What a speech you gave,' said the sarpanch. He spoke Hindi and possibly didn't know a word of English.

'Hello, sir, I am from *Dainik Bhaskar*. We would like to profile you for our Sunday magazine,' a reporter said.

I found my mother.

'Patna? Now?' she said.

'The Foundation people need me to sign some paperwork.'

'I thought they went to Gaya for the other programme.'

'Some of them did. Since they have announced the aid, I need to sign documents.'

'Go after lunch. Right now we have guests.'

'Ma, I need to go now,' I said.

My mother sensed something amiss.

'Where is that divorceé friend of yours?' she said. 'Saree and what all she wore today.'

'Her name is Riya, Ma. Not divorceé friend,' I said, irritated.

'I didn't make her a divorceé.'

'She's dying,' I said.

'What?'

I told her about Riya being ill.

'Poor girl. So young.'

'I have to go to Patna.'

'You are telling me or asking for my permission?'

'I will call you,' I said and left.

◆

Locked. That's how I found Riya's house. The neighbours had no clue.

'Madam is strange. I have never had a client like this,' said the broker, Hemant. I had called him in case he knew anything.

'What happened?' I said.

'Where are you?' he said.

'At her apartment. It's locked.'

'Wait, I need to come there anyway.'

Hemant arrived in twenty minutes.

'She called me last night. She said the keys will be in her letter box,' he said.

'Keys?'

Hemant and I walked over to the letter boxes in the building compound. He slid his hand in and drew out a bunch of keys.

'When madam called me yesterday, she told me she was leaving town. Needs to surrender the house,' Hemant said, panting as we climbed the stairs.

'Surrender?' I echoed stupidly.

'I told her there is a notice period. Her security deposit will be forfeited.'

'And?'

'She said she didn't care. She said the landlord could keep the deposit.'

He unlocked the apartment. We went in. Her furniture and TV were all there. I went to the kitchen. Everything seemed to be in its place, from the condiments to the appliances. The utensils and the gas stove were still there. I went to her bedroom. I only found her clothes' cupboard empty.

'She's left most of her goods here,' Hemant said. 'She said I could sell them.'

'She did?'

'Really, she did,' Hemant said, worried I might stake a claim. 'Madam said I could sell these goods to cover any costs of breaking the lease or finding the landlord a new tenant.'

'What else did she say?' I said.

'Sir, I can keep these things?'

'Hemant, tell me exactly what she said. Did she say where she was going?'

'No, sir. Sir, even the TV I can keep?'

'Hemant,' I said, grabbing hold of him by the shoulder. 'What else did she say?'

'She said she wouldn't be coming back as she has quit her job.'

'Did she say where was she going?' I said, shaking his shoulder.

'No, sir,' Hemant said, looking scared. 'Sir, you want some of these things? Really, I am not that type of person. She did say I could keep them.'

I ignored him and went to the balcony. I looked down at the street. I took out the letter from my pocket and read it again.

'I love you,' it said at the end. I had read that line over a hundred times on my way to Patna.

'Not fair, Riya,' I said out loud, 'not fair.'

'Sir?' Hemant came out to the balcony.

'If you hear anything from her, her company, her friends or anyone, let me know,' I said.

'Sure, sir. Sir, I will move her items to a godown. I can wait for some time in case someone comes for them before selling them off.'

'Whatever,' I said.

34

Chetan Bhagat's room,
Chanakya Hotel, Patna

'You okay?' I said.

He had paused to wipe his tears. I gave him time. He bit his lip but it was a losing battle. Soon, he was crying like a two-year-old, his tall torso slumped on the chair.

'I don't know why I'm crying. It was a long time ago,' Madhav said in between sobs.

'How long?'

'Two years and three months. Three and a half months, actually.'

'Since she left?'

'Yes.'

He excused himself and went to the toilet. I made two cups of green tea. We had finished our first cup of chai a long time ago. He came out in a few minutes. He had washed his face.

'Sorry,' he said. 'I lost it.'

'Here, have some more tea.'

I gave a cup to him. He took a sip.

'What tea is this?'

'Green tea.'

'No milk? No sugar?' he said. He looked at me like I was a vegetarian vampire.

'It's good for you,' I said.

'Is it? Anyway, thanks,' he said.

'So, Madhav. What happened then? You met the broker. You saw her empty house. Then? Did you try to find her?'

He nodded.

'I did. I called her company. They said she had submitted her resignation and left, letting go of all her benefits in return for a shorter notice period.'

'When did she resign?'

'A week before writing the letter to me.'

'So she knew she was leaving?' I said.

'Yes. When she told me to stay that night, she knew it was our last night together. She had planned it.'

He grew sad again.

'What else did you do?'

'I asked the company for the list of assigned doctors. I met them. They said Riya had come only once, when she first had a cough. After that she had preferred to consult with her family doctors.'

'In Delhi?'

'Yes. In fact, I went to Delhi.'

'To look for her?'

'I had to go there anyway, to complete the paperwork for the grant. I went to her house. She wasn't there.'

'You met her parents?'

'Her mother. Her father had passed away a month ago.'

He sipped his tea and turned silent.

'Did her mother know anything?' I said.

'No. She knew less than I did. According to her, Riya had called her and said she might do a meditation course. That is why her phone wasn't reachable, she told me.'

'You told her about the cancer?'

'Couldn't. I didn't have the guts to. I just expressed my condolences over her husband's death and left.'

'And you came back to Bihar?'

'Eventually, yes. Before that, I called every top hospital in Delhi to ask about Riya. Nobody knew where she was. I contacted her family doctor. He hadn't heard from her for years. I called her old friends from college. They had lost touch with her. I searched on the Internet; she wasn't on Facebook or any other site. I tried contacts at phone companies. I called the major yoga ashrams in the country. Nothing.'

His face fell. I could see he found this conversation difficult.

'I tried for three months. I hoped she would call me one more time before she left this world. She didn't.'

'You're okay now?'

'I was okay. Until these journals popped up. For the last two years, I have focused exclusively on the school. The grant has made us one of the best schools in the area. You should definitely come to visit.'

'I will. Madhav, you loved her a lot, didn't you?'

'She is the only girl I ever loved. I don't know if it is a lot, or less than a lot. I do know one thing, though.'

'What?'

'I will never love again. Ever.'

'Why?'

'Something is broken inside me. I don't have the equipment or wiring or whatever one needs to fall in love anymore.'

I stood up from my chair and went to the bedside table. He continued to talk, more to himself than me.

'I have my school. I have my mother. That is my life.'

I picked up the journals from the bedside table. I brought them to Madhav.

'So how did you get these journals?'

'Hemant called me. He had taken all of Riya's stuff to the godown to sell it. However, he had missed a wooden box in the far corner of the kitchen loft. The loft was a storage space in the kitchen to keep dry groceries. A company took the house on lease after Riya. They used the apartment as a guest house. They almost never used the kitchen. Two years later, the company vacated the apartment and a family of four rented it. The lady of the family found the box and handed it to Hemant. Hemant, in turn, called me and handed me the box with the journals.'

I placed the journals in Madhav's lap.

'Here,' I said, 'take these.'

'Why? I said I don't want to. I can't.'

'Just take them,' I said in a firm voice.

He kept his hand on the notebooks in his lap.

'I have marked out six legible entries. You need to read them, buddy,' I said.

'No, no, no,' he said and placed the books back on the dining table. 'I told you, I can't. I made myself get over her during these last two years. Now to read all this will only undo all that.'

'Trust me, Madhav. You need to read them.'

RIYA'S JOURNAL:

Legible entry #1

1 November 2002

This journal is a birthday gift from me to me. It is my fifteenth birthday. Happy Birthday to me. I feel odd celebrating birthdays now. I am not a grown-up, but I don't feel like a child either.

They say people write secrets in journals. Should I write one down?

They say I am so quiet. Silent Riya. Mysterious Riya. Shy Riya.

I don't answer them. All I want to say is, if you crush a flower before it blooms, will it ever bloom as bright later?

I was not quiet as a child. I became this way. Dad knows I changed. Dad knows I remember everything. Still, he pretends nothing happened. I do the same.

He hasn't touched me for the last three years. He dare not.

I don't know why I did not tell Mom. Maybe I didn't even know if it was right or wrong at that time. What could she have done anyway?

Dad gave me a gold necklace today. I returned it. I find it difficult to talk to him. He tries to reach out, but I avoid him. He says I am still his daughter.

I like writing in this journal. I am able to say things I never can otherwise.

My brother is an idiot. So are Chacha ji and Taya ji's boys. Spoilt brats, all of them. Just because they are boys, nobody tells them what to do. I hate these double standards.

Yeah, this journal does allow me to vent. Good night, journal.

Legible entry #2

15 December 2005

It's over. We are over.

Madhav and I, well, we never had anything as such. Whatever it was, it is over. He made me feel so cheap. All in Hindi. Crass Bihari Hindi. He's sick. I should have known. What was I thinking?

I actually hung out with him for a year. I let him kiss me. Yuck.

My friends were right. He is an idiot gawaar. I must have had a phase of insanity. Why else would I have even talked to him?

He was not fake, that's why.

But, all he wanted was to fuck me. Really, I know it sounds disgusting, but that is what he wanted. And imagine someone saying that to you in Hindi. Being told to fuck him or fuck off.

Well, mister, I am fucking off, for good. How dare you talk to me like that? I feel like smashing his head on the basketball court.

I told him I needed time. Lots of it. Well, he didn't want to waste time. Because his main purpose was sex. So he could tell his friends he nailed this rich chick.

Well, fuck off, says the rich chick.

Legible entry #3

4 September 2006

I said yes to Rohan. Yes, a month ago, when the proposal had come, I had called it the most bizarre idea ever. Rohan bhaiya and me? Had my mother lost her marbles? He was my rakhi brother, for God's sake. Not to mention I am just about turning nineteen and still in college.

But today I said yes. Well, it has been an eventful month. First, the gifts that arrived from London every week. Louis Vuitton handbags, Chanel perfumes, Omega watches—Rohan sent them all, not just for me, but the entire family.

My parents felt we may never get this good a match again. My mother said I didn't need to study more as Rohan's family was so rich.

I still didn't give in, until last night.

Yesterday, Rohan came down from London to Delhi. He came down for just four hours, only to see me. None of our parents know he did. He came and picked me up from Stephen's in the Bentley he keeps in India. We went for a long drive. He said he loves to travel, and I would make his best travel and life partner. He said he realized I was young, but I could continue to study in London. He had found out from Mom that I wanted to study music. He had brought a list of the top music schools in London with him.

Later, he went down on his knees. He took out a blue Tiffany's box. It had a giant three-carat diamond ring in it.

'It's still your choice,' he said. He put the ring back in the box and handed it to me. Finally, he said, 'Miss Riya Somani, the most beautiful person I know, inside and outside, since my childhood, will you marry me?'

So, dear journal, what's a girl to do?

That night, I took out the ring from the blue box and put it on. I showed it to Mom. She's still on the phone with Rohan's mother, hysterical with happiness.

I feel rushed, yes, but this time in a good way.

Legible entry #4 (Set of several entries from London)

4 April 2007

I came to London in the middle of the academic year for music schools. Also, they are so hard to get into. I have to prepare, apply, give tests. It is going to take at least eight months.

Rohan's mother wants me to meet her friends for dinner tonight. Every night there is someone to meet. These guys are social, and how. I told her I should stay back because Rohan was not in town, but she said I have to come.

Oh well, yet another party. Boring.

10 July 2007

Rohan travels all the time, and for a long time. He has just extended his trip by two weeks. I joined him for two days, and saw a bit of Istanbul. However, he's in meetings all day and it is no fun to roam around all alone after a while. Besides, Rohan's mom called me back. She was planning a party and the new daughter-in-law had to be there.

'So pretty,' one of her friends had said.

'Good you brought a girl from India. They listen to you,' said another.

6 September 2007

He came home drunk. He tried to hit me.

'Why didn't you take my call?' he yelled.

I was in music class. I had told him. I had messaged him right after.

'It's midnight, Rohan. What kind of business meetings happen so late?'

'Shut the fuck up, bitch. What do you know about work?'

'You will not talk to me like this.'

I turned around and walked away from him.

'You will not walk away from me like this.'

'You learn to talk and I will stay put.'

'I'm not drunk,' he slurred.

I turned to him. 'For your information, I'm twenty. I was studying in college. I left it to marry you.'

'You left it to live like a queen.'

'Rohan,' I said and paused to compose myself. 'I had a good life in India, too.'

'Somani Infra owned between three brothers versus my business? Girl, what are you comparing?'

'I am not comparing anything. I want you to stop making me out to be this gold-digger.'

He staggered and sat on the oversized grotesque sofa in the drawing room.

'Sit,' he said, patting the seat next to him.

I complied.

'Mom said you didn't talk to her properly when you were leaving home today.'

'Of course I did.'

'Is she lying?'

'I was late for class. She wanted me to go with her to the salon. I said we could go tomorrow.'

'You don't say that to my mother. Ever.'

'I had a class, Rohan.'

'What class? You haven't even got admitted to a college.'

'Yes, that's next year. I have joined prep classes for music. It isn't that easy to get admitted to one of these colleges. I've told you all this before.'

Rohan went up to the bar. He picked up a bottle.

'Stop,' I said and tried to take the bottle from him.

'What the fuck?' Rohan said. 'Let go. Now.'

He pushed me hard. I lost my balance and slipped. He bent over me.

'Don't touch me,' I said and pushed him away.

I miss home. I miss college. I miss not being told how to speak to someone else's mother.

Good night, journal. It is a good thing you aren't married.

7 September 2007

He has apologized. He said work stress was getting to him. 'I have a long way to go, Riya, I am nothing compared to the big hotel moguls of the world.'

'Why do you have to be a big hotel mogul?' I said.

But he began to speak of his mother. 'She's suffered a lot in life. My father did not treat her well. I want to be there for her.'

Hangovers make him senti.

14 January 2008

Wear only Indian clothes. Can you believe this? This is what Rohan's mom said to me today.

'If it makes her happy, do it. What difference does it make?' Rohan had said, as he chose from his two-dozen pairs of shoes this morning.

'Why?' I said. It isn't like I don't like Indian clothes. The point is, why does she get to tell me what to wear?

'You can get the best Indian designer clothes. You want me to send the hotel concierge? He will take you to the boutiques.'

'That's not the point, Rohan,' I said.

'Stop fussing. Her friends have certain expectations of her bahu. You trudged in yesterday wearing a short dress.'

'It was a regular dress, almost to my knees. Anyway, what if it was short? What is this? A family dress code?'

He snapped his fingers at me.

'Do it. Don't argue.'

This is what they call marital bliss, I guess.

18 March 2008

I made a mistake. A big, big mistake. I can't be in denial anymore. I made a mistake marrying Rohan.

11 June 2008

He slapped me in front of his mother, thrice. She didn't stop him. She kind of liked it. He even pulled my hair.

Should I go into the details? I don't think so. What is the point? Drunk husband, mother-in-law finding something to be pissed off about. This time it was about me seemingly ignoring her when she called me five times (I had headphones on, and was listening to my music tapes). Mother and son lectured me on how lucky I was, that Rohan was at least twenty times richer than my dad, and if I didn't behave there would be consequences.

But now comes the real news. Rohan was sleeping when his phone buzzed at 3 a.m. He didn't wake up. It buzzed again. I feared if he woke up he would fight with me again. I was enjoying the night's silence. So I walked up to the bedside table and picked up his phone to put it on silent. It buzzed again. A Whatsapp message flashed in the notifications. It was from someone called Kristin: Miss ur body honey. Wish I had u with me tonight.

Kristin had sent pictures of her body too.

I came back to bed. I didn't feel bad. In fact, I felt light. I had to make a tough decision and that decision had just been made for me.

Legible entry #5

13 June 2008

My marriage is over.

I left London without telling anyone and came home. I landed in Delhi this morning. When I told Mom everything, she wanted me to take the next flight back, and she had to call Dad. I told her I had decided I was not going back, no matter what Dad said.

'He seemed so nice,' Dad said at dinner without looking at me.

I explained Rohan to them. Rohan liked to conquer. Whether it is a hotel property or his wife, he liked the thrill of chasing more than what he chased.

'I said no to him. He had to have me. Once he did, he didn't care,' I said.

I skipped some stuff. I didn't say how he used to force himself on me when he was drunk. I didn't say anything about Rohan's mother asking her son to teach me a lesson, or about Kristin.

'Rohan's mother controls him. And she doesn't like me,' is all I said.

'Women have to learn to adjust, beta,' my mother said.

'Adjust? How does one adjust to violence?'

I lifted my left hand to show her the swelling. Rohan had pushed me and I had broken my wrist.

'What will people say?' Mom blurted out.

Let's find out.

Legible entry set #6

17 February 2009

Sometimes you need a knock on the head to come back to your senses. I received a hard knock today. I don't know what happened to me yesterday. I kissed Madhav on the roof of his haveli. It made me forget reality. I started dreaming.

And how the dream crashed. Just when those silly feelings of 'this seems so right' started to take root, Rani Sahiba brought me back to my senses.

The signs were already there. How could I forget those disapproving glances from her in the living room? How idiotic of me to open up to her. Just because she was Madhav's mom, I thought she would also accept my past like Madhav did? She fed me litti-chokha. It didn't mean she liked me.

'Are you the girl he was involved with in college?' she asked me in the school staffroom today, when Madhav went to take his class. I didn't know what to say. I had no idea what Madhav had told her about me.

'We were good friends, yes,' I said.

'And now?' she said.

'Friends only. Nothing else, aunty,' I said, a stammer in my voice.

'I know my son. He will get involved with you again.'

'Aunty, we do like each other but…'

'Stay out of his life,' she said shortly.

'Aunty, but…'

She stared at me.

'You are divorced. You must be desperate for another man. My son is handsome and a prince here. Of course, I can sense your plans.'

'Plans?'

'It is so easy for your type. One man didn't work out, so get another.'

If it were not Madhav's mother, I would have snapped back. I controlled myself.

'I don't want anyone,' I said.

'Then leave him. He is too weak for you.'

'I expect nothing,' I said. She handed me a tissue when she saw my tears.

'He does.'

Rani Sahiba folded her hands.

'He is all I have. If you stay here, he will never move on. You may be a big shot in Delhi. However, the Prince of Dumraon won't be with a Marwari

divorcee. Respect in society is also worth something,' she said.

I wasn't respectable, I guess.

'What do you want me to do? Stop meeting him?'

'That won't be enough. He won't stop chasing you. You have done mayajaal on him.'

Before I could answer, Madhav arrived. He pulled me by my hand to take me to the classroom.

Mayajaal, an illusory trap. Nice one, Rani Sahiba.

5 March 2009

I'm in Delhi. Dad passed away last night.

I saw him in the ICU yesterday afternoon. He could barely talk. He said I had to meet Gupta uncle, his lawyer.

I went to Gupta uncle's office. He told me my father had stashed away some money for me in a secret account.

'Don't tell your brothers or anyone at home. They may sue and the matter will be stuck in the courts for years,' Gupta uncle said.

I signed the papers. I remained silent during the funeral.

I was in two minds. I knew why Dad was giving me the money. It was hush money, money for me to go away from his mind, from his conscience, from his guilt. But I told myself to be practical. I will need the money where I'm going.

Also, maybe I was ready to forget and move on. Not forgive, but forget.

14 April 2009

I leave in three days. No more drama. No more dealing with another boy's mother. I don't want anyone's pity either. I am a divorcee. If that makes me tainted, so be it.

I am not upset with Rani Sahiba. I came to Patna to be alone. Madhav happened. Yes, he's nice. I know he loves me, and is falling for me more and more every day. I like him, too. Is that why I said yes to a job in Patna? Did I do so in the hope of meeting him again? Perhaps.

To be loved and to love is nice. However, right now, more than love, I want peace.

Madhav won't get it. He won't let go if I explain all this to him. I have been through it. He hasn't. He won't stop pursuing me. The simplest way out is if he thinks I am no longer an option.

I had a minor infection in Dumraon. So far, I have pretended it hasn't healed. Hence, when I leave, it will be more believable. Sure, he will be upset. However, he will get over it eventually and marry a princess sooner or later, who will come to him without a past, without deep dark secrets.

My fingers shake as I write this. I must stay strong. I have to type my parting note. I am faking my illness. Maybe I can at least be honest in my last letter and tell him how I feel about him...

He's coming home for the final rehearsal. It will be our last night together. Is it wrong if I make him stay over?

35

Chanakya Hotel, Patna

Madhav continued to stare at the last page long after he had read it, fists clenched.

'What?' he burst out and went silent.

He turned his gaze from the journal to me.

'What is this, Chetan sir?' he said.

'Your friend's journals, remember?' I said.

He slammed the notebook shut, and took rapid shallow breaths. He buried his face in his hands, ran fingers through his thick, uncombed hair. He remained still until I touched his shoulder.

'Are you all right?' I said.

He looked at me in a dazed way. His face had turned an intense shade of red.

'She's alive,' he mumbled.

'That is what it seems like,' I said.

'She's alive,' he said again. His body began to shake uncontrollably.

'So you see why I called you. You said she's dead. You wanted to throw these journals away.'

'How could she lie? Such a big lie...the bitch.'

He fought back tears.

'Madhav, you said you loved her. What kind of language is this?'

'I...I...' he said and stopped, unable to finish the sentence, the thought.

'You're in shock.'

'She always does this. She runs away. The only way she deals with issues is by running away.'

He broke down then, tears in his stubble.

'It took me years to get over her. I have still not healed. How could she...?' he muttered to himself.

'At least you found out,' I said.

'She didn't want me to. She wanted to dump me again.'

'She wanted to protect herself. And you.'

'Me? How did this protect me?'

'She didn't want to be a burden in your life.'

'Riya could never be a burden in my life. She *was* my life,' Madhav said matter-of-factly.

I handed him a tissue. He crushed it in his hand instead of wiping his eyes.

'Aren't you happy she's alive?'

'I should be, but all I feel is anger right now.'

'I can understand.'

'Two years. Not a single day when I didn't think of her.'

'What are you going to do, Madhav?' I said.

He ignored my question.

'When she left, I almost needed to be treated for depression,' he said, mostly to himself.

'You went through a lot.'

'Chetan sir, does what she did seem fair to you?'

'I guess not. But life is complicated sometimes. She seemed to have her reasons.'

'My mother? How is it even an issue? In fact, even my mother says Riya made me look more alive than anyone else.'

'Riya had a bad experience. Once bitten and all that.'

'I'm not Rohan.'

Like always, I had become over-involved in a situation. I needed to get home. It was Madhav Jha who had to plan what to do next.

He seemed lost in thought. I stood up to pack my bags.

'Can I stay for some more time?' he said.

'Sure,' I said, shrugging my shoulders. He went to a corner of the room to make a phone call. I zipped up my suitcase. He returned after a few minutes.

'I called her home in Delhi. Her mother says she has not heard from her in years,' Madhav said.

'She really has disappeared from everywhere,' I said.

I lifted my bag from the bed and placed it on the ground. I pulled out the rod of my strolley.

'I'm sorry. This is the only flight to Mumbai today.'

'Thank you for whatever you did.'

'I did nothing.'

'Can I accompany you to the airport?'

◆

We sat in the car in silence. He spoke after passing two traffic signals.

'I'll find her,' Madhav said in a calm but decisive voice.

I looked at him.

'Are you serious?'

'Yes.'

'Where could she be?'

'I have a hunch. She always used to mention her dream. To be a singer in a small bar in New York.'

'So?'

'If she has cut herself off from the entire world, wouldn't she finally want to pursue her dream?'

'How can you be sure? Where in New York? Or maybe she found another city? Or maybe she is doing something else?' I said.

'So you think I shouldn't look?'

'I'm just being realistic. Sorry, I didn't mean to discourage you.'

We remained silent for the rest of the drive. We reached the Lok Nayak Jayaprakash Airport. He helped me load my bag on the trolley. I told myself to withdraw from this situation. I couldn't.

'Keep in touch,' I said, as the security guard at the entrance checked my photo ID and ticket.

'I will, sir.'

'You really are going to look for her?'

'Yes, sir.'

'Even though you may never find her and end up in more pain?'

He nodded.

'I can't quit, sir. It's not in my genes to do so.'

36

After Chetan Bhagat left, I remained in Patna for a while. I met as many people as I could from Riya's past.

First, I went to her old office.

'She resigned but did not tell us her plans,' Mohini, her ex-colleague at Nestlé, told me.

'Did she seem sick?'

'Not really,' Mohini said.

I visited East India Travels, the agency Nestlé's staff used.

'You remember Riya Somani? She worked at Nestlé's Patna office two years ago,' I said.

'Pretty girl?' said Ajay, the young agent at the travel agency.

'Extremely pretty,' I corrected him.

'Madam did use this agency. Her father had become quite sick. Round trip to Delhi, right?' Ajay said.

'Yes, anything after that?' I said.

Ajay pounded his keyboard. He shook his head a couple of times. 'Anything?'

'Trying,' Ajay said and spoke after a minute. 'I have something. She took another flight to Delhi. One way. On 17 April 2009.'

I checked the screen. She had flown out the same day as the Bill Gates talk.

I went to the car-hire company. However, they didn't maintain old records so they had no idea.

I went to Kotak Mahindra Bank, where Riya had her salary credited. I met Roshan Joshi, the branch manager.

'Client information is confidential,' he said.

'She disappeared. I'm trying to find her.'

'Is she missing? Do you have a police report? We could help then.'

'She went on her own.'

'Sir, how can I reveal someone's bank account information?'

I hated doing this, but I called MLA Ojha from the branch manager's office. Ojha loved to do favours so he could ask for one in return later. He asked the Patna city MLA to give Roshan a call.

Five minutes later, I had Riya's accounts.

'Sorry, I didn't know you knew our MLA, sir…' Roshan said.

I scanned her statements. On 14 April, Riya had withdrawn the entire balance of three-and-a-half lakhs. The transaction had 'FX' written next to it.

'What is FX?' I said.

Roshan looked at the account statement.

'It's foreign exchange conversion. She has withdrawn the funds in another currency.'

'Which currency?'

'US dollars.'

'To travel to the US?' I said. The lamp of hope flickered in me.

'We don't know. Indians often take US dollars to whichever country they are visiting, and change it there.'

'She has travelled abroad. Right?'

'That's likely.'

I left the bank and called Ajay at East India Travels.

'Ajay, Madhav Jha here. I need to book a flight to Delhi, please.'

◆

'Ah, lucky, lucky girl,' Samantha said.

'Is she?' I said. 'Married at nineteen. Divorced at twenty.'

Samantha and I sat in the American Diner at the India Habitat Centre in Delhi. She swirled the straw in her orange juice as I told her Riya's story.

'That is indeed tragic,' she said. 'However, she is lucky to have you love her so much.'

I smiled.

'Madhav, most girls would kill for a lover like you. I would,' Samantha said.

'Thanks,' I said.

She took a deep breath. The waiter came with our food—a chicken burger and a large order of French fries.

'Anyway, so what can I do for you?' Samantha said, a fry in one hand.

'I have to find her. Nobody seems to know where she is.'

'That's not a great place to start. Any clues?'

'I have a hunch.'

'Like an intuition?'

'Well, a guess. A decent calculated guess. She could be in New York.'

'Oh, really? That's my city.'

'I'm not sure. I have to first confirm it is the US.'

'How?'

'The US consulate. I need to find out if they issued a visa to Riya Somani. Do you have contacts there, through your American circle in Delhi?'

'I do. But that sort of stuff is confidential.'

'I don't need details. I just need to know if they issued a visa to her and when.'

'It's…difficult.'

'That's why I've come to you.'

She finished every single fry as she considered my request. She took out her phone and flipped through the contacts list.

'There's Angela at the US consulate. We hang out sometimes. I can't promise anything.'

'That's fine. Whatever is possible.'

◆

'The best rural school in Bihar. That is super news, Madhav. You have any documents to show that the CM said that?' Michael Young, the CEO of Gates Foundation India, said.

I sat in his sunny office. It had a view of the trees on Lodhi Road. Over the last two years, I had interacted with Michael on several occasions, and received delegations on his behalf to my school.

'I have local newspaper articles. I can send you scanned copies,' I said.

'That would be wonderful. Little me will look good to my bosses in New York,' Michael said and winked at me. Americans can make you feel you are their best friend in the whole world.

'I need a favour, Michael,' I said.

'Sure.'

'I need to be in New York for a while. Can the foundation give me a job, an internship, anything for a few months?'

Michael raised his eyebrows. 'Really?'

'Yes. I will go anyway. However, it will help if I have a base there and some income to survive.'

'Bihar to New York. Is everything okay? You seemed so passionate about your school.'

'I am. I need to look for someone in New York. That's all. Of course, an internship would be a great experience.'

Michael tugged at his lower lip.

'Well, I will put you in touch with people in the US,' Michael said, 'and put in a word, too.'

'Thanks, Michael,' I said and shook his hand.

'No problem. Don't forget to send me the scanned articles,' he said.

◆

'The things you make me do,' Samantha said. She passed me a sheet of paper. It was early in the morning in Lodi Gardens, next to her office. Brisk morning walkers strode past us.

I looked at the sheet. It was a copy of a US visa.

'She applied, and the consulate granted her a visa on 5 April.'

'Thanks, Samantha.'

'My friend could get into a lot of trouble for this.'

'I owe you,' I said.

She looked at me with her deep grey eyes.

'No, you don't. Hope this is helpful.'

'It tells me my hunch could be right.'

'But it doesn't say which city in the US. Or if she went at all.'

'New York. She always wanted to go there.'

'Ah, no wonder Michael said you have applied for an internship there.'

ACT III

New York

37

'Name?' the officer at the immigration counter said.

'Madhav Jha,' I said, wondering why he didn't just read it off my passport.

'Mr Jha, what is the purpose of your visit to the United States?'

He flipped the pages of my passport, blank except for my new US visa.

To find the love of my life, I wanted to say.

'I'm interning with the Gates Foundation in New York.'

'Documentation, please.'

I took out a plastic folder from my rucksack. It had my internship offer letter, confirming my stipend of three thousand dollars a month. I also had certification from Michael's office, the cash advance the foundation had given me and my visa documents.

The immigration officer examined my file.

'Where will you be staying in New York, sir?'

'With friends. On the Upper East Side, 83rd Street and Third Avenue.'

The officer fumbled with my passport for a few seconds. He picked up a stamp.

The 'bam' sounded like a gunshot—to indicate that my race to find Riya had begun.

◆

I took a yellow taxi from JFK airport towards Manhattan, the main island that forms the City of New York. It was my first trip outside India and the first thing I noticed was the colour of the sky. It was a crisp, crystal-clear blue; one never sees such a sky in India. I can understand India is dusty, but why is our sky less blue? Or is it the dust in the air that prevents us from seeing it?

The second thing that hit me was the silence. The taxi sped on a road filled with traffic. However, nobody honked, not even at signals. The silence almost made my ears hurt.

Initially, I only saw row houses and brick-coloured warehouses, nothing quite as impressive as I had imagined. However, thirty minutes from the airport, the taxi reached the Brooklyn Bridge, over the Hudson River. One had to cross this bridge to reach Manhattan. The bridge resembled the Howrah Bridge of Kolkata I had seen on TV, only bigger and cleaner. On the other side, a thousand skyscrapers loomed. Literally one tall building after another dotted the entire city. We crossed the bridge and entered Manhattan.

'Welcome to The Big Apple,' said the taxi driver in an American accent.

'Are you from here?' I said.

'Now, yes. Originally from Amritsar,' he said.

I looked at the taxi driver's name: Balwinder Singh. Okay, not quite as exotic as I had imagined.

In Manhattan, I saw people, busy people. Early morning joggers, people going to office in suits, children on their way to school. The city seemed like a maze, with criss-crossing streets and avenues. If one were to get lost here, it would take years to be found again.

'It's all arranged in one grid,' the driver said. 'You going to Upper East, yeah?'

'Yes, please,' I said and handed him the address.

◆

'Madhav Jha. You made it,' Shailesh squealed in excitement as he opened the door.

I struggled to catch my breath. I had climbed three floors with a backpack and a heavy suitcase.

'These are pre-war buildings,' Shailesh said. He dragged my suitcase into the apartment. 'From before the Second World War. You get higher ceilings and more character. However, the lift breaks down every week.'

He took me to the guestroom of his three-bedroom apartment, which looked high-end and was done up in an ethnic Indian style with brass Ganeshas and Madhubani paintings of Krishna. Shailesh had done an MBA from Harvard after Stephen's. He had joined Goldman Sachs, a top Wall Street investment bank. He shared the apartment with his girlfriend, Jyoti, whom he had met at Harvard. Jyoti worked at Morgan Stanley, another Wall Street investment bank. The size of the apartment told me the banks paid them well. Dark circles under Shailesh's eyes told me they also made him work hard.

'M&A, that's mergers and acquisitions,' Shailesh said, telling me about his work. We sat in his living room. I had reached early, at 6.30 in the morning. Shailesh was ready for work, wearing a grey suit and a dark blue silk tie. He ate breakfast cereal with milk and slipped on his leather loafers.

'Sorry I'm rushing,' Shailesh said. 'Jyoti and I catch the 7 a.m. subway to work. Catch up in the evening, okay?'

'No problem,' I said. 'I need to rest anyway. I'm so tired.'

'Try not to sleep. It will help you adjust to the jet lag,' Shailesh said.

The ten-hour difference in time zones meant my body wanted to sleep while New York City had just woken up.

'Jyoti!' Shailesh shouted.

'Coming,' a female voice in a thick American accent came from one of the bedrooms.

'Shailesh, if you can put me in touch with a real-estate broker…' I started to say.

He interrupted me. 'Are you crazy? You're here for a short while. It's an internship, right?'

'Three months. I can't stay with you that long.'

'Why not? You relax here. I have to go to London tomorrow but we are definitely catching up tonight.'

Shailesh finished his breakfast and took the plates to the kitchen sink.

'You've changed so much, Shailesh. We sat in shorts doing adda all day in Stephen's. Now, suits, hi-fi banker life, New York City,' I said.

He laughed.

'Times change, lives change. You have to move on, pal.'

I thought about Shailesh's statement. I nodded, even though in half-agreement.

Jyoti, a thin, five-feet-six-inches-tall girl, appeared. She wore a formal black skirt and shirt with a jacket.

'Hi, Madhav. Have heard so much about you,' Jyoti said and

extended her hand. She sounded like Samantha, except she had brown skin and black eyes.

'Me too. Sorry to bother you until I find an apartment.'

'Stay as long as you want. Work keeps us so busy. At least someone can use the place,' Jyoti said and turned to Shailesh. 'You ready to go, honey?'

Shailesh nodded.

◆

I unpacked my clothes in the guestroom while making plans for the next couple of days; the internship did not start until the day after. I wondered if any live music bars would be open now.

I lay down for five minutes and woke up five hours later, disoriented. Jet lag had made me lose track of time and space. I needed a local SIM card. I checked the dollars in my wallet, picked up the house keys and left.

◆

Manhattan has a grid-like structure. Numbered streets run north to south. The wider avenues run from east to west. Shailesh's home on Third Avenue and 83rd Street was close to Central Park, which had its eastern side on Fifth Avenue.

The park, a landmark of the city, is three-and-a-half square kilometres in area and runs all the way from 60th Street in the south to 120th Street up north, and Fifth Avenue on the east to Ninth Avenue on the west.

The park helped me orient myself. Its southern tip had shops where I could buy a SIM card.

I walked west from Third to Fifth Avenue, and then down south twenty-three blocks from 83rd Street to 60th Street. In twenty minutes, I reached the southeast corner of the park. I found a row of shops, including a store called 'T-Mobile'.

◆

The T-Mobile salesperson offered me a SIM card with a 3G data plan. 'If you take a two-year contract, I can also give you a free iPhone.'

'I'm not here that long,' I said.

I agreed to rent a touchscreen phone along with a voice and data plan.

'It'll take twenty minutes to activate,' the salesperson said. I left the shop and walked back north towards Central Park. I had not eaten anything for hours. I scanned the various cafés and delis, each displaying their lunch specials. Most dishes cost close to ten dollars each. A van parked outside Central Park sold bagels, a doughnut-shaped bread stuffed with cream cheese or other fillings. It cost only three dollars, including a cold drink.

I got a bagel with cream cheese, tomatoes and onions. A giant-sized Coke came along with it.

I sat on an empty bench outside Central Park and watched tourists walk past. New York City looked beautiful and clean. The first day you spend out of India in a developed country takes a while to sink in. The swanky buildings, the smooth roads, the gleaming shops and the lack of noise (nobody blares horns for some reason) make you feel like you have entered a fairy tale where nothing can ever go wrong. I ate my lunch on the park bench.

A 3G sign on the corner of my phone screen indicated I had network. I typed in my first Google search: 'Live music venues in New York City'.

The Internet worked fine. The search results weren't fine. Literally thousands of places popped up. The first link directed me to the website of *Time Out* magazine. That site itself had a top-100 list of the best live music venues in the city. In Patna, you would be lucky to find one place that played live music. In Dumraon, the only way you could hear live music at a bar is if you yourself sang. In New York City, however, there is an endless number of places. I sat on the Central Park bench and examined the tall buildings around me. I felt small and insignificant.

It's a live music venue in one city, how difficult can it be? is what I had told myself before coming here. Now it didn't seem easy at all.

I went to Google Maps. It showed my current location as 59th Street and Sixth Avenue. It also showed me to be a three-kilometre walk away from Shailesh's house. A cold breeze penetrated my Biharstrength sweater. I crossed my arms and held them close to my chest.

You are so stupid, Madhav, I said to myself as I walked north on Fifth Avenue, along the edge of the park. On a whim, I had packed my bags and come to this cold city. A gust of wind left my face numb.

'I can't do this,' I said.

I took deep breaths. I reminded myself of old basketball matches, which I had won with sheer willpower.

One street, one avenue, one bar at a time, Madhav.

38

'You bagged a Gates Foundation grant. Incredible,' Jyoti said. We ate chapatis and chana masala for dinner at Shailesh's house on my first night in New York.

'My school did. They liked the good work the team had done,' I said.

'It's him,' Shailesh said. 'He cracked it. Bill Gates himself saw the school and proposed the grant.'

Jyoti said, 'Can this internship lead to a full-time job in New York?'

'I don't want a job,' I said.

'You're doing it for the experience?' Shailesh said.

'It's for... Well, there is another reason,' I said and turned silent. I looked at Jyoti.

Shailesh understood my hesitation.

'You want to tell me later?' he said.

'Buddy secrets, is it?' Jyoti smiled. I smiled back. Jyoti stood up to go to the kitchen.

'Whatever you tell me, I will end up telling her,' Shailesh said and looked at her. She blew him a kiss.

'All right then. Sit, Jyoti,' I said.

Jyoti sat down again, very attentive.

'I am here to look for someone,' I said.

'Look for?' Jyoti said. 'You don't have his contact?'

'Her. No, I don't. I'm not even sure she's here.'

'Ah, her. It's about a girl. Isn't it always?' Jyoti said.

'Who?' Shailesh said.

'Riya,' I said.

'Riya? Who? Riya Somani?' Shailesh said.

'Well, yes,' I said.

Shailesh let out a whistle.

'What the fuck,' Shailesh said. 'Really? You're in New York looking for Riya Somani?'

He started to laugh.

'Who is Riya Somani? Clearly she has created some excitement here,' Jyoti said.

'His...well, how do I say it? Well, kind of your ex-girlfriend, right?'

'Half-girlfriend. Ex-half-girlfriend,' I said.

'That was ages ago,' Shailesh said, sounding confused. 'Didn't she get married to her cousin in London or something? She dropped out, right?'

'It wasn't her cousin. It was Rohan, a family friend and rakhi brother. Not a cousin.'

I hate it when college rumours get blown out of proportion.

'Sorry, I don't remember the details. She messed with you, man, and flew away to London with her husband,' Shailesh said.

I smiled.

'There's more to that story. A lot more. Want to hear it?' I said.

Jyoti and Shailesh nodded. They listened with rapt attention.

I told them everything. I ended my story at 10 in the night.

Jyoti turned to Shailesh.

'I had no idea Indian men could be so romantic,' she said.

'What do you mean?' Shailesh said, looking wounded.

'You don't walk me to my office from the subway stop,' Jyoti said. 'And here are people coming halfway across the world to find lost love.'

'C'mon Jyoti. Everything is not an excuse to nag,' Shailesh said and turned to me. 'But, boss, you are mind-blowing. Still chasing that chick after, what, seven years?'

'That's so romantic,' Jyoti said dreamily.

'It's also stupid,' Shailesh said.

'Shailesh!' Jyoti said.

'I'm just being protective of my friend.'

'He's right,' I said, interrupting Shailesh. 'I am being stupid. But I can't help it. She means everything to me.'

'Everything? You thought she was dead. You survived, right?' Shailesh said.

'Survived, yes. Lived, no.'

Jyoti sighed. Shailesh gave up. He got us a bottle of red wine and three glasses. 'You guys have to wake up early,' I said as I took a sip. 'Feel free to go to bed.'

'No worries,' Shailesh said. 'What is your plan?'

'I will step out now.'

'Now?' Jyoti said, gulping down her wine.

'I will start with live music venues on the Upper East Side.'

'This late?' Jyoti said.

'Nothing starts before ten anyway,' I said.

I finished my glass and stood up.

'It's New York City. Every block has bars with live music,' Shailesh said.

'I'll have to visit every block, I guess,' I said.

'You are mad,' Shailesh said.

'Depends on how you look at it,' I said.

'Meaning?'

'You wake up at 6 and put on a suit. You reach office at 7.30 in the morning and work thirteen hours a day. Some may find that pretty mad.'

'I get rewarded for it, bro. In dollars.'

'Riya is my ultimate reward,' I said. Shailesh had no answer.

'You need a warmer jacket, wait,' Jyoti said. She rummaged in a cupboard and came back with a leather jacket with a down filling.

'Thanks,' I said. I walked out of the apartment and shut the door behind me. Inside, I could hear Shailesh say, 'You think he needs a psychiatrist?'

◆

Google Maps doesn't judge lunatic lovers. It simply gave me results when I looked for live music bars near me. The first suggestion was Brandy's Piano Bar on 84th Street, between Second and Third Avenue, a mere five-minute walk away.

I reached Brandy's, a tiny bar one would miss if one wasn't looking for it. A two-drink minimum policy applied to all customers. I didn't want to have drinks. I just wanted to meet the management and find out the list of singers.

'Sir, you need to order two drinks,' the waitress told me, chewing gum. I realized I would need a better way to do this. For now, I found the cheapest drink on the menu.

'Two Budweiser beers, please.'

A makeshift stage had a piano on it. I had entered during a break. Ten minutes later, a singer called Matt came and took his seat.

'Hi guys, lovely to see you all again, let's start with Aerosmith,' Matt said.

The crowd broke into cheers. I guessed Aerosmith was a popular band. Matt sang in a slow, clear voice. My English practice meant I could catch a few words: *'I could stay awake just to hear you breathing. Watch you smile while you are sleeping.'*

Customers swung their heads from side to side. Matt sang and played the piano at the same time. *'Don't wanna close my eyes, I don't wanna fall asleep. 'Cause I'd miss you, baby. And I don't wanna miss a thing.'*

I didn't want to fall asleep either. I wanted to stay up all night and look for Riya in as many bars as I could. I opened my Google Maps app again. The streets of Manhattan seemed manageable on the phone screen. In reality, this was a megacity of millions.

She may not even be in New York, a soft voice in my head told me. It was the only sensible voice I had left. As always, I ignored it. I focused on the music. I felt the pain of the singer who couldn't bear to sleep as it would mean missing moments with his lover.

I went up to the cashier and asked for the manager. When he arrived, I posed my standard list of questions.

'I've come from India looking for a lost friend. All I know is she is probably a singer at a bar in New York. Can you tell me who your singers are?'

'Too many, my friend. The schedule is on the noticeboard. You know her name?' the manager said.

'Her real name is Riya.'

'No such name, I'm pretty sure.'

'She may have changed it for the stage,' I said.

'That's a tough search then, my friend.'

'She's tall, slim and pretty. Long hair, well, at least when I saw her last.'

'This is a city of tall, slim and pretty people.'

'Indian. She's an Indian singer in a New York bar.'

'She sings Bollywood? I would check the Indian restaurants.'

'Unlikely. She liked Western music. Do you remember seeing any Indian singer at your bar?'

The manager thought for a few seconds. He shook his head.

'Sorry, mate. The schedule is there. See if something rings a bell.'

I walked to the noticeboard. I saw the timetable for various gigs all month. The singers' descriptions did not suggest anyone like Riya.

The waitress gave me the bill for two beers. She added a 20 per cent tip to it.

'20 per cent?'

'It's New York,' she said, glaring. I later learnt that tipping wasn't optional in New York.

I left Brandy's and visited a couple of other bars in the neighbourhood. There was Marty O'Brien's on 87th street in Second Avenue. It had more rock bands than singers. Uptown Restaurant and Lounge on 88th Street had its schedule placed outside. I could only find two female singers. Both were American, the doorman told me. The posh Carlyle Hotel, all the way down on 76th Street, had a bar called Bemelman's. Drinks cost fifteen dollars each, excluding the tip. I sat on a small couch in the corner of the bar and stayed away from the waiter to avoid placing an order.

The singer, a beautiful, six-foot-tall blonde American woman, sang a love song: '*I have loved you for a thousand years, I will love you for a thousand more.*'

A waiter came up to me to take my order. I told him I had to leave for some urgent work. I stood up.

'By the way, do you have other female singers here?' I said.

'A couple of them. They alternate.'

'Anybody who looks Indian?'

'I couldn't tell, sir,' the waiter said. Americans don't like to take a shot at answering questions they don't know—unlike Indians, who pretty much know everything about everything.

'Tall, really pretty girl who looks Indian?'

'No, sir. Only two black singers, and two Caucasian ones.'

Even at midnight, on a weekday, the place was packed. Everyone around me seemed incredibly happy. They clinked glasses and laughed at jokes. They probably didn't know of Bihar's existence. Neither would they know how it felt to love someone for a thousand years, as the singer crooned.

I did.

39

The Gates Foundation's head office in the United States is in Seattle. It is where Microsoft is based and where Bill Gates lives. Apart from that, they have an East Coast office in Washington. In New York, they often work with their partners on various projects. Since I had insisted on New York, Michael had given me a place on a Foundation project with the United Nations. The UN world headquarters is located in mid-town New York. On my first day to work, I walked to the 86th Street station on Lexington Avenue. I took train number four and got down at Grand Central Station on 42nd Street, walking half a mile to the massive United Nations Plaza complex. After a three-layered security process, I reached the office of the UNFPA, or the United Nations Population Fund.

'Mr Jha, welcome. Come in.' A forty-year-old black man twice my width met me in the reception area.

I entered an office filled with books and reports.

'Olara Lokeris from Uganda. Worked with the Population Fund for ten years. I will be your mentor.'

The Gates Foundation had granted 57 million US dollars to the UNFPA to educate youth on preventing HIV/AIDS in African countries. I had to make a report on the project's progress. Of course, I had no experience either in Africa, or in making a report.

'I run a school in Bihar, India. I'm sorry, but this Africa and HIV research is all new to me.'

Olara smiled. His white teeth glistened in his large face.

'Don't worry. Making reports is much easier than running an actual school,' he said.

Olara spent the rest of the afternoon explaining the various databases maintained in the project to me.

'Ghana, Uganda, Tanzania and Botswana are the four main countries of focus,' he said.

He briefed me on other logistical and administrative issues related to my internship. He also told me that work hours would be from 9 to 5, with a lunch break in between.

'First time in New York?' Olara said.

'Yes.'

'Good, I will take you out for a drink after work.'

'Sure,' I said.

'Any preferences?'

'Any place with live music,' I said.

◆

One month later

'Dude, no. Please. I can't take this,' Shailesh said. He pushed the envelope back towards me.

I had placed a thousand dollars inside.

'It's been a month, Shailesh. I feel obligated,' I said.

'Would I pay you rent if I came to Dumraon?' he said.

'No, but you are paying rent here. So let me contribute.'

'Don't be stupid. You are hardly here. You come home at 3 every night. You leave at 8. We barely feel your presence.'

Shailesh was right. We had not met the entire week, even though we lived in the same house.

'How's work?' he said. 'What exactly is your project?'

'Tracking the progress of AIDS awareness initiatives in Botswana.'

'Sounds noble.'

'I don't know about noble. All I know is I only have two months left and there's still no sign of Riya.'

Shailesh tilted his box of cereal. The box label said 'Cinnamon Toast Crunch'. Little sugar-coated squares fell into his milk.

'You are chasing an illusion,' he said.

'Maybe.'

'How many bars have you visited in the last month?'

I flipped through my notebook where I kept track of all my visits.

'Hundred-plus. Close to two hundred,' I said.

Apart from actual visits, I had also called up five hundred other music venues. Nobody had heard of a singer called Riya.

Shailesh gasped. He covered his mouth with his hand to prevent food from spilling out. He waited a few seconds to chew the contents in his mouth before he spoke again.

'Madhav, I love you as a friend so I am saying it. You have to stop this. She is gone. Wish her happiness. Move on.'

'I will. But only after I feel that I've tried my best. Two more months.'

'I would say end it now. And why go back in two months? Is there a chance of a full-time assignment with the UN?'

'I don't know. I've never really showed an interest.'

'Stop living in the past. Make a new life. Look for work here and meet other people.'

I smiled and nodded. He made sense. I was not interested in sense. He finished his breakfast. Slipping on his shoes, he said, 'Come out with us sometime. Jyoti has many lovely single friends.'

'Sure. Let me know if you're going to a live music venue.'

Shailesh looked at me and laughed. 'Mad you are,' he said. 'Anyway, I better leave or I'll miss my train.'

◆

I had a one-hour lunch break at the UN. Most days I ate a sandwich from the Subway or Starbucks outside. Since Shailesh had refused to take rent, I had enough money to even have a cappuccino later. I had found a fixed corner seat at Starbucks from which to make my calls.

'Hi, is this the West Village Talenthouse?' I said.

'Yes, it is,' an older lady with a heavy American accent said.

'Can I speak to the manager?'

'May I ask what this is about?'

'I'm looking for a singer.'

'We have lots of them. Did you check our website?'

'Yes, I did. However, I am looking for someone specific not listed there.'

'Didn't get you, honey.'

'Well, it's a girl. Indian-origin. She is in her early twenties. Her real name is Riya. I don't think she uses that on stage.'

'I can't help you with such limited information. Did you see her perform somewhere?'

'Well, no. Actually, she is an old friend. I am trying to locate her.'

'Sorry, getting another call, bye.'

She hung up. I had another sip from my Venti-sized cup, which held over half-a-litre of coffee. Americans are into size, whether it is their cars, bodies or food. I had ten minutes of lunch break left. I called a few more bars and one more talent agency. Finally, I made a route plan to visit six bars in the evening around the Tribeca area.

40

'No Indian singer here. I'm sorry,' she said.

I had come to Tribeca Nation, a small bar with thirty seats and a tiny stage for solo vocalists. The singer had just finished her performance.

I had gone up to her and told her I loved her voice. I asked her if she would have a few minutes to sit with me. She looked at me suspiciously.

'I just have some questions. Nothing else,' I had told her.

She ordered a Jack Daniel's whisky and Diet Coke, and urged me to try the same.

Erica was twenty-two years old. She was from Rhode Island, a state north of New York. She wanted to act in a Broadway play, and tried her luck at auditions during the day. At night, she earned a living through singing gigs.

'I finished high school and came here.'

I looked at her.

'No college, sorry.' She grinned. Over the past few weeks, I had learnt a thing or two about Americans. If they wanted something, they went for it. They didn't think about the risks so much. Which Indian parent would allow a girl to sing in bars at night after class XII, I wondered?

'I really need to find this girl,' I said, now two whiskies down and more talkative.

'Love. Makes us do crazy things,' she said.

'Well, I am going a little crazy.'

'Love.' She laughed. 'At least it keeps us singers in business.'

I gave her Riya's description.

'You spoke to agents?'

'As many as I could. No luck yet.'

'If she has a stage name, it can get quite difficult.'

'Well, she is Indian. I am hoping someone will remember her. I have two months left.'

'I'll let you know in case I spot someone.'

'That would be helpful.'

'I don't have your number.'

We shared contacts. She recommended other bars.

'Here,' she passed me a tissue she had scribbled names on. 'These are places that give new singers a chance.'

'Thanks,' I said.

'She's a lucky girl,' Erica said.

'It's me who needs some luck now,' I said.

◆

One and a half months later

'See you at Pylos then. At 7th Street and First Avenue. Eight o'clock.' Shailesh ended the call.

Pylos is a high-end Greek restaurant located in the East Village. Earthen terracotta pots with spotlights dangled from the ceiling. In Bihar, nobody would think that the humble matki could play chandelier.

Shailesh and Jyoti had invited me out to dinner. Jyoti had brought her friend Priya along, without warning me.

'Priya is a journalist with *Al Jazeera* in New York. We went to high school together,' Jyoti said. Priya looked like she was in her early twenties. Fashionable glasses, slim figure, attractive. She wore a navy-blue top with a white pencil skirt and a long silver chain that dangled down till her navel, which was visible when she stretched.

'This is Madhav. He's here on a United Nations project,' Shailesh said. Cue for Priya and me to shake hands and smile.

I told her about my internship and what I did back home in India.

'You run a rural Indian school? That is so cool,' she said.

'Thanks,' I said.

We ordered a bottle of Greek wine. We also asked for moussaka, which is sautéed eggplant and tomato layered with caramelized onions, herbs and a cheese sauce. A mountain-shaped dish, piled with vegetables, arrived on our table.

I ate a spoonful.

'This is like chokha,' I said.

'Chokha?' Priya said.

'It's a popular dish in Bihar. Which part of India are you from?'

'I'm from Minnesota,' she said. I realized that NRIs born in the US did not like being referred to as Indians.

'Oh,' I said. 'Anyway. This is similar to a local dish we have.'

'My parents are from Andhra Pradesh,' she said.

Shailesh refilled my glass of wine.

Jyoti ordered more food. We had a trio of Greek dips, consisting of tzatziki, a thick yogurt dip; taramosalata, a dip made of fish eggs; and melitzanosalata, made with char-grilled eggplants and extra-virgin Greek olive oil. It came with pita bread.

'I'm sorry, but this bread is also like our chapati,' I said.

'Yes, indeed. These are all flatbreads. From Greece and Turkey to the Middle East and all the way down to South Asia, flatbreads are popular,' Priya said.

'Is she Wikipedia?' Shailesh asked Jyoti and we all laughed.

'She is. Just be happy she's not discussing the Greek economic crisis because you came to a Greek place,' Jyoti said.

'Oh no, please. I read enough economic reports in the bank,' Shailesh said.

'Hey, I'm a nerd and a proud one. Cheers.' Priya raised her glass. All of us lifted ours.

'Don't worry, UN boy, I won't bore you with my little nuggets of wisdom anymore,' Priya said. She clinked her glass against mine.

The girls decided to make a trip to the ladies' room together. Why do they go together for a solo activity?

'Like her?' Shailesh said, after the girls had left.

'Huh?'

'Priya. She's giving you the eye, dude. Isn't she hot?'

'What?' I said.

'You play your cards right and she can be yours.'

I shook my head.

'I'm not kidding,' Shailesh said.

'Not interested.'

'I'm not asking you to marry her. Take her out, have fun. Loosen up.'

'Very funny. I hardly have any time left in New York. Only two more weeks.'

'All the more reason. Don't go back without some romance. Or a score.' He winked at me.

'I have a final report to finish. I haven't even started to pack. Plus, so many bars to go to.'

'You won't give up on this Riya nonsense?'

I kept quiet and finished my third glass of wine.

'You've visited or called over a thousand places,' Shailesh said.

'In two weeks it all ends anyway. I am tired, too. Just giving it my best shot.'

'Idiot you are,' Shailesh said.

We heard giggles as the girls returned.

'My friend here thinks you're a little serious. But hot in a brooding sort of way,' Jyoti announced.

Priya smacked Jyoti's arm.

'Shut up. You can't repeat a private conversation,' said Priya, blushing as she sat down again.

Shailesh kicked my leg. *Act, buddy*, he seemed to say.

The waiter brought us another bottle of wine. I poured my fourth glass.

'For dessert I would recommend a drained Greek yogurt served with fresh cherries, thyme-scented Greek honey and walnuts,' the waiter said. The girls swooned over the description and ordered two servings.

'Where are we going next?' Priya said.

'Well, we are the boring banker couple. We have early morning calls,' Shailesh said. 'So we will head home. Why don't Madhav and you check out other places in the neighbourhood?'

'Sure, I don't mind. I could show Madhav the East Village area around Pylos. I used to live here earlier.'

'Actually, I have other places to go to,' I said. I did have five places on my list tonight.

'Madhav, the lady wants to go out,' Shailesh said. He kicked me again under the table.

'Stop kicking me,' I said. The wine had made me more confident.

Jyoti looked startled by the sudden rise in my voice.

'I need to go. Thanks for dinner. What is my share?' I stood up.

My head felt heavy. I had drunk too much.

'Sit down, Madhav. We are trying to help you,' Shailesh said.

'What am I? A fucking patient who needs help?'

My wine glass slipped from my hand and fell on the floor. There was shattered glass all over the floor.

'You do need help, Madhav. You're losing the plot,' Shailesh said.

Customers at other tables were looking at us. A waiter came to remove the broken glass.

'We should go. Shailesh, did you pay the bill?' Jyoti said.

'Did I say something wrong?' Priya said.

'No,' Jyoti said to Priya.

'So what just happened?' Priya said.

'The boys go back a long way. They have their way of talking. Don't worry about it.'

Shailesh took hold of my upper arm. He dragged me out of the restaurant. The cold December breeze hit us all.

'You are drunk,' Shailesh said in a slow, deliberately calm voice. 'Let's take a cab home. We will drop Priya on the way.'

'I am not drunk,' I said, even though I found it hard to keep my balance on the icy street.

'You drank wine like water,' Shailesh said.

A yellow cab stopped next to us. The girls got in. Shailesh shoved me into the front seat. He sat behind with the girls.

'83rd and Third please, with a stop at 37th first,' Jyoti said.

I opened the front door of the car.

'I have to visit five bars,' I said and stepped out.

Priya looked at Jyoti, confused.

'You are drunk. Come back in so we can leave. It's cold outside,' Shailesh said, in a firm but annoyed voice.

'I am not drunk,' I screamed, stumbling on the road and falling on all fours. I twisted my right ankle and it hurt like hell.

'Can you cut the drama and come back in?' Shailesh said.

The girls saw me wince and were about to step out when Shailesh stopped them.

'Are you coming or not? I'm running out of patience, bro,' he said.

'I have to visit five bars,' I said again, still wincing from the pain of the fall.

'Chutiya,' Shailesh said. He slammed the door shut and the cab zoomed off. A few cold drops fell on my face. I looked up at the sky. Little white snowflakes were falling everywhere. A homeless man offered a hand to help me stand up. Only the most pathetic can help the most pathetic.

'I have to visit five bars,' I told the homeless man.

41

'I'm so ashamed, I can't even look at you guys,' I said, eyes down.

I sat at the dining table in Shailesh's house. I had brought muffins, bagels, cream cheese, fresh orange juice, takeaway coffee and fruit from Dean and Deluca, a neighbourhood deli.

Shailesh did not respond.

'When did you come back? And when did you get so much food?' Jyoti said.

'I came back at 6. I tried to sleep but the guilt wouldn't let me. So I went out and got breakfast.'

Jyoti said, 'You need not have bothered. We were so worried about you last night.'

'No, we weren't,' Shailesh cut Jyoti off.

I said to her, 'Sorry, Jyoti. I behaved like an ass in front of your friend. I embarrassed you guys. Luckily, I will be gone soon.'

Shailesh didn't say anything. He just stared at me without a word.

'Shailesh, I'm sorry. I had too much wine. I didn't know Greek wine was so potent.'

'That's not the point, Madhav. We all get high and have fun. You disrespected us. Priya felt horrible. You ruined a special evening.'

'I'm sorry. You are right.'

'Did you see yourself? Staggering on the road screaming "five more bars". What has happened to you?'

'It's sinking in finally. I might never meet Riya again. It is the realization that my effort was a waste. It got to me yesterday.'

'You are still visiting places. Five bars, five bars, you kept saying. What the fuck, Madhav?'

'I never went. I couldn't. I passed out.'

'How did you get home?' Jyoti said.

'I woke up shivering near a bus stop. Took a cab and came home.'

Jyoti and Shailesh looked at each other.

'You might be right, Shailesh. I may need a psychiatrist,' I said.

Shailesh gave me a sarcastic smile.

Jyoti took the cream cheese and applied it on three bagels. I took a sip of black coffee.

'Anyway, guys, I'm sorry I lost control. I hurt you guys, after all you have done for me. Enough is enough. No more visiting live music venues.'

'Really? Promise?' Shailesh took a bite of his bagel.

'Yes. I want to finish my final report. I want to see a bit more of New York, even though it's snowing and cold. More than anything, I want to spend my remaining free time with you both, because who knows when we will meet again.'

Jyoti smiled. She looked at Shailesh, gesturing for him to forgive me.

'And if Priya is brave enough to meet me once more, I will apologize to her, too.'

Shailesh stood up. He came around to give me a bear hug.

'Is it okay? Say something,' I said to him.

'Idiot you are, what else to say?' Shailesh smiled.

Bye, Riya Somani, I said in my head.

◆

'What size? Speak louder, I can't hear you,' I said to my mother over the phone.

I had come to a store called Century 21 to buy gifts for people back home.

'Take large size, and get me a cardigan with buttons,' she said.

I had brought candies for the entire school. It was not the smartest idea. I now needed a new suitcase just to carry the treats.

'Cardigan is done. Do you need anything else?'

'I need some bras. I heard you get good ones there.'

'Bye, Ma.'

◆

One week before the internship ended, I handed over my final report to Olara.

'Thank you, Madhav. I look forward to reading your work,' he said.

'Thanks, Olara. You've been a great guide these past few months.'

'Well, you are a bright man. Did you finally apply for a permanent position?'

'I leave for India next Sunday.'

Olara smiled and patted my back.

I returned to my desk. My phone had a missed call from a contact I had saved as 'Erica, Tribeca Nation singer'.

I called her back.

'Hi,' I said as she picked up the call.

'Hi. Mad-dav, right?' she said.

'Yes, the Indian guy you met at Tribeca Nation.'

'How are you? You were looking for someone, right?'

Warmth tingled through me. I told myself to calm down. I had promised Shailesh I'd quit.

'Yes. I was.'

'Any luck?'

'Nope,' I said.

'Okay, so I don't have much. This will confuse you even more. But there could be a new tall Indian girl who sings.'

'What do you mean?'

'I overheard.'

'Who from?'

'Customers at the bar. They spoke about this good-looking singer and were trying to guess her nationality. Indian features, but quite fair-complexioned, that's what they said. So it reminded me of you.'

'And? What else did they say?'

'They said she sang quite well. Jazz, a bit of rock…'

'What? No, I mean where? Where did they hear her? Did you ask them?'

'Well, yes. They said at the Union Square Farmer's Market on 14th Street.'

'Is it a bar?'

'No, a farmer's market is like a street fair. They have organic food stalls, and a couple of random gigs sometimes.'

'So what do I do?'

'I don't know. Sorry, they didn't know more.'

'Will the fair organizers know?'

'I doubt it. It's too huge a place. You can check. Take train number four to Union Square.'

'Okay,' I said.

'Sorry, Mad-dav. I said I would confuse you. But that day you said you don't even know if she is here. Well, she might be.'

'Thanks, Erica.'

42

Of course, my visit to Union Square proved useless. I didn't have a date or the exact location of the stall.

The farmer's market is put up in the Union Square quadrangle, a football-field sized area filled with over a hundred natural and environment-friendly product stalls. A few stalls featured performances ranging from juggling to music gigs. I passed organic honey and fruit-based soap counters to reach the fair office.

'Agents book the stalls. Then they call their own musicians on hire. It's quite impossible for us to trace them,' a lady at the fair office told me.

I took the subway back home. I felt stupid. I had wasted an evening I could have spent with my friends. I reached the 86th Street stop. I walked out to find the streets filled with snow. It was cold and dark. Still, under the city lights, New York, with its historic skyscrapers and modern neon lights, looked pretty. As I walked home, I passed restaurants with cosy interiors. Beautiful people chatted and laughed as they ate their dinner. I wondered if I would ever, even for one day in my life, be carefree like them.

◆

On my last Saturday in New York, I decided to visit the tourist attractions. I spent my morning visiting the Rockefeller Center, the Empire State Building and the Statue of Liberty. In the afternoon, I decided to splurge. I went to watch an NBA game.

'One ticket for the Knicks game, please,' I said at the ticket counter.

Madison Square Garden, also known as the MSG or simply the Garden, is a multi-purpose indoor arena in midtown Manhattan in New York City. Located between Seventh and Eighth Avenues from 31st to 33rd Streets, it is situated atop Pennsylvania Station. I had come to the Garden to watch a play-off game between the New York Knicks and LA Lakers.

The Garden cost nearly a billion dollars to construct, making it one of the most expensive stadiums in the world. I went inside, and was astonished by what I saw. It was the best basketball court and spectator stadium I had ever seen in my life.

The teams had towering players, many of them over six-and-a-half feet tall. The Lakers wore yellow kits with a purple strip down the side. The Knicks had on blue jerseys with an orange border.

I took my seat. It took me a minute to scan the huge arena and figure out all the complicated scoreboards. The crowd of nearly twenty thousand roared at every point scored.

I was in New York. However, I supported the LA Lakers. They had Kobe Bryant, one of the world's best basketball players and my favourite. He scored the most, over forty points in the game. I wondered if an Indian player would ever join the NBA.

The game ended with the Lakers scoring an easy win. The crowd, exhilarated from the game and the atmosphere, began to trickle out of the stadium. I followed them to the exit.

◆

As I came out of the MSG, I saw a couple of elderly people in jackets with the New York City Tourism logo, waiting near the exit. An elderly Hispanic woman walked slowly towards me.

'Tourist?' she said.

'Yes, well, sort of,' I said.

'How your trip goes? Me Daisy, from the Senior Citizens for NYC tourism. Sorry my English not good. I am Mexico originally.'

'My trip is going quite well, thank you,' I said. 'And your English is just fine.'

I could not believe I had commented on someone else's English. She held a bunch of brochures in her hand.

'May I ask the favour? Will you practise English me five minutes?' Daisy said.

I had to go home and pack. This was an unusual request anyway.

'I join adult school to learn English. To practise I volunteer here tourism department,' Daisy persisted.

'I actually have to go home.'

The older man with her took me aside.

'Hi, I am Doug, a supervisor for the senior citizens for NYC volunteer programme.'

I shook hands with him.

'Please spare five minutes for her. She lives alone. She needs to practise her English,' Doug said.

'Sir, my English is not so good. I am from India.'

'Indians speak good English.'

'Not all. I am also learning it.'

'You are speaking good English now.'

'Well, thank you, sir.'

'Someone must have taught you.'

I sighed.

'Five minutes,' Doug said.

I nodded.

Doug left me with Daisy.

'Hello, Madam Daisy. What would you like to talk about?'

'Would you like brochure? To see attractions of weekend?'

'Actually, I don't think so. I leave soon...' I said but she interrupted me.

'They free. Have look. We have discounted Broadway shows, a food festival, a jazz and music fest...'

'I will correct you. Please say, "they are free, have a look",' I said.

'Sorry, sorry. That I say.'

'I leave Monday. So I am afraid I won't be able to do much,' I said.

She looked disappointed. I figured she had to do her tourism job, too. She possibly had a quota of people she needed to distribute brochures to every day.

'Fine, I'll take them. Thank you.'

'Oh, thank you,' she said and cheered up again. 'You fill small survey for me. Two minutes.'

I put the brochures in my jacket pocket. She gave me a form asking basic details about my visit and myself.

'Can I leave now, madam?' I said, as politely as possible.

'Enjoy rest of stay,' she said and waved me goodbye.

'Yes, yes. Thank you.'

I left the MSG compound and came to the street. Peak hours

meant cabs would be stuck in traffic forever. I checked the time. It was 7 p.m. I decided to walk the four-kilometre distance from Madison Square Garden to Shailesh's house.

43

'Surprise!'

A crowd of people screamed as I entered Shailesh's house. Jyoti had arranged an unexpected farewell party for me.

'Wow,' I said as I entered the apartment. I found twenty guests, Shailesh and Jyoti's friends, waiting for me.

'Hey, Priya, good to see you,' I said, wondering if she would slap me.

'Hi,' she said.

'I'm really sorry about that night.'

'Just go easy on the wine,' she said and laughed. I smiled back at her. She was really attractive. Many men at the party had their eyes on her.

A black man came up to me.

'Olara,' I said and hugged him.

'Your friends are damn nice. They dug out my number and invited me.'

'I'm so glad you came.'

Jyoti dragged me away from Olara to give a short speech.

'I want to thank Shailesh and Jyoti, who hosted me, and treated me like family,' I said.

'Cut it out, let's party,' Shailesh interrupted me. He offered everyone tequila shots and turned up the volume of the music player. Conversations required people to shout. Male bankers huddled together to discuss expected bonuses. The girls made another group. They discussed the best value offers in town, whether on Netflix or Sunday brunch deals in Manhattan. I chatted with a few people.

'Gates Foundation. They are like huge, man,' one banker said to me.

'I just run a small school they fund,' I said.

'I need a Gates Foundation grant. Do they fund bankers who need an apartment in Manhattan?' said another. Everyone laughed.

I spoke to many of those present, but felt little connection with any of them. I stepped away from the crowd and sat on the sofa. I took out my phone to look at the pictures I had taken during the day. I had taken some inside MSG.

'You watched a Knicks game?' I heard Priya's voice from behind me.

I turned to look at her.

'Yes, I went today.'

'Nice pictures. Can I see?'

She sat down next to me. I flipped through the photos.

My phone vibrated. A message from 'Erica, Tribeca Nation singer'.

'Checking out the Jazz and Music Fest?' The message flashed as a notification and disappeared. The phone screen went back to displaying pictures again.

'Next?' Priya said as I didn't touch my phone for a minute.

'Priya, just a second. I need to send a reply.'

'Oh, sure, I will get a drink. Not for you, though,' she smiled, wagging a finger at me. I smiled back.

I composed a message for Erica: I leave Monday. Almost packed. At my farewell party now. Thanks anyway. ☺

She replied: Fly safe. Ciao. ☺

I looked up. I saw Priya engrossed in conversation with someone at the bar.

I shut my phone and placed it in my jacket pocket. I then realized that I was still carrying the brochures Daisy, the old lady, had given me outside Madison Square Garden. I read them one by one.

'CATS—the longest running Broadway musical,' said the first.

'Blue Man Comedy Show—combining music, technology and comedy,' said another.

One of the brochures was a sixteen-page thick, A5-sized booklet. It said 'New York Music and Jazz Festival Weekend'.

The room lights had been dimmed, making it difficult for me to read the text. I shifted my seat closer to a candle on the coffee table. '123 performers. 25 venues. 3 days. 1 city,' it said on the booklet cover.

The booklet opened with a two-page spread of the schedule of performances. It was arranged in three tables, one each for Friday, Saturday and Sunday. Each table had rows for the various time slots. The columns had the names of the singer, the venue and the kind of music and ticket prices. The next two pages had details of each venue. The remaining pages had a brief description of each singer, over a hundred of them. I read the first one:

Abigail—Grew up in Boston, degree in jazz music. Started out as a gospel singer. After singing in Boston for two years, she moved to New York. Boston Globe *called her voice 'smooth velvet' that can 'calm your soul'.*

I went through the names, mostly to pass time. I didn't really belong in my own party.

I skimmed through all the descriptions in the alphabetical list. I ignored all the male singers. Twenty minutes later, I reached the letter R.

Ray—A 'sparkling new voice on the NY scene' according to the Village Voice, *Ray would rather talk about 'where she is going' than 'where she comes from'. This tall exotic beauty 'sings as good as she looks' according to the* Daily News.

I stopped at Ray's description. I read it thrice. I flipped back to the schedule to see Ray's line-up. I looked under Saturday, which was today. My index finger ran down the schedule page.

'Blues, Soul and Contemporary, 10.00 p.m.–12.00 a.m. Stephanie, Roger and Ray, Café Wha?, $8 entry, two drinks minimum.'

I turned the page to look up the details of Café Wha? and strained hard to read the tiny print.

Café Wha? An old classic New York bar where many legends have performed in their struggling days. Mexican and American food options. 115 MacDougal Street, West Village. Subway 4, 5, 6. Bleecker Street F, West 4th Street.

'What are you doing, bro?' Shailesh squeezed my shoulder hard.

'Huh?' I said, startled.

'It's your party. What the hell are you reading?'

I put the brochure aside and smiled.

'Nothing. Just some touristy stuff,' I said.

'You're not drinking?' he said. He tapped his thigh in time with the music.

'No. You know me and alcohol.'

'I can handle you at home. Wait, let me get a drink for you.'

Shailesh went to the bar. I checked the time on my phone. It said

11.05 p.m.

I googled Café Wha?'s number and called them.

They took thirty seconds to pick up. It seemed like an hour.

'Hello. Café Wha?' I heard a cheerful male voice, barely audible due to the music in the background.

'Hi, I am interested in the Music and Jazz Fest performance tonight.'

'Yes, it's on now, sir. It's an eight-dollar cover charge. Two drinks minimum,' the person on the other side recited his rehearsed stuff.

'I wanted to know if there is a singer called Ray performing tonight?'

'Well, let me see. Yes, we have three singers. Hers is the last act. Should be on any time now. Sir, I need to hang up. It's really busy here tonight, and I am one of the very few servers.'

'Sorry, just one question. Is she there? Can you see her?'

'Huh?' the server said, confused. 'Well, I do see the singers near the stage. I think she is there.'

'What does she look like?'

'Sorry, sir, I hate to be rude but you want me to take your name down for reservations or something? Can't help you with much else.'

'Yes, just one last thing. Does she look Indian? It's really important. Please.'

'Hold on,' the server said.

Shailesh came up to me as I was on hold. He gave me a glass of champagne. I gestured a thanks to him. He gave me a puzzled look, wondering who I was calling at this time.

The wait seemed endless.

'Nothing, it is the travel agency who booked my return tickets,' I whispered to Shailesh, making up whatever I could on the spot.

'This late?' he said, surprised. I shrugged and excused myself to step aside.

'Sir? You there?' The man was back.

'Yes, yes. I am.'

'She's definitely not Caucasian white. She isn't black either. She could be Indian. Or I don't know, she's quite light-coloured, so maybe Spanish or mixed-race. Sorry, I can't…'

I interrupted him.

'Thanks. That's enough. I'm coming down. Can you hold a place for one? I'm Madhav.'

'Maad-what?'

'Just put me down as M. I'm coming.'

'You better be here soon. The acts end at midnight.'

Shailesh stood right in front of me.

'All okay with your ticket?' he said.

'Yeah. It's fine,' I said and paused before I spoke again. 'Shailesh, I need to get out.'

'Wha…?'

'Exactly,' I said. 'That's where I need to go.'

'Where?'

'I need to get some fresh air.'

'Have you seen the snow outside? Where are you going?'

He pointed to his balcony. Blobs of snow covered the ledge. Outside his apartment, a steady stream of snowflakes shot down from the night sky.

'I have a jacket,' I said.

Shailesh looked bewildered by my sudden desire for a night stroll.

'Madhav, what do I tell the guests?' he said.

'They will barely notice,' I said and left.

44

I stepped out of the apartment building. Cold winds slashed at my face. My phone showed the time as 11.12 p.m. and a temperature of 20 degrees Fahrenheit, or -6.6 degrees Celsius. People were all bundled up in gloves, caps and jackets. I saw a group of four friends walk towards the 86th Street subway ahead of me.

Fresh snow had made the pavements powdery and white. The group of four and I reached the subway stop. We took the steps down to the metro. Some African-Americans were coming up the steps.

'It's not coming, woo hoo, no train tonight…' said one of them in a drunk voice.

'How am I going to get my ass to Brooklyn?' his friend said.

'A hundred-dollar cab ride, baby. That ass deserves it,' another friend said. They all laughed.

I reached the customer services counter. A plump African-American lady from the Metropolitan Transit Authority, or MTA, sat inside. She made an announcement into a microphone.

'Ladies and gentleman, due to heavy snow, we are experiencing huge delays on all lines. A train is stalled in the network near Grand Central. We are trying to remedy the problem. We suggest alternative travel arrangements.'

I checked the station clock: 11.19 p.m.

Google Maps suggested the subway would have taken me to Bleecker Street in seventeen minutes. From there, it was a nine-minute walk to the café.

'How much delay?' I asked the customer service officer.

'Who knows, honey,' she said. 'It's snow. Half an hour, an hour, two hours. Take your pick.'

I ran up the steps and came out of the station. Cold air sneaked in under the jacket's collar and down my neck. The road had little traffic. I waited but no empty cab went past.

I asked a passer-by, 'I need to go to the West Village urgently. Where can I get a cab?'

'Want one myself.'

I checked the time: 11.25 p.m.

'Walk west to Fifth Avenue. You will hit Central Park. Try there,' someone said.

I took rapid strides to Fifth Avenue. I reached the periphery of Central Park, near the Metropolitan Museum of Art. Amber lights lit up the museum building. The falling snowflakes created a soft-focus effect.

Time: 11.31 p.m.

If I didn't get a cab, I would not be able to reach West Village before midnight. I couldn't see any cabs. I looked up at the sky to pray. Snowflakes fell on my face.

God, please, please, I said.

I looked around me. At least six more people waited for cabs. My heart sank. I wanted to cry.

One cab, please, I said, waiting for magic to happen.

No cabs.

Time: 11.34 p.m.

I reopened Google Maps. I checked the distance from my current location at the Met Museum to Café Wha? and chose the pedestrian option.

It displayed this: Walk 4.0 mi, 1h 10min

The route was simple. I had to go straight down south on Fifth Avenue for 3.8 of the 4 miles, and then turn right.

'Four miles. 6.4 kilometres,' I mumbled to myself.

An hour and ten minutes to walk, I thought. *If I ran, it would be less. If I ran like a mad dog with a pack of wolves chasing it, even lesser.*

'Madhav Jha,' I whispered to myself. 'Run.'

I remembered basketball. We used to run and dribble on court all the time.

A basketball court is not the same as six-and-a-half kilometres in minus six degrees temperature, my sensible mind scoffed.

'Don't think. Don't listen to sense. Just run,' I told myself and took off.

I ran so fast my surroundings became hazy. Central Park on my right and posh Upper East Side homes on my left whizzed past. My face became numb in the cold air. The jacket began to feel heavy as snow started to seep inside.

I had already spent the entire day walking, whether it was for shopping, walking over to Madison Square Garden or back to Shailesh's home. I had not eaten much all day either. My legs began to hurt.

'C'mon Madhav,' I panted, 'c'mon.'

Sometimes, when nobody is by your side, you have to become your own cheering squad.

I faked a dribble. It made me go ahead to catch my imaginary ball.

I checked the street sign: 67th Street. Café Wha? was near 4th.

'Don't look at street signs. Just run, Madhav,' I said aloud.

I passed a hotel on my left on 60th Street. It had an Indian flag hanging above the main porch.

'The Pierre: A Taj Hotel,' a sign said.

The Indian flag unleashed a fresh wave of energy in me.

'Run,' I said to myself. 'You can do this.'

I reached the most famous part of Fifth Avenue, with designer stores on both sides. Tiffany's was on 57th Street, Louis Vuitton on 51st. Riya's journals had mentioned these brands.

On 50th Street, I developed a nasty cramp in my stomach. I had to stop. I sat down in a squat and took a few deep breaths.

Time: 11.44 p.m.

'Damn. There is no time. Feel the pain later,' I told myself.

I couldn't move. I scanned the street for cabs. Nothing. I winced in pain.

On my right, I saw the NBA store. The store was shut. It had a huge poster of Kobe Bryant outside. 'NBA—where amazing happens,' it said.

'C'mon, Madhav. Be amazing.'

I stood up. Without thinking, I started to run again.

My legs and abdomen screamed with pain. My nose felt like ice. However, my head felt like fire. I ran, almost jumped with every stride, and looked straight ahead. Snow was in my sneakers, turning my feet cold and wet.

'Run, run, run,' I whispered with every breath. I reached a dead end at Washington Square Park.

'I'm close. Right turn from here.'

Time: 11.56 p.m.

I wanted to rest for a minute.

'No rest,' I scolded myself.

I turned right and ran.

The noise of music and the crowd outside made me stop.

'Café Wha?' The lit-up sign greeted me with its bright yellow letters. I pumped my fists.

45

I plonked my elbows on the usher's desk outside. I tried to speak. Snow fell out of my mouth.

'M,' I gasped. 'I booked a place for Mr M.'

I bent to cough. As my body shook, bits of snow fell off me.

'Easy there, M. Are you all right?'

I nodded.

'Your lips are purple. They may fall off, buddy,' the usher said.

I rubbed my hands and placed them on my mouth. Cold hands did little to warm up an even colder face.

The usher went through his register.

'Mr M, yes. But the show is almost ending. It's midnight. Last song probably.'

Time: 12.01 a.m.

'The singer is still there, right?' I said, still huffing and puffing as I spoke.

'Huh? Yeah, maybe just doing a bonus song or something. Entry is eight dollars, two drinks minimum. You sure?'

I slapped a twenty-dollar bill on his desk and walked in. I reached the bar area.

'Your two drinks, sir?' said a female bartender.

'Water and water.'

She gave me two bottles of water. I chugged them down in a flash.

'Where is the performance?' I said.

'Straight left to the concert area. Follow the music.'

I limped ahead. My legs had given way. I held on to bar stools and chairs to keep myself from falling.

The concert area was a dimly lit room filled with people. The crowd in front of me prevented me from seeing the stage.

I elbowed my way through the hordes of people to get ahead.

I heard a female voice.

'You're beautiful. You're beautiful.
You're beautiful, it's true.'

The bright spotlight on the stage contrasted with the dark room. It took a few seconds to spot the singer.

It was her.

Riya.

The water bottle fell from my hand.

She sang with her eyes closed, completely engrossed in the song. In a full-length, sequined black gown she looked more beautiful than what even God would define as beautiful.

Yes, Riya Somani, I found you.

She held an acoustic guitar in her hand. A male American pianist accompanied her on stage. She continued to sing.

'I saw your face in a crowded place,
And I don't know what to do,
'Cause I'll never be with you.'

My tiredness evaporated. No more aches and pain. Blood flowed through my body again. My face felt flushed and hot compared to the freezing cold a minute ago.

She sang from her heart. The crowd loved her and cheered. She opened her eyes between lines and smiled at the crowd's reaction. She had not seen me yet.

I removed my jacket and put it on a table. I walked right up ahead to the stage and stood before her.

'You're beautiful. You're beautiful.
You're beautiful, it's…'

Her voice vanished as her eyes met mine. The pianist looked at her surprised, wondering why she had missed her lines.

Riya stood up. The guitar looked unsteady in her hand.

The pianist filled the gaps with an instrumental interlude.

Riya put her guitar aside slowly. I continued to look at her.

We stood before each other, silent and frozen. The crowd began to murmur, wondering what was happening.

The pianist figured something was amiss. He took the mic and continued the song.

'You're beautiful, it's true.'

I just kept looking at her.

What all you made me go through, Riya Somani, my eyes said.

I'm sorry, her eyes said to me. A tear ran down her cheek. Mine too.

I thought I would have so much to say to her when I finally met her. I had mentally rehearsed it many times. I would be angry at first. I would shout, tell her how much she had put me through. I would then tell her what she meant to me. How I was not that jerk, Rohan. Or that others may have let her down, but I wouldn't. And that my mother could only be happy if I was. I had my speech all planned. However, neither of us said a word.

We just looked at each other and cried, and cried. After some time she stepped forward. That is all Riya Somani does. She gives you a little clue she is ready. You just need to be alert enough to pick it up. I opened my arms. They shook as she came closer. I took her in my arms.

'I… I'm sorry…' she said.

'Shh,' I said. 'Remember you placed a condition last time? No questions asked twice. I have one now.'

'What?' she said in the softest whisper.

'No questions at all. In fact, if possible, no words.'

She buried her face in my chest. I lifted her chin.

'Riya Somani, I love you. Always have. Always will. Please, never, ever leave me.'

She shook her head and said, 'I won't…I can't…'

I continued, 'Shh… Because next time I will find you again and kill you.'

She smiled and cried at the same time. Some of the crowd cheered, even though they were confused about what was going on. The pianist ended the song. The restaurant staff switched on the concert room lights. People began to make their way out.

I continued to hold her.

'Sorry, I left because I got scared…' she said.

'I know.'

'But how did you…?' she said.

'I said, no questions.'

'Just one last one.'

'What?'

'Why is your shirt so wet and cold?' she said.

I laughed.

'What?' she said.

'Nothing.'

46

'Upper West, 70th and 6th,' she said.

We were in a black Lincoln car, which the organizers had arranged for the singers. The car took us to her apartment on the Upper West Side near the western side of Central Park. I can't remember much of the journey except her face and the way it looked in the changing lights. And that the city seemed more beautiful than any other night in the past three months. I clasped her hand tightly and leaned back on the seat, just looking at her face.

◆

She turned the key and we were in her apartment. There were music posters all over the walls. The window faced the park, now dark, apart from the streetlights. She went to the bedroom to remove her make-up.

In the bathroom I undressed and noticed the bruises and blisters on my feet. My nose and ears looked raw and red. I took a hot shower. I felt like a pack of frozen peas being thawed.

I finished my shower and realized I did not have fresh clothes. A pink oversized T-shirt with a Dora cartoon hung in the bathroom. Perhaps Riya used it as nightwear. I put on the T-shirt, wrapped a towel around my waist and stepped out.

Riya laughed as she saw me in the girlie T-shirt.

'Sorry, I didn't...' I said.

She silenced me with a kiss. Her lips felt like warm honey. She kissed me for a long time, holding my face in her hands. Our tongues gently touched. I placed my left hand on her cheek. My right hand kept my towel in place.

She guided my right hand to her back. Her gown was backless, and I felt smooth skin.

She removed my pink T-shirt. I tried to remove her gown but it was too complex a garment for me to understand. I tugged at it, and then gave up.

She unzipped a side zipper and stepped out of it.

We embraced. We kissed. We touched. We caressed. We reached the bedroom, the bed. Our lips never stopped kissing. Our hands never stopped touching.

Every moment felt special as we made love. I entered her, and our eyes met. Both of us felt strong and vulnerable at the same time. I saw tears in her eyes.

'You okay?' I said.

She nodded. She brought her face close to my ear to whisper.

'More than okay. I'm great,' she said. 'And you?'

'More than great,' I said.

We cuddled afterwards. She slept. I didn't. I looked at her all night. I realized this only when daylight seeped in through the windows. I turned towards her. Her skin glowed in the morning light. Her eyebrows were still perfect. Her eyes were shut.

'You sleeping?' I asked her.

She nodded.

Epilogue

Three and a half years later

'It's easily one of the best schools I have seen,' I said.

'It was not like this seven years ago,' Madhav said.

I finished the tour of the Dumraon Royal School. Madhav had invited me as the chief guest for their annual day function.

I passed a music class, from where high-pitched notes could be heard. Madhav knocked on the door.

'Riya, Chetan sir,' Madhav whispered.

'Please don't call me sir,' I said.

'Sorry,' Madhav said.

Riya stepped out. Madhav had not lied about her looks. She had classic features and an elegant demeanour.

'Chetan sir, finally. Madhav has talked so much about you,' Riya said.

'No sir. And, trust me, Madhav has told me a lot about you too.'

She laughed. Madhav told her to finish the class and meet us outside.

'It's lovely here,' I said. We walked out of the main building into the school garden. Students had decorated the new basketball court with flowers. A function to inaugurate the court was scheduled for later in the evening.

'We wanted to call you earlier, but thought it better to invite you here when we had a basketball court,' Madhav said.

'The court is beautiful.'

'All the equipment is from the US,' Madhav said. 'Riya and I spend three months there every year. She does a few music gigs. I help out at the UN and also do some marketing of my rural tours.'

Madhav explained how they had started rural school tours, which included a stay in the haveli. People came from all over the world, allowing the school to earn revenue in dollars.

'Tourists spend a day with our kids. They teach them a class, share pictures or talk about their country. They say it is one of the most meaningful things they have ever done in their life.'

'That's innovative.'

'Students love it. They get an exposure to the world. Many tourists send regular grants or gifts to the school later on.'

'Where's your mother?'

'She'll come soon. She spends less time at the school now. Riya and I run it. Shyam keeps Rani Sahiba busy.' Madhav laughed.

'She is okay about Riya?' I said.

'You forget that she saw how I had become without her. She says she is happy to have her son back. Not to mention grandson. Her new darling.'

'How old is your son now?'

'Will turn two soon,' Madhav said. 'Here they come.'

I saw an elderly lady walk towards us holding a little boy's hand in one hand and a large tiffin box in another.

The school bell rang. Hordes of kids ran out. Riya joined us.

'Everyone's here,' she said.

Shyam extracted his hand from his grandmother's and came running up to his parents. He looked like a chubby baby version of Riya.

'Shyam is too tall and too naughty for his age,' Rani Sahiba said when Madhav had introduced us.

We sat in the amphitheatre seats of the basketball court. Riya served everyone a lunch of chapatis, daal and carrot-and-peas subzi from the tiffin box.

Shyam saw a basketball on court. He ran down the amphitheatre steps for the ball.

'Careful,' Rani Sahiba said.

'He's your daredevil grandson,' Riya said.

Shyam took the ball in his hand.

'Shoot,' Riya said.

Shyam took a shot. His little hands couldn't throw the ball high enough to reach anywhere near the basket. He tried two more times and failed.

He looked at his father.

'It's not happening,' he said.

'So what? Don't quit. It will happen one day,' Madhav said.